*For every single woman who has not let past abuse*
*define their futures. We're all in this together.*

# Deceitfully Damaged

*The Shadowed Souls Series Book Two*

## Abigail Cole

# Contents

# Avery

*"But now I think you might have been a part of this family all along."*

Those words flutter on the edge of my consciousness as I rouse from yet another fitful sleep. Huxley is flush to my back, his deep even breathing fanning my ear. I've been naturally waking around this time for the past few weeks, allowing me a fleeting moment of reflection before a new day of confusion and worry begins.

Time since Wyatt showed me the ultrasound in his pool house has passed quickly. That afternoon changed everything, and not in the way I'd hoped. I thought I had finally been gifted something in life that was real, someone who would always be with me. My twin. My own flesh and blood. The other half to my soul, apparently. Yet we've never been more distant and that's saying something.

Lying still in the dark and maintaining the pretence of sleep, I slowly build up the layers around my heart so it's buried far away from the surface. Huxley shifts and rolls over, his movement giving me the green light to launch myself from the bed without him noticing. Rolling from the mattress into a crouch on the floor, I peek over the duvet to check he's still asleep. The cover rises and falls smoothly over his new position on his left side, the wound on his collar bone practically healed now. Tiptoeing on silent feet, I pick up my phone from the bedside table and edge around the bed. I make it all the way to the bathroom door before his voice echoes around the walls.

"Where are you going?"

"I need a shower, is that a crime?" I huff bitchily and sag my shoulders. It's surreal how swiftly spending time in here has shifted from a pleasant oasis to a steel-barred cage.

"Do you want me to sit in with you?" He asks hopefully, pushing himself upright so his blonde hair tumbles onto his shoulders. The pink puckered scar is barely visible upon his broad chest as the sun begins to spill through a crack in the curtains. I know Huxley means well, and the puppy dog look in his eyes almost makes me say yes but I need some of my own space. His protectiveness is suffocating me.

"It's fine, I need a little time alone. I'll be back soon." I disappear through the door and lock it behind me, sagging against the wood on a sigh. Checking my phone, the screen illuminates with a selfie of Meg and I from a New Year's Eve party. Her eyes are glimmering to the purest shade of aquamarine in the flash, her red painted lips curved into a huge smile as I'm running the pad of my tongue up her cheek.

Unlocking it with my thumb, I open contacts to the 47 failed phone calls I've attempted to place to Meg so far and tap to add another. Holding the phone to my ear, bracing myself for the automated message *'Sorry, we are unable to connect your call at this time. Please try again later-'*, my heart jumps into my throat as the first ring sounds. With each one, I silently beg her to pick up and my excitement slowly ebbs into dread. Her voicemail begins to play, the sweet voice I yearn for promising to call back soon as I sink down until I'm slumped on the floor. The backs of my eyes sting with unshed tears as I try to keep my voice as level as possible.

"Hey Meg, I know you're still on holiday with your mum and I don't want to bother you. But it's been weeks and I really miss you. We've never gone this long without talking. It's like a part of me is missing. I feel so alone without you and there's so much I want to fill you in on. So, give me a call if you get a chance. I l love- "

A beep cuts me off and I lean my forehead onto my knees. Tears begin to fall onto my bare thighs, running a trail down to my skimpy pyjama shorts. I've managed to keep my emotions hidden by keeping distracted with helping Huxley recover but the flood gates are open now and I don't know how to close them. My body shakes violently with loud sobs I can't conceal. Distantly, the sound of the opposite door opening reaches my ears and causes me to glance through the watered glaze in my eyes to see Dax approaching.

Bending low to collect me from the floor, I slide my arms around his neck as he straightens with ease and bury my face in his black t-shirt. The firmness of his chest beneath the fabric pressed against my cheek, giving me the solid support I need. Striding into my own room, he sits on the edge of my bed and cradles me tightly while I use his warmth and scent to reign myself back in. His cologne is the perfect blend of sweet and spice, filling my senses with each deep exhale I force myself to take. Dax doesn't say a word, just holds me and rests his cheek on top of my head. His afro tickles my ear, making a smile a little.

Shifting my head so I can glance over his darkly tanned shoulder, I see ominous dark clouds filling the sky beyond my balcony. "Did he come home last night?" I ask quietly. Dax shakes his head and strokes my arm gently, causing goose bumps to rise beneath his touch. Sleeping next to Huxley is like having a radiator in the bed, but now I'm chilly in this flimsy vest and shorts combo. Dax's shoulder bunches as he reaches across towards my pillow, pulling the orange hoodie out from beneath it. The burn of a blush ignites in my cheeks in embarrassment as I accept Wyatt's hoodie from him with an awkward nod.

I know it's wrong to keep a piece of your brother's clothing hidden beneath your pillow so his scent is nearby if I should need it. I could justify it by saying I needed a connection to him, but I know Dax won't believe me. Wyatt and I were starting to bond and grow closer, but then he discovered what we were and went straight back to pushing me away. In fact, he seems to hate me now more than ever, judging by the way he bolted from the pool house, and has avoided me ever since. I don't care if we only smile in passing, he's supposed to be my twin and even if it doesn't feel natural, I want him in my life.

Slipping the hoodie over my head, I remain huddled into Dax until I hear the splatter of rain against the glass behind us. Looks like another day stuck in this mansion with four brooding guys. They are missing Wyatt as much as me, probably more in fact. The self-appointed leader of their group has gone AWOL and their dynamic has shifted massively. Huxley is hiding away, Axel and Garrett have coupled up so that leaves Dax to comfort me.

Setting me on my feet, Dax says he'll head down to start breakfast before slipping out of the door. Crossing the room, I stare longingly at the pool house beyond the window before slipping into my walk-in closet to find some sweatpants. Half of the clothes hanging across the left side are Meg's, making me pout further. Seriously, where is she? I'm worried something might have happened or that I am the problem. With all the craziness happening around here, I've considered Meg may have left to escape the drama but surely she could just call to tell me she's okay.

Yanking a pair of soft grey tracksuit bottoms from a hanger and pulling them on beneath the overly large hoodie, I twist my long hair into a bun and secure it with a band from my wrist. Spraying myself with anti-perspirant, deciding to have my shower later, I step into the hallway to see Axel and Garrett heading up the stairs. Thankfully, their attention is on each other, allowing me to duck back into my doorway unseen until they've rounded the hallway towards Garrett's room. I know, in their own ways, the pair only want to help but Axel will try to explore my feelings and Garrett will attempt to convince me threesomes are the best kind of release. Neither of which I'm in the mood for at the moment.

Walking down the staircase and entering the kitchen, Dax turns to hand me a tea with a wide smile. His pearly whites are perfectly straight and penetrating blue eyes shimmer slightly, giving me a wink as I accept the mug from his large hands. Perching on the stool across the island from him, I silently sip and watch him cook over the rim of my cup. With the others content to do their own things, we've spent a lot of time together lately so I feel comfortable letting my guard down in his presence. Dax moves around the island with a plate of pancakes for each of us, mine topped with bacon and syrup while his act as the base for a mountain of fruit. Tutting at his healthy choice, he sticks his tongue out playfully while sitting down beside me.

"What should we do today?" he asks just as I shovel a forkful of sticky goodness into my mouth. Holding my finger up to make him wait a moment for my reply, I almost choke trying to chew and swallow too quickly.

"You did that on purpose," I finally croak out, reaching to take a long drink of my overly sweet tea.

"Yeah I did," he chuckles, nudging my shoulder which causes the mug to miss my mouth and beige liquid to splash down my chin onto the orange hoodie. A moment of silence stretches between us until Dax bursts into laughter that I can't help to join in. Placing the cup onto the marbled surface safely, I lunge over in an attempt to wipe my face dry on his shirt but he's too fast for me. Dax's hands grip my shoulders to hold me at bay while I squeeze his knees in my fingertips. The resulting squeal belongs to a little girl, not the muscled basketball player beside me and I completely lose it.

Maybe because I haven't laughed properly in ages, but hysterics take a hold of me until I'm bent forward on the counter clutching my sides. His fingers grip my thighs, making me jolt. Cackling, I attempt to pry his iron clad grip from my legs with no avail. Dax abruptly withdraws his hands from me and straightens, as I wipe the tea from my face with the sleeve of the hoodie. Following his eyeline, I see Huxley standing in the archway with a pained look across his face.

"I thought you didn't want company." He looks between us accusingly. "But apparently, just not mine." His nostrils flare with a further crease in his eyebrows just before he turns to storm off without eating. Again. Huxley has been living off the bare minimum amount of food since he was shot, much to Garrett's approval since he gets seconds for every meal. A faint flicker of despair within my chest is quickly chased away by anger. Stabbing my fork into the centre of my pancakes, I jump down from the stool and head for the gym towards the back of the house.

I understand why Huxley is acting this way, but that doesn't mean I need to like it. He thinks keeping me hidden in his room is the best way to keep me safe. I've spent weeks taking care of him and aiding his every whim for the bullet he took for me. Soothed away every night terror, held him while he's cried, changed his dressings, even brushed his hair. I will always feel incredibly guilty about the events of that day but, surely, he can see it's time to get back to normal. There's been no sign of the intruders since, police still watch the house each night and there are now armed guards posted around the 6-foot stone wall surrounding the grounds. For my own sanity, I need to move on.

Music starts to play through the speakers as Dax passes me a pair of boxing gloves to use on the punching bag. He can be silently overprotective like that, but I don't mind since he isn't trying to guilt-trip me like a certain moping blonde. Peeling off the hoodie and chucking it over the pull up tower, I strap on the gloves as Dax moves around to hold the bag in place, only his afro visible either side of the red leather from this angle. Smirking, I throw the sole of my foot into the centre with as much force as I can muster to knock him off balance. A low chuckle sounds under the heavy bass as I continue to punch the bag over and over until the burn in my muscles levels out the one within my being.

Above Meg, and even Wyatt, I miss my mum. Discovering she was my birth mother this whole time was a punch in the gut and I've had to secretly mourn her all over again. She was the first person I learned to love, yet she was the one to abandon me. I have so many questions she held the answers to and for some reason decided to keep to herself. Why didn't she ever tell me?

Things might be easier if I could get a hold of Nixon and Wyatt wasn't avoiding me. He seems to sneak in while I'm asleep to grab fresh clothes and disappear by morning, according to Dax. My entire world has been spun on its axis. Just a few months ago, Meg was carrying a tall chocolate cake into the living room, with mum, Nixon, Susie and Jenson all seated on the U-shaped cream sofa, singing happy birthday to me. A sparkler fizzled on top in the shape of a 19 that was a bitch to blow out. Now none of them are here and I've realised Wyatt's birthday is at the end of this month – which means so is mine and I've just lost a whole year of my life. Crap.

# Wyatt

This is the life. High energy music seeps under the curtain from the club in full swing beyond, the sound of stomping feet accompanying the bass. Vibrant colours burst in rhythmic patterns behind my closed eyelids, like an internal never-ending kaleidoscope. My mind feels light and empty as I roll my head across the back of the velvet sofa, enjoying the high from the tablet I swallowed a little while ago. I don't even know what it was, but it's fucking incredible. The small tremors that took a hold of my body soon morphed into this blissful numb feeling with faint tingles dancing around my skin similar to pins and needles.

The scent of weed travels across from the next booth over, signalling I'm not alone in having a good time. "The devil's lettuce," I muse to myself, chuckling quietly with a stupidly large grin across my face. Sighing contentedly, I stretch my legs wider and slouch down a little further to accommodate the blowjob I'm currently receiving. I've spent my days and nights doing whatever the fuck I want for a while now, not sure how long since I don't even know what day it is. Only sneaking back to the mansion if I have no other choice i.e. need to grab some cash or rotate sneakers. Each day has been mine to seize, any way I see fitting, and it's been glorious. Crashing celebrity-exclusive parties, placing high bets at casinos, going back to a different chick's hotel room each night. She-who-will-not-be-named is actually a Hughes, which relieves me of my adopted babysitter bullshit. The truth will set you free and all that jazz.

My fingers are threaded through the black hair of a random woman I picked up walking through the seedy club, her head bobbing up and down on my dick. Her brown eyes, dark hair and multiple face piercings were the polar opposite to the figure haunting my dreams each time I close my eyes, which made her perfect in my opinion. The fact she had drugs stashed in her cleavage and was desperate to suck me off were bonuses. Through my daze, I can barely feel the effort I'm sure she is putting in but I still don't make her stop. This is worlds away from the straight A, respected, upper class guy I was a few weeks ago - which is exactly the point.

Recent revelations have forced me to get my priorities in sync, number one being to stop lusting over my twin sister. Fuck it, I promised myself I wouldn't think of her. Opening my eyes, I focus on the woman kneeling between my legs. Clutching the back of her head, I encourage her to go deeper, hopelessly trying to banish the blonde mirage appearing in front of me. She moves faster, her black hair covering my thighs like an ink spill as she takes me all the way in the back of her throat, but any ounce of pleasure I might have felt through this high has gone. Her thickly outlined eyes flash up to me, a trick of my mind seeing them as blue in the strobe light that passes over the curtain. My dick jumps excitedly at the notion and I hate myself even more.

I tried so hard to keep my distance when I thought she was adopted, but the more I pushed her away the more I wanted to pull her close. She was the forbidden fruit I couldn't resist, and when I think how close I came to acting on my urges I feel sick. Bile rises in my throat, the effects of the drug instantly wearing off. I grip the sides of my head as my mind begins to spin with all the thoughts I've been suppressing. I didn't want to think about her until I could control myself and now her blue beautiful eyes are all I can see, no matter how many times I blink.

"I need another one of those pills." I rasp, nausea flipping my stomach as I push the woman off me. Releasing me with a 'pop', she looks offended as I hastily tuck myself back into my boxers.

"You shouldn't take more than one at a time, that shit is strong." She warns but I roll my eyes, sensing her game. Pulling a roll of money from my pocket, I bend forward to reach into her cleavage that's fully on display in the low V in her red top in hunt for the packet she pushed back down earlier. Locating the small plastic bag, I pull it free and shove the roll of money into its previous hiding spot. There're 7 more small pink pills within, which should be enough to see me through this bad patch I'm having. I may be temporarily unstable, but I'm not stupid enough to get addicted. By the end of the summer, I'll have dragged the pieces of my broken soul back together and return to finish my bachelors since they only way I'm going to succeed in this life is through my own perseverance.

Noticing brown eyes staring at me with concern, I school my features and straighten my shirt. "Why are you still here? Get the fuck out," I bark and point to the closed curtain. The metal studs in her eyebrow and either side of her nose shift simultaneously with her frown as she picks herself up from the floor and storms out. I stare at the pills for a while longer, twisting the packet between the fingers of my right hand. Deciding not to risk it and remain plagued by my thoughts, I shove the bag into my pocket and recline back.

This area is dimly lit by a red bulb beneath a tacky frilly lampshade hanging from the ceiling. The only other furniture apart from the sofa I'm sitting on is a leather stool pushed into the corner for lap dance purposes. The booth is one of many with the intention of enticing old, rich men back here. The undercover hooker I picked up must have been thrilled to have a client in the first half of his life for a change. Anyone who comes to 'Hellhole' knows this back-alley club is a front for a brothel. That's the reason I came. Despite having the time of my life lately, keeping up the pretence that I'm carefree is taxing.

I wanted to go somewhere hidden where I could let my guard down, just in case this exact thing happened. Lifting my glass of whiskey from the flattened arm of the sofa, I cross my ankles and down the liquid.

I can't think of a time I've ever been alone like this. The day I started Waversea college I met Huxley and the others came soon after, so it feels strange to be here without my boys. From the sounds of the orgy taking place a few cubicles down, Garrett would be in his element here. But I can't call them. They would be here within the hour, trying to 'fix' me. The truth is, I don't want to be fixed, I want to ride this storm and feel every ounce of self-loathing because I deserve it. I'm twisted in ways I didn't even realise; I need time to be reckless and banish the darkness within before I hurt someone I care about. Eventually, I'll be able to return home without looking twice at *her.*

Standing, I button my black slacks and stride towards the curtain. Shifting the heavy, purple material aside, the crowd of dancing bodies filling the entire space becomes visible, spilling from the dancefloor so they are unavoidable. There were burgundy armchairs surrounding low tables lining the left side of the club when I entered that aren't visible now. A glint of metal in the flashing lights draws my attention to a fully uniformed police officer in the centre of the throng, his shirt unbuttoned as he spins handcuffs around his index finger.

Shaking my head, I start to push my way in the direction of the bar. Hands grab at my white shirt, stroking my biceps and yanking on my loose tie. Pushing my hands in my pockets so no one can steal my cash or recently purchased drugs, I use my shoulders to barge through the sweaty swarm and find a recently vacated space at the granite surface.

Signalling over to the bartender, a short, fat man in a sharp suit stumbles into my side. His drink splashes across my front, the shirt material sticking to my abs as the clear liquid soaks in. I throw him a filthy look which he blanches at and raises his hands in apology, a Rolex slipping down his chubby wrist. The gothic prostitute that was just on the end of my cock slides her arm around his shoulders and leads him away, glaring at me as she passes.

Turning back, I find the bartender standing eye-level in front of me, drying a glass and looking impatient. His rolled-up sleeves reveal a colourful array of tattoos on both arms to match the one poking out of the collar on his neck. A brunette top knot sits above his head. "Bottle of Jack," I demand rather than ask. My mood has soured and I'm glancing around for the right kind of pick-me-up.

"You got some ID kid?" He shouts over the music, causing my jaw to clench. I could walk into a store and buy a gun easier than I can get a fucking drink. Pulling a $100 bill free of my pocket, I slam it on the counter deciding this bottle will be to go.

"Sure, name's Benjamin Franklin." I sneer. After hesitating for a second, which I give him props for, he slips the note into his pocket and lifts my drink from the shelf. Placing it down with a glass, he removes the cap before sliding it towards me.

"Enjoy, Benjamin." He smirks, walking off. I lift the bottle to take a long swig, enjoying the spicy burn as it glides down my throat. Setting it down, my eyes find their own reflection in the mirrored wall behind the bar. The emerald orbs are the only part I recognise of myself, causing me to think it's some kind of trick of the mirror or my mind. Shifting my face side to side, I realise it is in fact me.

I look drawn, ill even. Deep crevices hang below my eyes, my cheeks looking hollow and pasty. My hair is an overgrown mess, sticking out in all directions from tugging my hands through it. The open-top buttons of my shirt reveal hickeys lining my neck and the glimpse of a scratch across my chest. I look like shit. Like some STD-riddled sleaze who's crawled out of the gutter in search of my next victim or a hit. What would my mom say if she could see me like this? I'd like to think she'd be disgusted in the way any parent would be, but let's face it – I was always a disappointment in her eyes and she'd probably been too busy pawing over Avery to even notice. Fuck it, I thought of her name.

I watch like an outsider as the walls slam down over my expression, my eyes harden as my posture grows rigid. It always comes back to her. All my shortcomings and failures. Everything I yearned for and lost. The pulsing vein in my forehead I thought I had learnt to control returns with a vengeance. If I clench my jaw any longer, I'm going to crack a tooth, but I can't move. It's as if I'm frozen in place and time as this anger fuelled asshole she turned me into.

My hand tightens around the neck of the whiskey bottle, reminding me it's still there. Gripping it tightly, without taking my eyes off the pitiful reflection, I launch the bottle across the space dividing us. Hitting its intended target, the image of me multiplies dozens of times over while the rest of the mirrored wall splinters and falls. Shelves filled with countless bottles crash to the ground loudly over the music and shrieks fill the air as chaos breaks out all around me. But I can't take my eyes off myself, because in this moment I see who I am inevitably destined to be. An unloved fuck-up.

# Meg

Huffing, I lean my forearms on the timber railing and stare longingly at the horizon. Another day in paradise, and I can't wait to leave. A salty breeze tingles my nostrils on a deep inhale as I try to ease the tightness of my chest. Rhythmic lapping of waves in the distance are only broken by the occasional squawk of a seagull hovering overhead and diving into the sea in hunt for its breakfast.

Rounding the porch, I hop down the steps and walk across the golden sand. My bare feet sink slightly with each step towards the shore as I enjoy the cool gentle winds before the sun rises and brings the scorching heat. Too bad I don't tan like my mom, who looks worlds away from my pasty skin at the moment. The sky blends from the palest pinks to purest blues which has me pulling my phone out to take another photo for the 'Avery Collection.' The day I can actually share the images with her can't come quick enough.

Avery would have loved it here, and I wish for the millionth time I'd begged my mom to bring her along. Every mile that stretched between us had wretched out another piece of my heart, leaving a trail from here to Atlanta. I know we are in California somewhere, but with the days of driving and three motel stopovers, I lost track of exactly whereabouts.

To make matters worse, mom had insisted we left town that very night and conveniently didn't pack my charging cable. I'd practically jumped from mom's Land Rover as we pulled up to a red traffic light in a town during the last leg of our trip. After finally arriving at this extremely well-hidden coastal retreat, mom began exploring the secluded beach outside while I was sitting eagerly on the wooden floor of my chosen bedroom, cradling my phone like the most precious thing in the world as the screen finally came to life. And low and behold – no damn service!

Checking my ponytail is secure after I haphazardly threw my hair up earlier, I adjust my sports bra and stop at the water's edge. Pushing my phone back into the hidden pocket of my black lycra leggings, I roll my neck and start to stretch my arms in large circles. The freezing water laps against my toes, an enjoyable shiver rolling through me since I'll be sweating soon. Stepping forward into a lunge, I continue my usual lacrosse warm-up routine, making sure every muscle is properly stretched for my morning jog.

Starting the run slow, my feet slap against the recoiling waves as I follow its edge along the darkened sand. Before long, my arms are pumping and breath is visible in heated puffs. My calves burn as I push harder, my mind drifting to wonder what Avery is up to right now. Atlanta is three hours ahead of here, so she would be on her second cup of tea by now. I hope she's managing to hold her own with a house full of men, although even Wyatt had seemed to be softening before I left.

I skid to a halt seconds before colliding with the high metal fence marking the edge of the rental's property. I'd been so caught up in my thoughts, I almost hadn't noticed I'd already ran the two miles. Looking up, I see a bird fly overhead, having the freedom to travel beyond the fence. Not for the first time, I wonder if this 'vacation' is more of a prison sentence.

Grabbing for my phone, the screen lights up with a notification of a voicemail and my stomach plummets. No no no. I've trekked up and down this godforsaken beach countless of times trying to find signal, but somehow Avery managed to get through and I missed it. Tears fill my eyes as I desperately tap the screen but I have no bars again, I can't even listen to the voicemail she left. Falling to my knees in the sand, I hover over the device and pray for a miracle. I just need to know she's okay.

As the sun peeks over the sea, I give up hoping I might get to hear my best friend's voice and rise with my mood soured. Banishing my troubles, the only way I know how, through exercise, I push myself to my limits running back towards the house. My feet fly over the sand as the sun rises higher in the distance. Returning to the spot I stood in previously, I bend to rest my hands on my knees, gulping in mouthfuls of air and focusing on evening out my erratic heartbeat.

Glancing back at the house, I can't help my scowl. No matter how much I've tried to enjoy myself, a niggling feeling is keeping me in a constant state of unease. In all of its luxury, something about the house feels off. Mom makes good money, but surely almost three weeks here has amounted to a small fortune, yet she still hasn't given a clue as to when we might finally return home.

Both stories of the exterior are painted a powdered blue, with the loft bedroom I have claimed poking out at the top. Huge bay windows cover every back wall, ensuites included, to allow all rooms the spectacular views of a seaside sunset. I don't know why we needed to travel so far for a rental with six bedrooms but maybe it was all that was available at such short notice. Noticing mom's shadow pass by the kitchen window, I stroll to head back inside.

"How was your run?" Her cheery voice greets me as I walk straight for the fridge, grabbing a bottle of water from inside and downing half its contents. Already in her bikini top and linen shorts under a silk kimono, mom places a frying pan onto the electric hob. The rich glow to her skin from sunbathing blends with her free-flowing brown locks.

"Same as yesterdays." I answer blandly, leaning against

the granite counter and deciding to keep my voicemail a secret for now. With the protective way mom's been acting, she might confiscate my phone if she thinks I can use it for anything other than photos.

Contrasting with its surroundings, the interior of this place is magazine worthy. Pristine white cupboards line the kitchen wall, a double door chrome fridge matching the shiny appliances covering the counters. A shiny glass table fills the centre of the room with enough chairs to seat twelve comfortably.

"Well don't just stand there, fetch the bacon and eggs." She orders, despite the fake smile she's grown accustomed to wearing lately. Huffing, I take my time guzzling the rest of my water and refilling it from the tap before opening the fridge again. Returning with her ingredients, I hop up onto the counter beside the hob and watch her make our breakfast.

"Mom, seriously, when can we leave?" Her smile falters as she clenches her jaw impatiently. I know she is worried about the break-in at the Hughes' mansion, but how can we know what's happened since then? Maybe the intruders have been caught and charged already and there's no need to stay here any longer.

"I will have to return to work soon, but not yet. You should be having the time of your life. No school, no stress. What more could you possibly want?"

"Erm, Avery mainly. I don't think you understand the connection we have mom. I feel physically sick we haven't been able to–"

"Stop being so stupid!" She shouts, her brown eyes flickering furiously at me before she schools her features. Sighing deeply, her smile reappears and she leans over to grip my hand. "I'm sorry. I just want to keep you safe. As soon as I hear word we can return, we will."

"Hear word from who?" I question, wondering if she has a means to contact the outside world. By the roundness of her eyes, she hadn't meant to say that out loud. Flicking her hand through the air to end our conversation, she busies herself cracking eggs into the pan while I hop down to make some coffee. It's not like I have anything else to be doing.

Switching on the coffee machine, mom mentions there should be some more long-life milk in the pantry. Opening the glossy white door, I flick on the light and search the dozens of shelves within. Rummaging through the hundreds of tins and cartons, I find it odd there are still enough supplies to last months. Seriously, who kits out their holiday home like an apocalypse bunker and fails to install Wi-Fi?

"What shall we do today?" Mom asks as I return to make our drinks. She plates up scrambled egg and bacon onto bone-china plates and carries them over to the table with a stack of buttered toast. Following with two mugs of streaming coffee in my hands, I sit beside her and shrug.

"I'll probably chill indoors; I want to start rereading The Secret Garden." Mom rolls her eyes, moaning I should get some more sun - which would be true if I didn't burn like a crisp despite smothering myself in factor 50. After we've finished eating and taken turns washing up and drying, I'm more than ready to lose myself in my book. Mom slips her feet into her palm tree patterned flipflops and lifts her overly large beach bag onto her shoulder, complete with a stripy rolled towel poking out the top. Retrieving two bottles of water from the fridge, I place them into the bag and kiss her on the cheek.

"Maybe we can play a few board games this afternoon?" She asks hopefully. Keeping my smile in place, I nod even though I'm sick to death of playing board games with Coronal Competitive over here. Watching her leave, I sigh and let my shoulders sag. It's getting tougher by the day to see the love in her actions and not resent her for them. Jogging up the stairs, I open the door to the mini library/study.

A polished mahogany desk rests against the huge window, a similarly coloured leather chair pushed underneath and facing outwards. A fireplace sits on the right, which I presume is only for display since I haven't seen a chimney sticking out of the roof. Crossing the spongy cream carpet, I smooth my finger over the various tattered hardbacks lining the left wall. The bookshelves stretch from the floor to ceiling and have been filled with first editions. Whoever owns this place certainly is trusting. Finding the book I saw in here yesterday, I grip the aged cover gently and try to remove it from its dusty spot.

Albeit stiffly, I manage to wiggle the book a quarter of the way out before it jams. Another slight tug releases a click and an unlocking sound behind me. Turning slowly, I don't see anything out of place to begin with but on a second glance, a faint shadow of a line on the opposite wall is just visible. Glancing out of the window to check my mom is still sunbathing in the centre of the sand, I edge across the room. Prying my fingernails into the grove, a section of the wall begins to move outwards, moving the fireplace with it. I have to use my strength as I continue to shove it open until the inside is revealed.

The inner wall is a metal door, fit with a medieval style steel bar for sealing from the inside. Flicking the light switch on the inner wall, I find a small bunker within. A set of bunk beds with, what I presume are, vacuum packed sheets on the end of each mattress sitting against the left wall. A flimsy curtain hangs at the foot of the bunk, which screeches in protest against the metal pole supporting it as I pull it aside. The sight of my own reflection scares the shit out of me, my wide pale eyes staring back. Beneath the mirror is a compact toilet and sink, reminding me of a portaloo.

Stepping back and tiptoeing further inside, I find cupboards filled with similar long-life goods, as downstairs, and a first aid pack. A laptop and landline phone sit upon a small desk with a foldaway chair in the corner, which I rush over to. Lifting the phone to my ear, my heart bursts as a dial tone sounds from the receiver. Without sparing too much time on why a 'coastal retreat' needs a panic room or who might be listening in, I quickly dial Avery's number which I know off by heart. Anticipation thrums within me, causing me to shake slightly as the phone rings for what seems like hours. Finally, a muffled voice sounds through the other end in a curious 'hello?"

"Avery!" I scream.

# Wyatt

A loud bang jolts me from my sleep, the fluorescent overhead lights disorientating me as my head seizes tightly. Trying to sit up, my back aches from the twisted position I was lying in upon a wooden bench. Hands grab my shirt, dragging me upright from the bench and causing me to groan at the swift movement of my protesting body. Attempting to shove the overweight brute away brings my attention to my bound wrists behind me in painfully tight metal cuffs. Shoving me out of the cell, the uniformed dirtbag pushes me along a dimly lit hallway which gives my eyes a chance to adjust to the vice tight grip inside my head.

A guard dressed in black pushes the door open at the end of the hallway, glaring at me in disgust as I walk past. Squinting, I find myself being prodded through a busy police station. Stacks of paperwork rival towers of empty donut boxes on dozens of desks. Officers either scowl or completely ignore me as a strong hand grips my shoulder and pushes me through another set of metal doors. After removing the cuffs, he barks at me to sit down before leaving the interrogation room.

I round the table in the centre, rolling my wrists and twisting my back. Catching sight of myself in the two-way mirror, I can see why so many people looked upon me with such distaste. Even I'm appalled by my own reflection. My once-white shirt is covered in filth and blood which I'm going to guess is mine judging from the line of disposable stitches running across my temple and into my right eyebrow. Many of the shirt's buttons have been ripped off, my belt is missing and I realise I'm not wearing shoes. My hair resembles a bird's nest while my eyes are more bloodshot than green right now.

The door to my left opens to reveal a short Latino woman, seemingly with a chip on her shoulder if her rigid posture and grimace are anything to go by. Her navy uniform hugs her frame tightly and a shiny badge sways from her thick black belt. A similarly dressed male cop I recognise from somewhere trails in behind her and shuts the door.

"Master Hughes, is it? Take a seat." The Latino points to one of the collapsible chairs around this side of the table. Not having much of a choice, I fall into the closest chair despite the pain shooting through my back. My head is spinning slightly but I keep a calm expression on my face. Sitting opposite, she opens the brown folder she carried in and places it on the table. A mug shot I don't remember having taken is clipped to the inside cover, apparently before I was cleaned up since a blood smear covers my right cheek.

"Hughes as in Nixon Hughes? He owns the mansion up in Brookhaven?" The male cop asks. I nod slowly, trying my best to place his thinning hair and rounded belly. He makes a low whistle and smirks at me. "I didn't even know he had a son. I wonder what your old man would make of your overnight accommodation here."

"If you manage to contact him, feel free to ask." I reply bitterly, ignoring his previous comment. Little Latino, as I've decided to call her, clears her throat to regain control of the conversation.

"Master Hughes, you've been arrested for damage to private property, possession of drugs and assaulting a police officer. These are very serious charges." Staring at the picture on her file, I search my brain for the events that led me here. There was the emo hooker and her drugs, the fat rich guy and the mirror. Sliding my eyes to the male opposite me, a smile pulls at my lips. I remember him now.

"How fortunate you were so close by. What were you doing in Hellhole, Mr-" I lean forward to read his nametag, "Phallus?"

"It's Phillis you little shit, and I was undercover hunting for scum like you." He sneers, something resembling pink icing stuck in his overbite. Rolling my eyes and crossing my arms over the disgustingly soiled shirt I'm still wearing, despite however long I've been here, I lean back and ignore the rest of their waffling. Little Latino plays good cop and tries to reach my conscience as I laugh internally. I couldn't give less of a shit if they locked me up and threw away the key. In fact, it may be preferable since my life is rapidly swirling down the crapper and, bonus, I wouldn't have to see Avery for a long time.

"Don't say another word," the door bursts open with a loud clang. A bulky, dark haired man in a pinstripe navy suit strides in with a black briefcase in his hand. Chunky gold rings adorn his meaty fingers, a shiny gold watch to match poking out from his cuff. He casually takes a seat beside me, not seeming phased by the glowers he's receiving from across the table.

"Who the fuck are you?" I finally break the silence. I place him around mid-30s as his blue eyes slide to me.

"Jeremy Charlton, your lawyer." He extends his hand which I hesitantly shake, still confused as to why he's here.

"Did my father send you?" The easy smile on his face doesn't falter, but he doesn't answer my question either. Opening the leather briefcase, he pulls out images on PC Phallus raving it up in Hellhole and slides them across the metallic surface.

"My client was detained while the arresting officer was intoxicated, which makes his statement inadmissible in court. For all we know, you could have planted the drugs on my client in a bid to boost your career," he glares accusingly at the sweating man across from him. PC Phallus blubbers and grunts incoherently in anger, his face turning a beetroot red. "As the son of a billionaire, I'm certain you wouldn't want your boss to find out about this, so why don't we agree that my client walks out of here with his record intact and he, in return, will not press charges." My attorney cocks his eyebrows at me in question to his statement, so I shrug and nod. Following his lead, we both stand and exit the room without another word.

Ignoring the still present scowls as I stroll across the building, noticing my phone in a clear evidence bag on the edge of an empty desk. Swiping it, I push the double doors leading onto the main street outwards and breathe in deeply. The crisp air outside fills my lungs, the sun peeping around tall buildings. Charlton clears his throat as I begin to walk away, gesturing for me to slide into the black limousine parked against the sidewalk. His driver, dressed in a black suit and flat cap, flicks his half-finished cigarette to the floor and squashes it beneath his shiny loafer.

"Since when do attorneys offer to see their client's home or ride in limos?" I question. He pulls the door open with an easy smile, waiting for me to duck inside before following and slamming the door shut. The driver takes his seat up front and rolls up the dividing window in the centre.

"I'm not your attorney and you're not going home." Charlton chuckles as the limousine lurches forward and speeds away from the precinct.

∞∞∞

Pulling into a curved driveway, the vehicle circles a fountain to pull up beside a huge mansion. Twice the size of the one I grew up in judging from this angle. The curved doorway is surrounded by exposed, grey brick while the rest of the building is covered in a rich wood color. Darker grey tiles lie across the roof, which are visible by a sloped garage alongside the house.

Following Charlton out, I step onto the concrete and stretch my neck. Except for two toilet stops, we have been in the limo all day, allowing night to have nearly fallen. Thankfully, the mini bar was fully stocked and my road trip companion was friendly enough, filling me in on the Lakers/Celtics game last night and directing the driver to the closet drive thru, so I wasn't bothered where I was going. Another mile between me and my old life is nothing but a blessing in my eyes.

As soon as I close the door, the limo pulls away towards the garage. Two hugely muscled guys dressed all in black exit the mansion and make a bee line for me. Charlton steps aside as I'm roughly patted down, although where or what they think I'm hiding, I don't know. I removed my tattered shirt in the limo, so Mr Handsy only has my trousers to grope, my phone hanging loosely in the side pocket. Grunting, he slowly rises to his full height and stares down at me. His brown eyes assess me closely for a short while, then gestures to follow as he turns away.

Small lanterns either side of the main door flicker to life in the fading light of the sky as I pass. A vast staircase fills the centre of the hallway, gold banisters complimenting the sparkling chandelier high above. Open archways either side of the hallway lead further into the lower level, the same cream glossy wood flooring throughout. The guards lead the way toward the right, Charlton's shoes clicking loudly beside me as we stroll behind.

Meandering through a seemingly unused living room, Mr Handsy knocks upon a mahogany door and waits to be permitted entry. Once a voice sounds from within, he pushes the door open but nobody moves. All sets of eyes turn to face me, Charlton giving me a nudge with his shoulder so I enter the dimly-lit room.

I'm plunged into darkness as a click signals the door closing behind me. Straining my eyes, the outlines of a sideboard and desk tell me I'm in an office as I shuffle towards the armchair I noticed while I still had the light of the hallway to aid me. Finding the velvet material with my outstretched fingers, I round the chair and sit down to focus on the shadowed figure across the desk. Only the occasional orange glow from a cigar and his heavy breathing alerted me to his presence, as well as the air of danger he's shrouded in.

The silence stretches between us, my impatience starting to flare up but I bite my tongue. My instincts are telling me, despite the obvious cloak and dagger routine, this man isn't someone to trifle with. His watch ticks with each passing second, a rhythm I start to twitch my toes along with. Shifting forward across the desk dividing us, the man flicks on a lamp that stings my eyes momentarily.

Blinking to clear the spots from my vision, I settle upon the figure before me. His thinning slicked-back hair is a pale shade of grey, his skin scared with years of drug and alcohol abuse. Also topless, blurred and faded tattoos litter his sagging frame that must have once held muscles to rival the guards outside put together. A horizontal scar lies across his upper left side, judging by his age probably from a pacemaker being inserted. Fear freezes my blood flow like liquid nitrogen as I consider that this man could be a future glimpse of who I'm going to become.

"I've looked forward to meeting you Wyatt." His croaky voice fills the air, shaking me from my internal panic.

"How do you know my name? Why am I here?" The answering chuckle I receive is anything but reassuring. Lifting the lid on a personalized cigar box, a capital P showing through the glass on top, he slides it towards me in offering with a metal cutter. I shake my head slightly, more focused on what he has to say.

"When you've lived as long as I have, you learn who to keep tabs on. I'm man enough to admit Nixon Hughes almost had me fooled, along with the rest of the world." Creasing my eyebrows, I wonder which one of those sentences to focus on first. Has this man had his goons follow me, and if so for how long? And how does he know my father?

"Forgive me, you seem to know a lot about me but I'm unsure who I'm speaking with." I tread carefully, not wanting to become one of his guard's punching bags today. I haven't minded coming here, but suddenly I think I may be in over my head and don't have a way to get back home. Hell, I don't even know where I am.

"Where are my manners? Ray Perelli." He announces, as if the name should mean something to me. My blank expression causes him to frown. "He really didn't tell you anything, did he?"

"Who?" I ask, utterly lost now. Fatigue is starting to seep into my bones, the headache I'd managed to shake taking hold again. A bath and comfy bed would do me wonders right about now. Leaning forward into the light, his faded turquoise eyes contain a surprising amount of venom for his age.

"Your so-called father took something very precious to me long ago. There's a war coming between our families, and you have a choice to make, son. You're either with me or against me, and trust me when I say – you don't want to be against me."

# Avery

"Meg!" I scream in excitement. "Oh my god! I've missed you so-wait, why are you calling me from a blocked number?" Darting into my room, I lock the main and bathroom doors and throw myself back onto the bed. My hair spills all around me as I twist strands through the fingers of my free hand.

"It's a long story and I don't know how much time I have. Something weird is going on Ave, my mom is acting so shady and this house is like a secret lair or some shit. The cupboards are stocked with food and water for months so we never leave. I don't know what's got mom so spooked, but this is more than just worry for my safety." Her voice comes out in a rush of hushed whispers. My eyebrows crease as I try to understand what she's talking about.

"Wait, you're not on holiday having the time of your life?" Her scoff sounds through the headset. Sensing I'm not going to like what I'm about to hear, I shift my arm to fiddle nervously with the hem of her grey college sweatshirt, that I happen to have paired with my cropped lycra pants today.

"Absolutely not. I'm so bored and I want to see you. Hopefully, I can convince mom to let us leave soon." The sadness in her voice magnifies my own. At least when I thought Meg's absence was due to her having a lovely time away, I was able to console myself with thoughts of her travelling, climbing mountains or riding an elephant or something equally exotic and ridiculous.

"Hang on, rewind. Where exactly are you?"

"In some overly fancy beach house in the middle of butt-fuck nowhere. We drove through California, but that's where I lost track. What's strange is my mom knew the way here without needing my phone's sat nav, not that there's any signal to use it anyway. She's normally terrible at directions." Her voice trails off in thought, apparently hearing how odd it all seems now she's saying the words out loud.

"Dammit, it's not even like I could find you if I tried. Surely the beach is nice though right - if it's not a pebble one and the sand is the right texture. We both know you're a complete sand snob." A small breathy chuckle echoes in my ear, causing me to smile slightly. A lump is rising higher in my throat but I focus on keeping my tone light and even, not waiting her to know how lonely I am without her.

"Oh, it's a perfectly soft consistency. But it's just not the same without you. I wish you were here Aves. There's no technology either, not even a crappy old TV. If I have to play Monopoly one more time, I'm going to scream." The fact Meg isn't holding back her feelings is more than telling something really isn't right.

"But you're calling me so there's at least a phone. How come you didn't call sooner if you were this unhappy?" I try not to sound bitter, but my voice holds a trace of accusation that I internally berate myself for.

"That's the thing. I just found this creepy panic room hidden behind a false door. There's a laptop here, maybe I can find a clue as to where I am." I hear the tapping of keyboard keys and clicking of a mouse in the background. I desperately want to help her, but I feel so useless from here. Mentally clutching at straws, a glimmer of an idea filters into my mind.

"Oh, I think Dax knows some hackers - it's how he found me at the tattoo shop that time. Send me an email, I'll see if he can get an IP address or whatever from it."

"Oh god," she quickly changes conversations, the usual light tone to her voice returning, "I'm being so selfish! How are things with the guys? Wyatt behaving himself?" Unable to hide my scoff this time, I roll over into my stomach and push my hand into my hair.

"Wyatt's MIA. I'll fill you in when you get back, but I haven't seen him since about the time you left. The guys are fine, except Huxley who's struggling to readjust to normal life." I sum up as basically as I can, not wanting to burden her with my issues when she seems to have so many of her own right now. It's rare for Meg to talk so much so I'm more than happy to be the only one offering advice for a change. "Listen, don't worry about me. I'm fine and will be waiting here for you to get back. Please try to enjoy your time away, for the both of us. You'll be longing to go back when college starts again in September."

"Only if you're with me. I love you."

"Love you Meg." I disconnect the call, a single tear falling down my cheek. All this time I'd been holding onto the hope that at least my best friend was having a lovely summer, but it turns out she's as much at a loss as I am. It's always been this way between us though, almost as if we can sense the other's emotions. If I'm ever having a rough day, Meg will instinctively know to call or visit.

I hold my phone for a little while longer, waiting to see if an email might come through. By the sounds of it, something is definitely wrong with wherever she is staying. A panic room, no signal and Elena knowing her way without need for directions – all very suspicious. But what can I do other than lie here like a lemon and hope she comes back to me soon?

Sighing, I push myself back to my feet and head for the bathroom. Twisting the key and pulling on the handle, the door bangs against a heavy weight on the other side and a groan sounds. After hearing a shuffling inside, I'm able to open my door fully to reveal Huxley. Chocolate brown eyes land on me without a trace of apology as he teases a green and black stiped tongue piercing between his white teeth. His blonde waves are way past his shoulders now, giving him a lion's mane vibe that I would be digging if it weren't for the scowl on his face.

"Who were you talking to?" Huxley crosses his arms over a clean white t-shirt, refusing to back down despite being caught snooping. His stance widens in green checked pyjama trousers with bare feet poking out from beneath.

"Erm… excuse me?!" I ask in disbelief. Who the hell does this guy think he is? "That's absolutely none of your business." My face transforms into a mask of anger, letting him know just how much he is royally pissing me off.

Sighing and rolling his eyes, as if *I'm* the problem here, Huxley props his hip on the marbled counter. "How can I keep you safe if you withhold information from me?"

"I don't need you to keep me safe!" I shout for what seems like the hundredth time this week, flapping my arms about. I'm seriously done with having this conversation over and over. I've been more than patient, trying to coax his stubborn ass out from the walls he's built around himself. At one point, I was sure there was a romantic connection between us but that's well and truly fizzled out now. Sighing with exasperation, I turn to leave when his deepened voice finds me.

"I took a bullet for you." There it is. The ultimate guilt trip card he's been playing for weeks. If I could change anything about that day, I'd have gladly jumped between Huxley and said bullet - and I would have had twice the balls whilst healing too.

"Oh, did you? You haven't mentioned it before," I look over my shoulder to say, my voice laced with sarcasm. Pulling the door shut between us, I walk straight out of my room, knowing he's less likely to follow this far from his new-found comfort zone. First, he insisted I continued to sleep in his bed, then it was sitting on the counter while I showered and now, he's listening to my phone calls. Well fuck that. I've never belonged to anyone, and I'm certainly not going to play girlfriend now – especially when I don't even get the make-up sex after these petty arguments.

Jogging down the stairs, the 'ding' of the elevator shaft arriving chimes below. At least now I know Meg is thousands of miles away, my heart can stop filling with hope every time I hear the sound and I don't have the twisting in my gut when she doesn't walk out. Rounding the banister, I find all three of the house's other current occupants readying to step into the elevator, all in hoodies, sports shorts and sneakers. Upon seeing me, matching smiles break across all of their faces. One of these hunks would bring a girl to her knees, but when all three of them look at me that way, I have to resist the urge to melt into a puddle on the marble flooring and force my feet to move in a straight line.

"Hey, we were just heading out for some groceries. Since there's nothing else to do, we figured we'd save both Susie and our sanity for a little while." As acting head of the household (which is hilarious since he's never fricking here), Wyatt must be the one to allow Susie to return to work. Until said blessed event occurs, our cook has been running around doing our shopping, cooking batches of reheatable meals, the laundry and any errands we need. I reckon she's as bored as we are at the moment.

"Oh please, *please,* take me with you!" I beg, pressing my hands together in prayer and fluttering my eyelashes. Garrett kicks his foot out to stop the sliding doors from closing and mock bows as I smile and skip past. Joining me inside the metal walls, Axel's fingers slide into mine as Dax slips his arm around my shoulders. Usually I'd push out of this protective bullshit, but in light of Meg's misery and my run-in with Huxley, I'll take any small slither of comfort I can get right now. Garrett steps in and finally lets the doors close, transporting us down into the underground garage.

As the boys cross the darkened space, each light flickering on with the sense of moment below, I quickly dive into the closet to my left. Ignoring the heaps of jacket and coats loaded onto brass hooks along the side, I rummage through various storage boxes beneath to find my matching white Converse. Pushing my feet inside, I jog over to the burnt orange Nissan as the engine roars to life.

Dax is in the driver's seat, one arm slung across the wheel while the lovebirds are whispering in the back. Sliding into the passenger seat, Dax accelerates the second my door is shut. Hastily buckling myself in as we emerge from the underground ramp onto the gravelled driveaway, I glance over the shadows falling upon the bushes lining the front of the house on instinct. Nothing seems out of place, but these days I am trying to be extra vigilant.

Bright amber eyes catch my attention in the side mirror, a mischievous smirk on Axel's face matches the look Garrett is giving me in the rear-view mirror. They are both looking at me like they did that day I entered Axel's room. The image of Garrett roughly gripping my hips and ramming into me from behind while Axel tugged on my hair as I sucked him off flashes to mind, causing my cheeks to heat and core to pulse.

Clenching my thighs together tightly, I attempt to casually slide down from their eyelines to hide the blush, although the chuckle that sounds behind tells me they know just how much I'm affected by their mind games. I don't think I'll ever get used to having the attention of so many hot guys at once, not that I'm particularly complaining. Although I'd be lying if I said I wasn't counting down the days for them all the return to college and for my life to resume some type of normality.

# Axel

Spooning the last chunk of cookie dough from the ice cream tub, I lean over to Avery and pop it into her mouth. Her bright blue eyes twinkle in the fading sunlight and her smile warms me from the inside out, despite the chill descending upon us with the last glow of the sun. The sun setting over Atlanta has been stunning from this hilltop we found, hues of red and orange bleeding into the sky which already has a few stars shining through. But still, none of it compared to the blonde sitting beside me. Lights begin to appear amongst the shadowed buildings far below as we dangle our legs over the ledge.

"This was exactly what I needed." Avery sighs contentedly. I think this afternoon was what we all needed. Grocery shopping consisted of Garrett piling items high in the trolley, while Dax pushed it with Avery leaning over the bar. Every time Gare was distracted by another aisle of sugar snacks, I would slip out some of the high-calorie rubbish he doesn't actually need and snuck in actual food we can cook with. Apparently, I'm the only one trying to maintain our strict nutritional diet the basketball coach usually has us on, if it wasn't for me and the list I'd made, we all would have been on popcorn for breakfast and pop tarts for dinner for the foreseeable future. Although, I have to admit his idea to grab some cooked pizzas from the ready-made counter and tubs of ice cream for an impromptu four-way date night was a hell of an idea. But remembering to buy some plastic spoons was all me and I want full credit for that.

"How come you didn't go to college with Meg?" Dax

breaks the silence, his eye line tracing the lettering on Meg's grey sweater Avery is wearing. 'ATLANTA' sitting central is bold red, above a circular logo of two lacrosse sticks forming an X with a ball in the bottom section. Avery looks down herself before shrugging and focusing back on the horizon.

"Not really a people person, I guess. Mom and Nixon liked having me there when they weren't working and I got to do lessons in my pyjamas." she smirks, but my frown is mirrored in Dax's face. Garrett moans sensually from behind us, sitting on the hood of Huxley's car and fully invested in his fourth pizza. Even though I know his reasoning and I'm more than used to it by now, it still baffles me how Gare's first priority will always be food. We could be in a room of America's hottest models butt naked, but for Gare the buffet table would still win every time.

"Don't you worry you've missed out on living a normal life?" Dax asks quietly, his hesitation evident by the shy side glance he gives her. Avery simply laughs dryly.

"I've lived enough to last me a lifetime and nothing about it has been normal. If I can hide away and enjoy the rest of my days in peace and solitude, that'll be good enough for me." I stare out into the night sky, wondering if she really meant that. Avery's been through more shit than all of us combined, but I had expected her resilience to blur into all aspects of her life. From that statement, it almost seems to me like she's given up on attempting to have a future, and for such a free and strong spirit, that seems like a crime to me.

"Surely there's more you'd want to experience. To see the world, achieve amazing things, be loved and have a family?" I ask, unable to help myself. Her head turns my way as she seems to consider my question.

"Every day I continue to wake up is another fight I have to face. It shouldn't be a mission to simply get by, but to me it is. I've been broken and never properly put back together. So no, I don't want to be loved. My life was ruined for me; I refuse to

waste energy trying to fix it for the sake of those around me."
Her eyes shine with the truth that she genuinely believes her
words.

"It doesn't have to be that way." I clasp her chin and pull
her towards me. Placing my lips softly on hers, I kiss her for a
long moment before pulling back. I've never been one for pretty
words, so hopefully my actions speak for themselves. There's a
whole world out there, and if it doesn't have Avery in it then
there's no such thing as justice.

Avery links her fingers through mine and leans into me,
her hair tickling my arm in the gentle breeze. Glancing over her
head, Dax's face is covered by shadows as he stares out at the
horizon, his posture rigid as he hugs his knees into his chest. I'm
about to ask if he's okay when Garrett throws himself between
him and Avery with a thud.

Slipping his arm around her waist, he drags Avery
roughly from my body and into his. The dents appearing in his
cheeks taunt me with a shit eating grin as I roll my eyes. A
choked noise comes from Avery as she elbows Gare's chest and
rises from his hold. Without a second glance, she retreats back
to the Nissan and slams the door shut once inside. "Nice one,
asshole." Dax grumbles, brushing down his shorts as he stands
and leaves too.

"What did I do?" Gare asks me, although his smirk tells
me he knew exactly what he was doing, ruining my moment
with Avery. For someone who shares partners so easily, Garrett
can be a possessive prick. Whether that power move was out of
jealously for Avery's or my benefit though, I'm not sure.

"You can be a real cock sometimes, you know that,
right?" I can't help to smile back when he's giving me that look –
all dimples and a cocked eyebrow. The engine begins to rumble
behind us, signalling it's time to leave. I rise to my feet, offering
Gare my hand to pull his heavy weight up.

"Thinking about my cock again?" he winks and strides

away while I flip my middle finger up at his retreating back. "I saw that," he shouts over the sound of Dax revving the vehicle impatiently and I chuckle as I follow.

Sitting on my open window ledge, I watch as a group of guards walk across the manicured lawns towards other members of their team for the midnight cross over. I could never have a job that required standing on high alert all night, I need my sleep but I guess someone has to do it. From this distance, they all appear the same - huge tanks of men, dressed all in black. Guns strapped across their uniformed bodies glint in the moonlight as they walk past the darkened pool house.

My thoughts drift to Wyatt, wondering where he is or what he's doing. Ever since we met, he has been the one to insist our group stays together and, failing that, in constant contact with one another. He hated being forced to come home for the occasional holiday, saying he felt guilty for leaving his real family back at college without him. Seems like that doesn't matter to him anymore, since I welcomed Avery into our fold. And rightly so - I stand by my decision. Not because she's his real sister, because she deserves a place to belong with like-minded people who understand her. I'm sure he'll come around once he's had time to adjust but I really miss his presence.

Shuffling within the room alerts me that Garrett has returned from his midnight snack hunt. Pulling the window closed, I turn and walk across the room while he stuffs a cracker into his mouth. "Where did all the M&M's and Cheeto's go?" he mumbles. I shrug, switching off the bedside lamp and slipping into bed, needing to hide my terrible poker face.

Gare dives into bed with all the grace of a small elephant and rolls over to hug me. Even though he can't stop the night terrors plaguing me each night, just having him right there when I wake up is more than enough until the next night rolls around. His arm slips beneath my head as his chest meets my back, our legs tangling together. Inhaling and exhaling deeply, I ease myself into a calm state, attempting to keep the bad dreams at bay, even though it's never worked before.

*"Axel honey, come on in. Don't be shy." No, please no. Looking up and down the hallway, I briefly consider running but I've tried that before, the outcome is the same. Running a hand through my hair, I release a sob at its silky texture. I'm not that boy anymore, but I still don't know how to get out of this never-ending loop. Bracing my hand on the handle, I shudder slightly as I turn the nob and open the door into the ballroom.*

*The space is filled with women of all ages in fancy ball gowns. In unison, they turn to glare at me. Gloved hands ball into fists, perfectly painted lips sneer. A walkway down the centre of the crowd has been left clear for me, my mother waiting expectantly at the podium on the other end. A sparkling champagne coloured dress hugs her surgery perfected body, her usual pearl necklace hanging around her slender neck.*

*Stepping onto the shiny floor, my shoes echo loudly in an otherwise silent space as I make my way towards her. With each step closer, my mother's hands begin to change to a deep shade of crimson. The stain grows until I reach the raised platform, stopping just short of her wrists. Following my eyeline, she smiles wickedly and lifts a skinny index finger to paint the color across her lips.*

*"This is all your fault," she smirks down at me. Confusion seeps in with a feeling of unease as I look around. Pale, bare feet poking out from behind mother's dress catch my attention. Sidestepping the opposite way, I find Avery's blonde hair fanned around her as she lies lifelessly on the stage. Making a move to rush to her, hands grab me from behind and pull me backwards. Arms hook across my chest*

*with impossible strength yanking me further away from Avery and
my cackling mother.*

*"It's all your fault!" the crowd shout and jeer over and over
again. I try to set my feet so I can't be moved anymore but it doesn't
work and soon I'm too far back and too surrounded to even see the
podium. I reach out desperately, tears filling my eyes as I scream her
name. I've failed her again, like I do every night in every scenario.
I'll never be able to save Avery when I can't save myself from these
visions. The first tear spills from my eye and everyone freezes, my
mother suddenly appearing before me. Her dark hair has started to
fall from her flawless chignon and the bloodstain has smeared from
her lips across her cheek.*

*"You see, you are weak. Real men don't cry, which is why you
will forever be stuck as this pathetic, little boy."*

I shoot upright in bed, forcing Garrett to flinch. My skin is
clammy as I run a hand over my shaved head instinctively. Gare
slips his arms around my middle but I shake him off, keeping my
face angled away from him. "It's okay," he soothes, rubbing my
back. I spin around in the hazy light of morning and glower at
him angrily.

"No Garrett, it's not okay. Real men don't cry and they
don't screw other men." I regret my words immediately at the
flash of hurt reflected in Gare's hazel eyes, but clearly my subconscious was trying to tell me something. It's my own mind
that conjures these images and words each time I close my eyes,
these are my thoughts. I try to rise from the bed but Garrett's
hand clamps down on my bicep to keep me in place.

"Now, you listen to me." He grips my face roughly and
forces me to face him. His eyes are churning with emotion like a
wild hurricane is trapped within them. Shifting his body so we
are directly opposite each other, he grabs my hand and pushes it
down on his left pec forcefully before copying the action with
his palm on my chest.

"This is real. It may not be some poetic love story like

in the movies. It's twisted and dark and something no one else will understand, but this is us and it's 100% real. I will be here to kiss away every nightmare, hold you every time you cry, love you because you don't know how to love yourself. And I refuse to let you self-sabotage what we've got going because, for the first time in my life, I actually feel something I've never felt for anyone."

I stare at him in stunned silence. I honestly didn't think Garrett thought about anything other than his dick and his next meal, not particularly in that order. He didn't specifically say those three words, but he definitely insinuated he loves me. I try to think of something to say back but there's only one word filling my mind – why? I don't have anything to offer him, just a broken shell of a man. The tears from my dream finally fall, rapidly soaking my cheeks.

"Make the pain go away" I beg, tremors still having a slight control over my body. Garrett strokes his fingers up my arms and gently takes a hold of my face between his hands. Looking deep into my eyes as the sun's rays spill through the curtain, he whispers "I'll do my best," before his lips connect with mine.

# Wyatt

Stretching across the wide mattress from the ends of my fingers to the tips of my toes, I sigh contently. I haven't seen Ray since the evening I arrived, but the last two days have been pure bliss. Despite the small army of guards I've seen walking through the mansion, other than bumping into Charlton on occasion and the staff, I've pretty much had this place to myself. It occurred to me rather quickly this is probably an easier way for whoever Ray's 'family' are to keep watch over me. But as long as they keep the food and booze coming, I'm happy to play along.

A knock sounds at the door, announcing breakfast bang on time. "Come in," I shout and pull the cover tightly around my waist. Rachel, the live-in cook/cleaner pops her head around the door with a large smile. Nudging the way in with her hip, she easily balances a tray in one hand and a glass of cranberry juice in the other.

"Did you sleep well?" she asks, her perfectly curled brown locks pulled into a ponytail at her nape. I nod and accept the tray with a thanks, groaning in delight at the smell. Fried eggs on toast with sausages wrapped in bacon, just the way my mom used to make. On weekends, when she wasn't travelling the globe to film the latest blockbuster movie, mom would cook me a breakfast like the one in my lap, before a day filled with one of our adventures to the forest or beach. Rachel hands me the glass and produces two small tablets from her apron's front pocket, stroking my hair softly as I pop them into my mouth and guzzle down the juice.

"That's a good boy. You need your vitamins," her kind smile brings my own out. A sense of calm and peace fills me at her presence. "Ray would like to see you this evening, so make sure you freshen up and take your pick from the clothes in the wardrobe." I nod, the motion making my hair bounce upon my head. As Rachel backs out of the room, I toss my head side to side enjoying the way my hair flops from ear to ear.

Remembering the breakfast in my lap, I tuck in and moan in between mouthfuls. Rachel's cooking isn't exceptionally different from Susie's, but I don't ever remember enjoying her food this much as a child. Each mouthful is a burst of flavor, overriding my senses so I don't hear the sexual noises I'm making until I've swallowed.

An image of Garrett flickers to mind as I think how much he would enjoy being here, waited on hand and foot with as much food as he could want. My mood sours, realising I haven't thought about my brethren in days. How could they have slipped my mind like that when they've been an integral part of my life for years? Reaching over to the bedstand, I pull out the drawer to grab my phone.

The battery is extremely low, flashing red but the screen lights up long enough to show I have hundreds of missed calls, voicemails and messages. Using my thumb, I scroll down the list getting the gist of every message despite flicking through quickly. Even Avery's name in amongst them, making my appetite flee completely. How dare she ruin my breakfast when I'm over here, doing my own thing. Pushing the tray further down the bed, I toss the phone onto the bed as I rise. Crossing the room butt naked, I walk into the ensuite for a cold shower.

Why does she have to crawl so deeply beneath my skin, taunting me with the life I could never have? I didn't want her as an adopted sister and I definitely don't want her as my fucking twin. I want her in the most forbidden way, making me the monster of the century. Literally no better than the bastard that hurt her as a child, which is why I've decided I can never see her again. Pretend she doesn't exist so I can actually move onto someone else, someone perfectly uncomplicated and available.

Stepping into the spray, my body barely registers the freezing temperature the dial says it should be. My skin feels taut and numb. After working a lather into my hair, I continue to wash my body with the remaining suds. Unnerved by the lack of feeling anywhere, I start to scrape my nails across my skin in various places to try to find a spot where I'm not completely desensitised. Giving up, I wash out the shampoo and exit the cubicle. The mirror hanging opposite shows red scratch marks covering my body, some deep enough to draw pricks of blood. Yet I don't feel a thing. My eyes are bloodshot with haggard bags hanging darkly beneath them, my whole face appearing aged despite the fact I've never felt better. Wrapping a fluffy towel from the warming rack around my middle, I go in hunt of fresh clothes.

The wardrobe is full of dry-cleaned items in plastic sleeves filling the top rail and rows of smart and casual shoes lined along the base, fortunately all in my size. Ignoring the various fancy suits, I reach for a white polo and the only pair of dark jeans. Once dressed, I rub the towel over my dripping wet hair until it's in a damp mess. Smoothing it back with my hand, I head to the drawers and shove some socks onto my feet before leaving the room.

Practically skipping from my assigned room, I hop up onto the golden banister and slide all the way down. Landing on both feet at the bottom, I raise my arms above my head and puff out my chest like an Olympian. Rachel walks through the hallway, clapping enthusiastically. My lips curve up into the wide smile that appears whenever she's around. Offering her my arm, the shoulder height brunette accepts and I escort her to wherever she is headed.

Rachel must be in her sixties, the ease in which she carries herself around the mansion speaking of years of service here. Beneath her white apron, a black dress sits on her rounded frame, featuring baggy short sleeves and a white collar. Her feet are in black, flat pumps allowing her to move about the house silently.

"Why don't you spend some time in the games room today?" She asks, leading me past yet another unused living area. This one has a deep red corner sofa in front of a vast fireplace, filled with logs and begging to be lit. The east side of the mansion is much bigger, featuring a massive dining room, ballroom, library, indoor gym complete with pool and sauna, even a home cinema. One day I'm going to own a home like this I've decided, paid with money I've worked my ass offfor and earned myself.

Pulling me to a halt in front of a black door I've yet to explore, Rachel pushes down the handle and reveals the goods inside. Black out curtains are drawn, the space only lit by long blue bulbs trailing the edges of the ceiling. In the centre, a black and red gaming chair with an attached metal footrest is fixed to the floor. I've read about the new 4D Turbo simulation chairs, but I hadn't realised they'd been released yet. The wall beyond holds three large screens, a low cabinet beneath holding various game consoles. On top of the surface lies a range of equipment from controllers, headphones and a VR headset.

"Holy shit! My boys would love this!" I yell, swiftly moving to grab a controller and leap into the gaming chair. When Rachel had said 'games room', I'd envisioned a poker or ping pong table, but this is epic. How have I been here two days and I'm only being shown this room now?

"Well, it's all for you my dear. You can have everything you've ever dreamed of if you side with us." She whispers close to my ear from behind. Her fingers soothe into my hair, gently caressing me as I switch on the PlayStation. The screens light up with a surround view of the war-style game I've chosen, a vibration sifting through the chair beneath me at the first sound of gunfire. "I'll bring you some snacks," Rachel promises as she leaves me to it.

Speakers all around the room immerse me fully into the game, the overhead lights flickering in time to the bullets and bombs landing all around me. The first round I merely stand in the middle of the battlefield, sacrificing myself as the other online player's target practice. Each time the chair vibrates, I enjoy the one sensation my skin has felt so far today as well as marvel in how hi-tech every element of this room is considering the house's owner is almost on his deathbed. Reaching for the headset and slipping it over my ears, I soon find myself welcomed into an online team where I can begin to show my real gaming talents.

"Get out the way you stupid mother- "

"Wyatt my dear, Ray is ready to see you now." A soft voice in the doorway pauses my shouting but also puts me off so my character on screen is shot clean through the head by a sniper. Dumping my controller onto the surface and spinning, I see Rachel has changed into a casual denim jumpsuit, announcing the end of her shift for today. She delivered homemade pizza to me earlier, amongst the bowls of popcorn and crisps that kept appearing. The sun is no longer trying to seep in around the curtains and I stifle a yawn. Silently promising to come back and spend the night in here, I stand and stretch before following Rachel to Ray's office.

After being permitted entry, I stroll into the room and take my seat like last time. Once again, only the lamp lights the room but I reckon Ray is deliberately trying to project a menacing vibe.

"My apologies for not calling for you sooner, my life has always been... hectic - for lack of a better word. I do hope you're enjoying your time here with us?" I hum and nod, sitting on my fidgety fingers that are itching to get back to the PlayStation. The outline of Ray's sinister grin catches my attention. "Have you thought any more on my proposition to join our family?" I shrug, the scent of a recently smoked cigar making my head a little woozy.

"Meh, why not? It's not like I have another family waiting for me." A stab of guilt strikes my heart at the mental image of my Shadowed Souls. I made them my family when my own failed me. But realistically, how long are they going to stick around? After college, we'll all venture into our separate jobs, make new friends, promise to stay in touch but the time between calls and meet-ups will get longer until eventually, they have their own lives. Wives and kids, and no room for me.

"I like you Wyatt, I'm starting to think we should have approached you years ago." A croaky cough across the table turns into a heavy splutter as a wrinkled hand reaches for a glass of whiskey. Slowly downing the glass' contents, Ray sighs and murmurs 'that's better.' Damn, this guy is so cool.

"What do you want with me exactly? Surely I'm not here just to eat your food and enjoy the amenities of your home." Ray shakes his head slowly, an evil glint to his pale eyes.

"Whether you choose to join us or not, I've brought you here for what you deserve. The truth. I'm about to tell you everything Nixon has ever kept from you. Your whole life has been a lie, son, but I have the power to set you free."

# *Avery*

Kneeling down in the soil in my denim shorts, I stare up at the tall honey blossom tree at the edge of our property. My mum would bring me down here on sunny days like this, to sit beneath the pastel pink canopy with a picnic basket and woollen blanket. The dirt surrounding the trunk lies in a perfectly neat circle, as I requested of the gardener last week.

Opening my tote bag, I pull out a small metal spade and begin to dig. Working my way further into the soil, I make a cylinder shape around three-foot deep from the surface before I'm satisfied. Placing down the spade, I reach into my bag and pull out the long urn I had intended for mum. The biodegradable container was to be planted with the seeds of another honey blossom by the three of us in our own personal ceremony, far from the cameras and tabloids. I'd hoped this would have given Wyatt the closure he clearly needs and would have bound us all closer together. Surrounding this tree with mum safely beneath it, we could have finally been the family she'd always wanted us to be. But it's too late now.

Opening the urn, I look through the items I've spent all morning collecting to fill it with. A pathetic attempt to recreate her aura really, but I needed to do this for my own benefit. In all this time, I haven't had the opportunity to say goodbye properly, especially since Wyatt robbed me of that chance. Her ruby teardrop earrings are delicately placed on the fabric of her favourite teal and gold scarf. The photoshopped picture from Nixon's office showing her cuddling me with Wyatt curled around the edge. I can't see the other items stuffed in the bottom but I know the page from her favourite book, Henry James' 'The Portrait of a Lady', a ticket from our last musical, and wedding ring are down there.

Securing the lid tightly in place, I slide the container into the hole I've created in the earth and begin to cover it using my hands to push the soil back in place. I haven't prepared anything to say, but the moment seems to need some sort of speech. The wind has eased and the leaves in the tree have stopped rustling, the garden around me waiting in silence for my next move. I can almost feel a presence beside me as I stare of the mound of dirt.

"Oh, mum. I'm probably talking to myself, but I have to believe you're around me. It's the only way I'm getting by at the moment. I want to make you proud and be all the things you'd dreamed for me, but I don't think it's possible. I think we're both going to have to settle for me being satisfied with how I am now. Placid. Content.

I have been broken for so long, it was only you that made me whole. When you were holding my hand, life came so much easier. No one other than you and Meg saw the real me, but she's not around either at the moment. Everyone expects me to just move on, forget about you and look to the future but it's so much harder than they realise. Especially when Wyatt is in such denial about his own feelings. I really wish you'd told me the truth, not that it would have made much difference. You were my mum in all the ways it mattered; I don't need a piece of paper to tell me what my heart already knew.

I'm sure you're watching me from the other side, I need something to believe in. One day we will be together again, somewhere our souls can run freely. Until then, I pray that you rest peacefully."

Taking the last object from my bag, a decorative plaque, I push the pointed end into the heap. The black granite shines in the sunlight, gold letters etched into the stone. Her name is scripted beautifully over the inscription *"The tears in my eyes I can wipe away but the ache in my heart will always stay"* with golden roses either side. I sit a while longer staring at the bark in front of me, remembering the way she would drop everything to simply hold me every time I needed a hug. No words were needed, she would comfort me silently with her actions.

A large shape rustling against the bush beside the stone wall makes me jump to my feet, fear leaking into my bones as I realise I'm out here alone with nothing to protect myself. A guard in a dark navy uniform raises his hands defensively and mutters an apology before walking back the way he came. Leaning against the thick trunk until my heart stops racing, I glance around the open space stretching before me. Lush green covers the lawn all the way back to the mansion, ideal for the marquee summer parties mum would have been hosting around this season.

Each year, a huge white tent would in in the middle of the grass kitted out with a temporary dance floor and small orchestra. Cream covered tables displaying an array of fancy French delicacies and filled glasses of champagne would line the back, for all those posh snobs that can't afford to put on a pound but drink like sailors. As an adopted teen, I'd hated those fundraisers for the various orphanages the Hughes donated to. Although I understood the cause better than anyone, these were the only times I felt like my adoption was a power move to promote their charity work as I was paraded around in gorgeous summer dresses and dainty jewellery.

The only saving grace was Meg, who was also forced to attend and dress in similar attire. There's a framed photo on my vanity from such an occasion when we were 15. Meg and I are wearing matching white halter necks adorned in a sunflower print and my mum standing in the middle, hugging us into her sides. Her dress is stunning, a fitted black maxi dress with pink lilies floating across the bottom and a thigh high slit. The sun is shining brightly upon the three of us, mimicking the glow of mum's wide smile. Even though I hadn't wanted to pose for it at the time, that has to be my all-time favourite photo – the two people I love most in this world in one single image.

Collecting my bag from the ground, I blow the plaque a kiss goodbye and trek back across the grounds towards the mansion. It's a beautiful summer's day, warm enough to brown up my tan but not too hot that I'm streaming in sweat. There's not a cloud in sight in the flawless blue sky. I ignore the multiple guards lining the wall, trying to pretend there's not still a threat out there somewhere. Surely if they still wanted me, they would have tried to attack again by now – but we can't relieve the guards until we have news from the police they've been located.

Rounding the pool house, every window teasing me with the darkness inside, I hear the repetitive sound of a basketball bouncing. Throwing my bag onto the sun lounger Wyatt always favoured, I walk over to the high fence surrounding the basketball court and watch Dax dunk the ball into the hoop. Regaining control of the ball, he dribbles up and down the court while I enjoy the view far too much.

Wearing blue shorts, white sneakers and nothing else, I drool over the rippling muscles covering his abdomen. With each twist of his deeply tanned body, his chest flexes in time with his rounded biceps. Even the hardness of his calves are affecting me as he runs across the tarmacked surface. His icy blue eyes catch sight of me, halting his solo game as he catches the ball and walks towards me.

"Have you been staring at me for long?" He cocks a brow, looking down on me through the gaps in the fence. I feel the blush lining my cheeks but hope I can pass it off as slight sunburn. Dax rests his fingers on top of mine, that are poking through the metal separating us.

"Of course not, I noticed your game kinda sucks considering you play on a team." Throwing his head back on a laugh, his huge blonde afro bounces around his face wildly. Retracting his fingers with a slow stroke against the lengths of mine, he beckons me to enter the court.

"You have the talk, but let's see if you have to balls to back it up, shall we?" Bouncing the ball towards me as I enter, I catch it easily with a smirk. Dribbling the ball in a circle around him, I stop when we are face to face again and give him a cocky smirk.

"Did you really think I lived in a mansion with its own personal court, and never practised shooting a ball?" I mock, turning to throw the ball towards the hoop. Bouncing off the backboard, it slips into the net with a satisfying 'swoosh'. Grinning to myself that I managed to pull that off in his presence, I don't hear Dax move behind me until his whisper breathes into my ear.

"No using the backboard in my rules." His hands smooth around the front my t-shirt, holding my flat stomach as he presses his body against my back. Suddenly hot for a very different reason, I focus on keeping my breathing even which Dax makes really difficult by running his tongue up the shell of my ear.

"Are there any other rules I should know about?" I manage to ask without a quiver to my voice, needing a moment to compose myself. Shifting his hands, one trails up the inside of my arm before coming to rest lightly across my collar-bone while the other winds around my body to hold my hip in place.

"No more rules, but if I catch you using that backboard again, travelling with or carrying the ball, there will be punishments." He breathes seductively, grinding his groin against my ass. In the next second, he's halfway across the court retrieving the ball while I'm left clenching my thighs and really wanting to do any and all of the three things he just told me not to.

Never one to back down from a challenge, like the one shining in his eyes, I step between Dax's smirk and the hoop.

Keeping my eyes focused on his body language, I notice a slight jerk in his right knee. Following my instincts, I lunge right while he fakes left and steal the ball from right beneath his huge hand. The shock on his face makes me laugh as I step out of his grasp and shoot the ball straight over his head. The orange sphere circles the hoop twice before dropping through the middle.

Collecting the ball, I round the court while bouncing it beneath my palm to resume the position Dax was just in. Pretending to yawn, he stretches one arm behind his head while the other hand trails down his washboard abs to the waist band of his shorts. Pushing the material down slightly to reveal a hint of blonde curls nested underneath, my mouth goes dry at the display. Biting my lip hard enough to split it, I do what any logical, rational person would in this situation.

Throwing the ball into his gut, Dax grunts as I retrieve the ball from the ground and continue to make my way to the hoop. Lifting the ball above my head with one hand to aim, Dax plucks it from my grip and chuckles as I attempt to get it back. Lowering it back into my reach, I try to swipe it but he's too fast for me, twisting around to shoot the ball straight into the net.

Running towards the ball, Dax grabs my waist and tosses me aside so he can get there first. "No fair!" I shout, not that I'm surprised. Every time I've seen the guys play ball together, they always play dirty. But if that's the way he wants it – I'm about to make this game fricking filthy. Heading back over to the fence, I grip the hem of my t-shirt and pull it over my head. Luckily for me, I spent the first half of the morning practising ballet so I'm still wearing a black sports bra that really enhances my cleavage.

The resulting 'thump, thump, thump' as the ball Dax has dropped bounces away is music to my ears, having the exact affect I intended. Feigning innocence, I roll my shoulders and twist my torso while Dax's jaw trails the floor as he advances on me.

# *Dax*

Holy shit. Nearing Avery, who is holding her leg behind her pretending to stretch, I can't take my eyes off her curves. She is rounded in all the right places with a tight cinch to her waist. Decorative black ink draws a path up her inner arms and intricately patterned teardrops on each of her ribs poke out from the sports bra. Her hair is floating around her like a sheet of liquid gold as I get close enough for her to look up at me. Fluttering those naturally thick eyelashes as me, my fingers itch to touch her.

Avery is her own brand of sex on legs, but to me the most appealing part is how she doesn't give a shit what anyone else thinks. The world is full of too many fakes, smothered in make-up or hiding behind fashionable clothing. Avery wears whatever is comfortable and carries herself with confidence. A refreshing rarity in my eyes. The tattoos lining her body speak of her resilience to anyone who might attempt to bring her down. She will always survive and adapt, not that I'll ever let harm come to her as long as I'm around.

Unable to hold back any longer, I bend to grip the back of her thighs and lift to trap her between the fence and my body. I've forced myself to hold back from my desires thus far, especially since Garrett has been hounding her like a dog in heat almost every day, but from the persuasive look in her eyes, I'm not sure why I did. Pinning her in place with my hips, my dick rapidly hardening between us, I let my hands roam her creamy thighs and exposed mid-section. Smoothing my thumbs along the edge of the fabric, I explore the line beneath her heavy breasts and she pushes her chest out ever so slightly. Sliding a hand around the back of her neck, I pull her into the kiss I've been dying to give her each time she walks into a room.

Soft touches of our lips soon turn heated, forcefully crashing against each other in a bid to get closer. Avery's nails scrape gently across the top of my back while her other hand grips my hair. Holding my head firmly in place, she eagerly pushes her tongue into my mouth. A low moan escapes me as our tongues duel and fight for control. Arching her back, she presses her chest against my bare one in a way that has me growling. Pushing my hands between us, I fondle her luscious tits through the thin material separating me from them. Avery squirms and groans as I massage her breasts in time with grinding my now painfully hard cock against her core. The heat radiating from her centre makes my mouth water with anticipation, thirsty for a taste of her knowing it'll be the sweetest nectar in the world.

Returning my hand to her thigh, I drag my thumb along the incredible softness lining the inside until I reach the edge of her denim shorts. Sensing Avery's impatience by the iron grip her legs tighten to around my waist, I slip my thumb under the thick material to feel a lacy fabric underneath. Avery gasps into my mouth as I push the pad of my thumb roughly onto where her small bud should be, her groan telling me I've found the right spot. Rubbing the material against her in small circles, Avery bites down on my bottom lip and grinds against me. Pushing both hands through my overly long hair, her nails draw lines across my scalp in a way that makes my toes curl.

"Avery," I rasp against her mouth, beginning to spiral too far into lust to remember I'm not this kind of guy. I don't sleep around like the others; I believe in having a meaningful connection before I take a girl to bed. And for someone like Avery, that has never needed to be truer. She deserves to be cherished and adored, although I'm not sure she has realised that yet. Retracting my thumb, her protesting whine almost has me ripping the shorts from her body and doing exactly what I've been daydreaming about for weeks. Using my hands to support her while I reluctantly step back and settle her down onto the ground, I fiddle with a strand of my hair.

"I'm sorry, I shouldn't have crossed that line." I breathe, starting to wonder if I made the right choice. But how can I take what she's so willingly offering when she won't be receiving the real me in return? "I think, now more than ever, what you need is a friend." A flash of confusion passes through her features, which I hate myself for, but is quickly replaced with an understanding smile. After heading to collect my discarded basketball, I offer Avery my arm like the gentleman I was raised to be. Linking her arm with mine, we start to walk to the edge of the court. "Come on, let's find some lunch."

∞∞∞∞

The soothing sounds of piano filter through the kitchen as I finish preparing our sandwiches. A hauntingly, beautiful harmony grows louder as Avery loses herself to the piece, the robust notes beginning to grow into a crescendo. Placing the two plates across the island for when she's finished, I pad across the kitchen and lean against the open archway. Finding Huxley slumped on the sofa with his back to the piano, I now understand why Avery began to play. She has used the power of her music to reach Huxley many times in the past couple of weeks, reaching him when words cannot.

The piece continues to build, the melody stirring feelings in my own chest. Her fingers, which are poking out of my burgundy hoodie that she seems to have found and helped herself to, fly over the keys rapidly as she stares out into the gardens, seeming to know the composition off by heart. Each note seeps further within me, coiling around my soul and starting to rip it from my very core. As soon as the harmony's first point of intensity has been reached, the music rolls into the next dramatic peak, dragging my heart from my chest and slamming across the marbled floor.

Garrett and Axel appear over the upstairs railing, also pulled from their room by the most intense piece we've ever heard Avery play. Her hair shifts in time with the violent jolts to her upper body, every part of her being travelling through her fingers and projecting into the melancholic vibrations. Catching Garrett's eye, I gesture with my chin to Huxley. Nodding, he slips his hand in Axel's and guides him down the stairs on silent feet. Rounding the living room as they reach the lower level, the three of us close in from different ends of the sofa and set ourselves down either end of Huxley.

On instinct, he makes a move to leave but both I and Axel plant a hand on each of his thighs to keep him firmly in place. His posture is stiff but he remains, staring straight at the unlit fire place in front. Dark semi-circles hang beneath his eyes which illuminate the hollowing in his cheekbones beneath the mess of his blonde waves. Even his arms look skinnier than I remember, the short sleeves on his blue t-shirt appearing baggy around his biceps.

Eventually, the soul-crushingly divine piece softens to its final stage, a flowing string of notes to ease the raw ache I now feel inside. The music comes to a stop, but no one moves. Like mine, Huxley's chest is heaving slightly from that mid-afternoon emotional rollercoaster. Avery appears on the other end of the U-shaped cream sofa, slipping herself into the tiny gap Axel makes for her by Huxley's side. Leaning her head on his chest, the TV mounted on the stone wall opposite flickers to life as Garrett channel surfs from his position next to Axel.

Settling on the movie 'Man of the house', we all remain

together for longer than we have since that day at the pool house, letting Tommy Lee Jones whisk away our worries for a short while. Although, I can't fully enjoy the peace in the room without Wyatt being here. At least when he popped back in the dead of night to change, I knew he was still alive but lately there hasn't been any sign of his stubborn ass. I've left so many voice-mails, but he hasn't responded to a single one. If he doesn't let me know he's safe soon, I'll consider calling the police.

Garrett is the first to rise from the sofa, going in hunt for food no doubt. I've been scared to move in case it jars Huxley into leaving, and it seems I was right. The second Garrett is out of view, Huxley launches himself from the sofa and disappears upstairs. His door slams shut a few seconds later and Avery sags into his vacated spot with a sigh. I know she blames herself for Huxley's personality shift, little does she know he lacks resilience. He may not have a healthy relationship with his parents, but he's never wanted for anything or suffered a type of trauma like the rest of us. Until now, I suppose. Shifting over and widening my legs, Avery lies her head upon my thigh. Her hair spills over my lap, combing my fingers through its silky length. Axel takes her feet and pulls them onto his lap, stroking his thumbs across her ankles.

"M'Lady," Garrett returns, handing her the plated sandwich I left in the kitchen earlier. Avery sits upright to accept the plate with a huge smile.

"Aw wow, thanks Garrett. I'm starving." She gushes, moaning in delight as she takes her first bite. Tossing himself down in his previous place and tucking into my sandwich, I glower over at his stupid dimpled grin. Throwing me a wink, his arm slips around Axel's shoulders and focuses on the movie's credits like it's the most fascinating documentary in the world. Shaking my head, Avery giggles as my long curls tickle her cheek which has Garrett's smile slipping.

If I weren't against violence, I would have launched him

across the room for that little trick. But there's one thing I took from my upbringing and that's aggression is never the answer. No matter how many countless beatings my father delivered to me for flunking school, getting a B on a test, showing him up in front of his high society pals, I refused to change. I laugh when I'm happy, cry when I'm sad, place myself in other's shoes and show empathy more than not. To the emotionless robot who raised me, I'm the worst type of son. But this is who I am, who my mother wanted me to be and I won't apologise for it – no matter how 'weak' it makes me seem. He thought sending me to boarding school was a punishment, but instead it was a god-send. I refuse to use my fists to gain respect, because to me that seems like the true nature of a coward.

The day drags into evening, the sky beyond the French doors darkening. Axel has offered to cook tonight so he is in the kitchen with Garrett leaning across the island, watching his every move and probably drooling. Shifting to see if Axel needs any help, Avery's hand quickly clasps my forearm so I turn back to look at her with a quirked brow.

"I completely forgot to ask you for a favor. You know when you tracked me down at the tattoo studio with the help of some hacker friends, are you still in contact with them?" She nibbles her bottom lip nervously while I stare at her curiously and lean back again.

"I'll call my cousin and find out what he can do. What do you need?" Avery plays with the hem of my hoodie she's still snuggled up in as she fills me in on her conversation with Meg. Panic rooms, stocked cupboards and no internet? Alarm bells sound inside my mind and I instantly wonder if she did forget to ask me this or if she was stalling because she knows how strange it all sounds.

"Elena must be really worried to keep Meg hidden away for so long. Do you think she knows something we don't?" I ask, glancing past Avery's face to the guards pacing around the garden. Following my eyeline, a shudder passes through her and she turns back with a haunted look in her clear blue eyes. Shrugging, Avery tucks her knees up to her chest beneath the hoodie and slowly leans into my body. Instinctively, I wrap my arms around her and place a kiss on the top of her head. "I won't let anything happen to you," I promise, silently praying I can live up to that statement.

# Meg

Breaching the salty surface, the burn in my lungs starts to fade as I gasp in mouthfuls of clean air. Seagulls fly overhead in the sky, heading towards the heavy grey clouds rolling this way. A deep rumble in the distance tells me I need to get out of the sea before the storm hits. Diving back into the icy water, I kick as fast as my nearly frozen legs will move, coming up for air every few powerful strokes of my arms. The beach is in sight when the rain hits, pelting mini bullets of water down onto me. Finding the seabed beneath my feet, I push myself up and wade the rest of the way to shore.

Not slowing once back on land, I grab the towel I'd left on the sand and force my legs to carry me towards the beach house. Leaving the violent crash of waves behind, the calm sea I had entered turning turbulent, my feet hit the wooden porch steps. Taking a second to collect myself before bursting into the house, I lean against the blue exterior and watch the dramatic weather shift from the safety of the porch's timber cover. The dense sheet of rain is now hiding the sea from my vision, a bright flash lighting the landscape briefly. The back door beside me flies open and my mom's hand flies around the corner to latch onto my arm, dragging me inside.

"What were you thinking swimming in that?!" She shouts, pointing her finger towards the doors glass panes after slamming it shut. A puddle starts to form at my feet, my hair dripping onto the lino floor. Thunder rumbles around the building, rivalling the rain's noise.

"Well obviously it wasn't raining when I initially went into the water. It's not like I can rely on my weather app to tell me these things anymore, is it?" I glare at her accusingly. Mom's brown eyes narrow in the way they do when she's about to shout at me, so I turn to leave. Careful not to slip on the wet patch I've created, I rub the ends of my hair with the towel.

"I'm doing this for your own good, you know!" Mom's voice finally finds me halfway up the stairs. Leaning over the banister, I see her retrieving a mop from the skinny cupboard beside the fridge.

"What about the good of Avery? You abandoned her therapy sessions when she probably needs them the most!" I shout back, stomping up the two flights of stairs to the top level which holds my bedroom. The converted attic is huge, the king size bed seeming small in the centre of the room. The ceiling slants into the middle, reminding me of the tent we spent many summers in whilst camping. My shoulders sag with a long sigh, knowing I need to fix things with my mom soon. I understand a shooting and near kidnap at my best friend's house has panicked her, but her actions are rather extreme in my eyes. I've tried relentlessly to explain my connection with Avery over these past few weeks, but she refuses to listen.

Not being with my best friend is physically hurting me, an ache in my chest that grows each day. Our connection isn't one I can put into words because it hardly makes sense to me. It's as if Avery was hand crafted and placed in my life to show me what true love is. Not the kind my mom can give me, love in the sense that my soul has bound itself to hers, I need her in my life for it to be complete. And never before has it been so apparent, I rely on her as much as she does me.

Stepping into my personal bathroom, I switch the shower onto scolding hot and peel off my black swimsuit. Steam thickens the air, fogging the large oval mirror above the basin. Dumping my costume into the bathtub to deal with later,

I release my hair from its ponytail and step into the spray. Warmth immediately soaks into my skin, drawing the chill from every cell in my body and swirling it down the drain. Taking my time, since I don't have anything else to, I wash the shampoo from my hair and smooth a handful of conditioner through the long lengths. Leaving it to soak in, I shave my legs and wash my body twice before rinsing it out.

Not able to stall any longer, I flick the shower off irritably and emerge thoroughly scrubbed. Combing through my hair in the mirror, an edge of sadness lines my pale blue eyes. If we don't leave soon, I'll run back to Atlanta – Forrest Gump style. A rounded window in the slanted roof shows the rain has stopped, the sun poking through the clouds to brighten the bathroom. After drying my hair with the travel hairdryer I brought, I hunt down some tracksuit bottoms that are fluffy on the inside and a black tank top.

Everything is quiet in the house as I pop my head out of my door. Padding across the hallway on bare feet, I go search for my mom, hoping I can finally make her see sense. She must need to get back to work soon, which I will try to use to my advantage. Failing to find her in her bedroom, I head for the kitchen instead. Halfway down the second staircase, I see her feet poking out from a checked woollen blanket on the sofa. Her dark hair is strewn across the arm, huddled beneath the blanket and fast asleep.

Realising I have a limited amount of time without her breathing down my neck, something the lack of sunshine has prevented these past few days, I tiptoe back up the stairs and slip into the study. Quickly locating the decoy book upon the shelf, a soft click sounds which has me darting across the room to pry open the secret wall. After my phone call with Avery, mom had shouted my name and forced me to abandon my mission, anticipation eating away at me ever since.

Pushing the wall closed behind me this time, a trio of

silver bolts shoot back into place and lock me inside. My heart quickens as I fear I'm stuck until I notice a large red button on the inner wall to my left, hopefully able to release the locks. Not wasting another moment, I power up the laptop and take a seat in the office chair. My fingers shake over the keys slightly as a password protected screen appears, although I knew this would appear from locking myself out last time. Thankfully, red text below the empty box tells me I am allowed another three attempts. Despite the lodge's name, hand painted onto a slab of rock and propped by the front door, not working the last time, I type 'Avalon' again in hopes it was correct but case sensitive. The text box shakes slightly as a red X appears and takes my attempts down to two.

Glancing around the small room, I look for a clue the owner may have planted but, like the rest of the house, everything in here is completely impersonal. Thinking of the house and its surroundings, I vaguely remember a sign hung to a tree that signalled for us to leave the main road and venture onto a rocky, dirt path. Dense woodland on either side barely left enough room for the rented Range Rover to pass through, leaves scraping the window as my mom eased the vehicle along at 5mph. But that was miles away and the forest's name has slipped my mind.

At a loss, I pick up the laptop and look underneath but I don't know what I was expecting. The password isn't likely to be taped there for any of the guests staying, with a passion for Frances Hodgson Burnett's novels, to find. Close to giving up, I check the laptop over again before placing it down and pressing a button to release the disk drive. To my surprise, the automatic tray slides out to reveal a white disk with letters and numbers written directly onto it with a marker.

BH/404/31KM

Figuring it can't be that simple but trying anyway, I type the code into the password box and tap the enter key. My attempts reduce to one and I curse myself. Staring at the combination, something starts to jar in my mind. I was forced to do a home project in my last year of high school Geography, which I hated since all I wanted was to spend my time on the lacrosse pitch instead. But some of those useless facts have stuck with me over the years; one in particular being that 31km is the distance between Brookhaven's furthest points. Factoring in that BH is extremely close to the city's name and 404 is my area code, I start to type the city's name. Hovering a finger over the enter key, I close my eyes and press down.

No way. The screen unlocks through my cracked eyelid and my heart jolts in excitement. A generic blue background appears with a small spinning circle by the mouse's arrow signalling something is happening. Windows begin to pop up before me until ten in total cover the screen, each starting in black before changing one by one to a monotone image. Confusion bleeds into dread as my eyes land on the image of my mom sleeping on the sofa downstairs, the slight rise and fall of the blanket barely visible. The time in the corner of each window tells me these images are a live feed from cameras I hadn't even noticed were present. Each of the six bedrooms, the kitchen, living room, outside the front door and back porch are visible and I have a sudden panic as to who else can access this footage.

Clicking the X's to close all windows except the one featuring my mom, so I can keep an eye on when she wakes, I run my finger over the mousepad to click on the settings. Selecting internet, any traces of hope I felt scurry away as no available connections are found. Hanging my head, I allow myself a moment of self-pity before deciding my original plan (convince mom we should leave or run home) is my best and only option. Refusing to pass up an opportunity to hear Avery's voice, I lift the landline receiver to my ear as mom starts to sit up on the sofa. Stretching her arms above her head, she swings her legs onto the floor and looks around. Slamming the phone back down, I close the window and power off the laptop before leaping from the chair. Hitting the red button on the wall with my fist, the locks are released and I slip outside, pushing my back against the wall to close it just as mom rounds the corner.

"There you are. I must have dozed off. How about we make dinner and then play some Scrabble?" She asks smiling sweetly, her eyes still slightly glazed with sleep.

"Sure," I reply, returning her smile and leading her out of the room, thankful I can keep the panic room a secret for a tiny while longer.

Tossing onto my other side, I throw the cover off my sweaty body and fist my hands in frustration. Every time I close my eyes, I think about some pervert leering over a screen watching me sleep. I tried all evening to sneakily spot the hidden cameras but I can't find a trace of them without making it too obvious I know exactly where they are. My only saving grace is that the bathroom is apparently off limits, but I can't hide in there any longer without seeming suspicious. Rising from the bed, I walk over to the huge window covering most of my slanted ceiling. Opening the latch and pushing the glass outwards, the cool night's air surrounds me as I gaze out to the sea stretching across the horizon. A perfect luminescent circle is reflected in the still water, a mirror image of the moon directly above. I haven't given this place credit for its beauty or serenity; it's difficult to see what's right in front of me when I'm more focused on what's missing.

A noise similar to a harsh 'shh' filters up to me, making my eyebrows crease as I lean over the window frame to look below. I can't see anything out of place but I'm sure I hear a deep murmur that has me darting back into my room. Pushing my feet into Ugg-style slippers and throwing a baggy hoodie over my head, I creep from my room and down the stairs as quickly and quietly as I can. Every room I pass is dark, the last step of the bottom staircase groaning beneath my foot and causing me to freeze. After nothing happens, I continue through the living room and into the kitchen.

"She's asking so many questions," my mom's voice beyond the back door has me ducking and shuffling across the open space until my back meets the cupboard doors. Her shadow moves against the closed blind, as the moon helps to make out two figures.

"I understand but she needs to stay here." A deep voice replies. My heart is thumping around my rib cage like a balloon that's been released before it has been tied. I think I know that voice, but I can't place it. A strange sense of déjà vu washes over me, a memory I'd long forgotten playing out before my eyes. That deep rumbling voice, mom's hushed whispers, light seeping beneath my closed bedroom door as I pull my unicorn duvet over my face and push myself into a mountain of stuffed teddies.

"How long do you intend to keep us hidden?" Mom's impatient voice pulls me back to the present, the realisation she too is a prisoner here unnerving me. Slowly rising to my feet, I square my shoulders and brace myself. I'm getting answers, tonight.

"Don't take that tone with me, Elena-" I whip the door open, a shriek of surprise leaves mom as she clutches her chest with wide eyes. A tall shadowed figure turns to me, grey visible at his temples. Pushing his hands into his slacks, he shifts so the moon's rays fall over his face to reveal icy blue eyes that soften as they land on me.

"Nixon?"

# Wyatt

Tapping my foot on an expensive Persian rug, I hold back the sigh that's lingering on my tongue. Ray promised me the truth tonight, but so far I've had to sit here and watch him puff on a cigar for longer than my patience can handle. Every so often he coughs excessively, banging his fist in the centre of his chest but still refuses to put the cancer stick down. Being stuck in this darkened room without any ventilation, the smell is making me feel nauseous and lightheaded at the same time.

Other than a sideboard on my left, the desk separating us and our two chairs, there's nothing else in the office as far as I can see. I'm beginning to wonder if Ray's fondness of the dark is due to a medical issue or if he's embarrassed he hasn't decorated recently. Finally, he stubs out the short remainder of his cigar and focuses on me. I lean in at the same time Ray does, thinking he's about to bring some clarity to my confusing life, when he reaches a shaky hand for the glass decanter on his desk.

Watching him attempt to lift the heavy container is painful, so I stand on a huff and ease it from his fingers. After pouring the amber liquid into an empty glass beside the ashtray, I hand it to him and resume my seat. Ray smiles at me in the lamp's glow, lifting the glass to his aged lips and downing the liquid. After planting the glass down, he gives a stiff nod just in time, since I was about to scream for him to get the fuck on with it.

Pulling open a drawer on his side of the desk, Ray pulls out a brown envelope and flicks open the lip. Carefully sliding out an aged piece of paper, he pushes it across the wooden surface towards me slowly. I lean forward, squinting in the light to read the tiny writing. It's the birth report from my birth date. After reading the hospital's heading, I glance up with a cocked eyebrow for him to explain.

"Twenty years ago, this month, Catherine Hughes gave birth to twins." Sighing deeply, I wave my hand in the air, feeling deflated his 'big news' was something I already knew. Pushing the paper back towards him, I slump back into my chair. So much for getting answers.

"I already know Avery is my twin," I manage to say evenly, despite the vomit that rising in my throat at those words. Ray chuckles deeply, causing me to frown in suspicion. I would think he had a screw loose if it weren't the perfect clarity in his eyes.

"Read the report." is all he says. Reaching for it back and scanning the document, I flick my eyes from the hospital name to the date and down to the description typed beneath. My gaze snags on the short paragraph, ice filling my heart.

*Dear Mr and Mrs Nixon Hughes,*

*We would like to congratulate and thank you for choosing to use Piedmont's maternity centre. On 19th July 2001, a set of healthy female twins were delivered naturally at 4:11pm and 4:36pm. Baby A weighed 6lb 5oz and Baby B weighed 6lb 1oz at time of birth. Neither new-born required specialist treatment and have successfully breast-fed within hours of birth. On this basis, we are pleased to discharge you today. From the entire team here, we hope you leave with the knowledge we all hold you in our prayers and wish your girls the best fortunes in life.*

*Your Sincerely,*
*Dr Fawcett.*

"I don't understand," I trail off, although I understand perfectly. Dread has taken a hold of my body, keeping me tightly rooted in place. The paper starts to crinkle in my clenched fist so Ray leans forward with surprising speed to snatch the page from my grip.

"Avery was never the adopted one in your household, son. You were." After forcing the creases from the paper, he slides it back into the envelope and returns it to the safe hiding spot within his drawer.

"But, why?" is all I can think, slowly forcing myself back into the leather armchair. It doesn't make any sense. To adopt their real child after pretending I was legitimately theirs. Unless I was such a disappointment, they couldn't bear being stuck with me any longer. I wasn't good enough.

"A long time ago," Ray recaptures my attention with his low tone, "Nixon Hughes murdered my daughter in cold blood. She was the light of my life. And the sole heir to my legacy. So, I made Nixon a promise. That the day he was gifted a daughter, I would return the favor. Apparently, that fateful day arrived with not only one, but two daughters I could use to exact my revenge. It seems he thought he could outsmart me, hiding the girls they bore and taking in a boy instead. For years I wallowed in my grief, consumed with the fact I'd never get vengeance. Until they brought her back."

My mind is starting to spin, the light in the room becoming fuzzy. Images of my childhood start to play through my mind, searching for clues to support Ray's allegation. But my fath- Nixon was the doting dad when he was around. Even if my birth right was a lie, that doesn't sound like the father I grew up with.

"Why not come for me? Did it really matter what gender their child was?" I ask, wondering if that's the real reason I'm here. But surely, it that was true, I'd be dead by now - not feeling bloated and pampered.

"There's a certain bond between a father and his daughter. Although I'm sure he adored you to the best of his blackened soul, can you honestly say he doesn't love Avery more?" My nostrils flare as anger rises. He's right. She was instantly welcomed into our house, showered with compassion. Even though I received anything I desired, it was only with material objects. She got mom's sole affection. Father's undivided attention. And now it makes sense since she was actually theirs and I was the fraud.

"So, who's the other twin?" I seethe, needing to know which other girl in the world deserves my home more than me.

"That's where you come in. We can't locate the other one." Reaching into his pocket, Ray pulls out the latest iPhone. The wrinkles on his face are illuminated by the bright screen as he taps the device with his index finger. After holding it to his ear and requesting to 'send her in', we sit in silence while I wait for someone to enter.

I mentally run through as much of my childhood as I can remember, trying to find another girl my parents showed any interest in but there's no one. Maybe they only took Avery back after they discovered the abuse she was suffering, but if the other one is living a perfectly happy life – she could be anywhere in the world.

The door opens behind me, but I don't turn to see who is entering. Focusing on the mix of emotions battling with each other, mainly rage and a hint of self-worthlessness, a dark figure rounds the room to stand across from me on Ray's left.

Glancing up, my eyebrows crease. "You?" I breathe in surprise. Her mousey brown hair looks almost black in the darkened room, covering her shoulders. Her Prada knee-length coat is tied tightly at her waist with a fabric belt, cinching her waist. She takes Ray's hand in a comforting squeeze before releasing it, regaining her full yet short height to face me.

"Hello, Wyatt." Detective Vincent says blandly, almost seeming bored. I start to splutter out a range of questions all at once, but she holds up her palm to silence me. "I understand your confusion. I didn't lie when I said I promised to find Sydney's killer – but I've also been working as a double agent for Mr Perelli for many years. The FBI are, in fact, hunting for solid proof that Nixon was in Chicago at the time of her murder, but our cause goes beyond that. My connections are particularly useful in allowing Perelli's men to enter and exit the Hughes' property without being seen to find the information we desperately need. I realize this is a lot to take in, but time is of the essence. With Cathy's death, Nixon is the only one with the information we need now. We have been unable to locate him for months."

"You shot Huxley?!" is the first thing that springs to mind, quickly followed by my curiosity around my mom's car crash. Although killing her would seem counterproductive to their whole scheme that's been 20 years in the making.

"Well, not me personally." She mumbles. "But yes, I helped stage the intrusion. The break-ins were merely distractions so I could obtain warrants to search for evidence for Nixon's location and the 'Hidden Hughes', as we've been calling her." The detective rests her hand on Ray's shoulder as my eyes trail down to where her shiny badge would be sitting on her hip beneath the coat.

"I'm afraid casualties come with the territory. That particular...member of my family is fairly new and not fully trained in our ways yet. Don't fret, he has been properly punished for the headache that incident has caused us and will be more prepared next time." I feel my eyebrows pull together. 'That incident' came within two inches of killing one of my brethren and I can't help to feel the guilt that blooms in my chest from his words. None of this really has anything to do with me, yet I followed my father's instructions to stay in Atlanta. I dragged my boys into this, put them in harm's way.

"If I'm joining your family, I need you to promise me my boys will be kept out of all of this. None of them get hurt or are used as a pawn to gain what you want." Ray's head bobs slowly in the lamp's glow and I trust he is a man of his word. I mean, he's been nothing but completely honest about everything this far and I have a feeling family means everything to him. Sighing, I lean forward to rest my elbows on my thighs. "Tell me what you need me to do."

"I will need you to return to your former life for a short while, find information on the missing twin, and then bring Nixon and Avery to me. After that, you'll be welcomed back with open arms and have a place with us for the rest of your days." The plan sounds simple enough, despite the discomfort I will feel at being back in Avery's presence.

She is no relation to me after all, which in one way is a huge relief but, in another sense, it's my own personal form of torture. I practically have a green light to act on my instincts to throw her against a wall and kiss her the way I've been yearning to do. To sink my dick nine-inches deep as she finally accepts all of me in the way I've craved. But now more than ever, I can't have that.

She was supposed to have the life I led. It wasn't enough she took the love of the only parents I had ever known, she had to taunt me with her perfectly blue eyes and golden hair. Her faint freckles and plump lips. Gloating in my face this entire time that she was meant to take my place. And now she's going to pay for it. Her and her stupid twin will learn what it means to steal from me, and I will relish every second of it.

"What do you need my father for? Surely Avery is your target?" I seethe. The old man's lips turn up in a smile although there's no humour in his gaze. Just pure rage that mirrors the fury I'm feeling within.

"Because Nixon will be chained down to watch me slit Avery's throat, of course. That small slither of revenge is all I'm still clinging onto my feeble life for."

# *Avery*

Lying on my stomach across my bed, my legs swing to and fro as I mindlessly scroll through Facebook. Everyone is posting photos of their perfect summer break, from European holidays to picnics in parks with their friends. All of my 'friends' on the app are mostly people I've met through Meg, either from her team, sorority, or some of their many house parties. An image pops up of Angelica, the girl's lacrosse captain, surrounded by children in adorable sports kits in the mini lacrosse camp she runs each summer. Meg usually volunteers to help out, my heart tightening as I realise I'm not the only one missing her.

Refreshing my emails for the millionth time and checking through the junk folders, just in case Meg has managed to message me and I've missed it, I huff loudly when I find nothing from my best friend. Tossing my phone onto the pillow, I throw my head down and groan into the covers. I don't think I've ever been so bored in my life, and that's saying something. There's only so many times I can swim the same pool, eat the same food, play the same video games. If I don't hear from her again really soon, I'm booking a flight to California and walking the entire 840 miles of coastline until I find her.

A soft knock sounds at my door before it's swung open, the sound of Axel moaning at Garrett reaching my ears. Rolling over on my mattress, my jaw drops at the sight in front of me. Both guys are wearing dark slacks and dress shoes, shirts clinging to their ripped forms with the top few buttons left open. Garrett's pebble grey shirt is rolled up at the elbows, his biceps straining against the material, while Axel's lilac one is buttoned at his cuffs. The hunger in my eyes is reflected in Garrett's hazel ones as he glances over my oversized t-shirt and panties combo like a predator who has found his prey. Axel's hand grips his forearm, pulling him back as if he could read Garrett's mind.

"What's the special occasion?" I ask, swallowing loudly. Whatever is going on here, I was in from the second I set eyes on them. Both pairs of eyes drift to my exposed thighs, goose bumps lining my skin in anticipation. Garrett's too busy licking his lips at me in that sexy practised-in-the-mirror kinda way to respond, so Axel takes the lead.

"We have a surprise for you. Meet us downstairs when you're dressed." Flicking my eyes between the two, I am desperate to know what they have planned but I can already see they won't tell me. I rise from the bed, Garrett stepping towards me on instinct but Axel pulls him back towards the door, whining like a dog the entire way.

I turn towards my walk-in closet as soon as the door clicks closed, excitement filling me. Standing in the centre, I stare at my clothes wishing I'd asked for a dress code. Or a time limit, for that matter. It's mid-afternoon so I can't see many places matching their smart attire being open, but just to have somewhere to go is enough. They can take me to Subway in my fanciest dress for all I care. Channelling my inner-Meg, since I'm useless with selecting outfits for myself, I lift multiple hangers from the rail before changing my mind and putting them back.

Settling on a knee-length bodycon dress, I pull the t-shirt over my head and replace my underwear for something a little more satin and much more revealing. You know, just in case. Slipping into the hunter green dress with intricate black beading swirling in patterns up each side to accentuate my curves, the colour causes my mind to shift to Wyatt. Where is he, and when is he eventually going to come home? We have so much to talk about and the longer he avoids me, the bigger the chasm between us seems to grow.

Emerging from my wardrobe, I sit down at my vanity and take the time to apply makeup for the first time since we all went to Sinergy. That night feels like a lifetime ago now and so much has changed, barely any of it for the best. Not one for contouring, I apply a mineral powder to my face and work carefully on a smoky eye like Meg would have done on me, before adding mascara to complete the look. Using a dusty pink colour on my lips, I brush out my long hair and finish with a light sprinkling of hairspray. Pushing my feet into skinny, black heels, thankful I was bored enough to shave my legs this morning, I walk from my room and head for the staircase.

Glancing over the banister, I can only see Axel below, waiting for me patiently. Gliding down the curved staircase with as much grace as I can muster in these neck-breaking heels, Axel extends his hand to help me down the last step.

"Wow," he breathes, raising his eyebrows as he looks me up and down. Pulling me into his body, he gently tucks my hair behind my left ear and bends to place a kiss on my neck. "You look beautiful," he whispers in my ear. Stepping back, Axel keeps a hold of my hand as he guides me into the corridor. I start to pause at the elevator doors, expecting us to head for the underground garage but he continues to pull me along with a smirk.

"Where are you taking me?" I ask, but he doesn't answer except for the grin spreading across his face. His shaved head sharpens his cheekbones and jaw line, making him the ideal sitter for a portrait with his clear-cut angles and sparkling amber eyes. Bringing me to a halt outside the studio door, a thumping of heavy bass vibrating under the door, he rasps his knuckles against the wood and clutches my hand a little tighter. From the stiffness to his shoulders, I'd say he's nervous.

The door opens inward to reveal Dax in a similar fitted navy shirt and suit trousers. The smart outfit on his body is a complete contrast to the wildness of his huge afro, and I wouldn't have him any other way. His piercing blue eyes trail my body in a similar way Axel's did, his cheeky smile growing even further. Stepping out of the way for us to pass, it's then I see the room beyond.

My dance studio has been converted into a full-on night club. Black fabric panels cover the mirror wall and window at the far end, flashing neon lights trailing the edges of the wooden floor. The central light socket has been replaced with a disco ball, reflecting the multicoloured stroke lights being projected from a pop-up DJ stall in the corner. Garrett has taken pride of place behind the booth, my name on an LED screen rolling across the front on repeat. A table draped in black along the right side holds the entire house's stock of alcohol by the looks of it and white beanbags have been placed around the dance floor.

"How... did you guys do all of this?" I ask over the music, walking further inside so Dax can shut the door, concealing the glare of daylight.

"We snuck in a crew to assemble their equipment, but it was all my idea." Garrett's voice booms through a microphone he's holding to his mouth. A chunky headset covers his ears so he must have guessed what my initial question should be. Returning to fiddling with switches, his brown hair flops back and forth as his head nods to the beat. Axel strides towards the drinks table and pours a round of four shots, clearly ready to kick this party into gear. Catching Dax's eye, I mouth "Huxley?" His eyes soften as he glances to the ground and shakes his head a little. Axel hands us each a strangely green shot and carries the other over the Garrett, us following behind. Holding his shot glass in the centre, Garrett shouts into the microphone despite us standing right in front of him.

"To making Avery smile," he winks at me as we all clink glasses and down our first shot of many. Setting both of our glasses onto the booth, I reach deep into my cleavage, much to everyone's excitement and produce my phone. Flicking the camera to selfie mode, I twist so Garrett is in the background in his DJ get up and pull Axel back from walking away. Locking my arm around his, he grins sheepishly at the screen whilst Dax shifts in beside me. His rounded afro blocks Garrett from view, who leans over to knock him out of the way. Once everyone's in the frame, I slip my hand south to grab Axel's junk so a huge smile spreads across him face as I snap the shot.

Giggling to myself, I plant my phone down on the booth and turn towards the dancefloor. Slipping his hand into mine, Dax leads me into the centre of the room as Calvin Harris' 'We Found Love' starts to blast through the speakers. Pulling me into the cage of his body and wrapping his arms around my shoulders, I can't hide the smile he draws from me so easily. Placing my hands on his firm chest and looking up, the coloured patterns passing over his face lure me into our own moment, away from the rest of the world.

Hands find the dents of my waist from behind, Axel's fingers trailing over the bead work on my sides. Dax pulls away, clearly not one for sharing, my hand stretching after him as he turns away. My pout is quickly retracted when he returns a second later with a bottle of champagne in one hand and rosé in the other. Opting for the wine, I raise the bottle to my lips to take a long swig whilst Axel grinds against me.

The mix of alcohol and flashing lights start to affect my rational thinking, giving myself into the beat of the music and escape the guys have provided me with. Before long, my hair is sticking to the back of my neck and my shoes have disappeared, although I can't remember removing them. Garrett has fabricated in front of me, his shirt unbuttoned as he too lets the rhythm take over. Lost in his own world, I catch a glimpse of the Garrett I saw when he first kissed me – no acting or playing up to his audience. His body moves fluidly, his face relaxed and eyes closed, a bottle of rum gripped in his hand.

Axel walks over to me delicately holding another shot in his fingers with a smirk in place, magnified by the neon lights. I stop bouncing on my heels as he trails a finger up my throat and gently pushing my chin upwards, lifting the glass and pouring its contents into my open mouth. Licking my lips after swallowing, Axel bends his head to trail the same path with his own tongue. My dulled senses come to life, electricity humming through the air, so potent I swear I feel my hair starting to stand on end.

Needing to distance myself from this trio of hot and sweaty men, I signal for a timeout and edge away from the dance floor. Collapsing onto a beanbag, my chest heaves as I try to catch my breath around a fit of giggles. My head is woozy in the best kind of way as I watch the guys jump enthusiastically to a new beat. Axel has loosened up more than I've ever seen him, his arms thrown around his best friend's shoulders as they sing 'I'm the real Slim Shady' at the top of their lungs. A smile is glued to my face, my cheeks starting to ache from holding it in place. This is the first time I've seen the guys actually enjoy themselves the way I'd imagine they do regularly at college. I quickly reject the thought of them returning to Waversea and leaving me behind so I don't ruin this moment right now. I need to cling onto the small slithers of happiness while I can, otherwise there's nothing dragging through each day.

Two heavy weights chuck themselves onto bean bags around me, jarring me from my darkening thoughts. My grin is instantly back in place, thankful that right here and right now, this devilishly handsome bunch have gone through all this effort just to lift my spirits. Dax spreads his legs as he leans back comfortably, his knee knocking mine. Axel is over by the drinks table while Garrett's eyes have zeroed in on me like laser beams. There's no hint of smile on his face, the seriousness to his features reminding me of our threesome weeks ago, and the monster that lurks beneath his striking surface. Leaning closer to me, he places his palm on my ankle and slowly trails his hand up my calf, over my knee and beneath my dress.

"What are you doing?" I flinch, pushing his hand out and glancing over at Dax. His head has lolled back against the white fabric, his eyes closed in an alcohol induced coma. Smirking at me, Garrett tries again to slip his hand between my thighs, but I shake my head holding my dress firmly in place. Even if Dax has passed out and probably knows of my history with Garrett, I'm not going to have sex with another guy right beside him. For some reason, Dax's opinion matters to me and I won't compromise it. Sensing my hesitation, Garrett leans further across to whisper in my ear.

"My room, 5 minutes." Rising from his seat, he lifts Dax into his arms and throws his bulky frame over his shoulder. Striding from the room as if he's not carrying almost 200 pounds of muscle, he disappears though the doorway, leaving me with Axel. Glancing over, I jolt to find his cat-like eyes focused intently on me, glowing with passion that makes me clench my thighs together. Sauntering over at a casual pace, my eyes drawn to the shift of his powerful thighs through the tight material of his slacks, I swallow loudly to my own ears. Holding out his hand, I don't hesitate to accept and allow him to pull me to my feet.

# Garrett

Slipping from Dax's room after throwing his body onto the bed, my blood is raging at a fever level with need to share Avery with Axel again. Fisting my hands at my sides, I try to keep my legs from running down the hall. Knocking my bedroom door open hard enough for it to bang loudly against the wall, I find the pair waiting on my bed patiently. Axel's fingers are fiddling with Avery's hair, her chest lifting and falling with anticipation.

As I enter and slam the door closed, the two of them stand together and wait for my instruction. Their actions have my dominant side roaring to life, a voice in my head screaming to bend and break them both until they've felt the true extent of the pleasure I can gift them through pain. But I can never fully let myself loose like that, and by the warning in Axel's eyes, he knows I was briefly considering it. The part of me that knows Avery can't handle the real me is chased away by the fact she's here for a second round, knowing what she's letting herself in for.

"Undress her," I order, forcing my back to press against the wall. Axel takes his time, giving me a show as he draws a path up her legs with his fingers. Reaching the edge of her dress, he eases it upwards, revealing her creamy skin bit by bit until the green material is pushed over her head. The black ink of her tattoos blend into the black satin bra, lace tracing her full breasts and the curve of her hips before tilting over the apex of her thighs.

Not one to wait for my next command, Avery takes her turn, unbuttoning Axel's lilac shirt painfully slowly and rising onto tiptoes to push it over his shoulders. Flicking open the clasp of his belt buckle, she smoothly pulls it free from his trousers and turns to face me. Threading the tail into the buckle, I watch in fascination as she pulls the loop smaller and repeatedly winds the leather back on itself. Pushing her hands into each hoop she's managed to create, Avery takes the loose end of the belt in between her teeth and pulls securely. The strap tightens around her wrists in makeshift handcuffs and my dick bulges painfully behind my zipper.

Lunging forward on instinct, needing to act on the way she's just sacrificed herself to me, Axel quickly steps in to block my way. Clasping the back of my head, he drags me in to kiss him first so I can vent some of my pent-up frustration on him first. The beast inside is clawing to burst free and sink my teeth and dick into Avery simultaneously, despite the tiny voice in my mind telling me to savour it, worship her. Smashing my lips against Axel's, sure there will be bruises left, I push my clenched fists against his exposed abs as his nails deepen into my nape.

A small figure pushes her way between us, signalling she doesn't need Axel to defend her - although in this moment, I'm glad he did. Axel and I take what we need from each other, our fractured parts binding together to form one, albeit deformed, complete soul. We know each others needs and limits, whereas Avery is fresh meat walking towards her own slaughter. Breaking our kiss, I glance down into the blue eyes separating us and send a brief, silent prayer she's ready for this because there is no going back for me now.

Dipping low, I lift her arms over my head with her restricted hands stuck behind me and grip her thighs as I stand. Trapped between the two of us, Axel's hands help support her ass, kneading and massaging the perfectly rounded cheeks with more care than I could muster in my little finger in this moment. Nibbling at her neck and jaw, sure to leave a few marks along the way, I trail my mouth to her lips and push my tongue straight inside. She moans into my mouth, the intensity I'm feeling rocketing sky high as I grind her against Axel. Knowing she is sandwiched between two rock hard cocks and that Axel's ripped body is on the other side does unknown things to me, a shudder rolling down my back deliciously.

Extracting my tongue from the twisted tangle around Avery's, I push her into Axel and duck beneath her arms. Continuing to lean her back into him, Axel lowers himself down on the edge of the bed and plants Avery down into his lap. Yanking my shirt from my body, thankful the buttons were already undone or I would have torn them clean off, I hastily step out of my trousers and boxers. Axel's hands have moved around to grip and tease Avery's tits through the thin fabric of her bra, the tips of his fingers dipping beneath to graze her nipples. Fisting my dick in my right hand, I wait for the moment she gasps and arches her back to guide her mouth onto my purple helmet.

The first swirl of her tongue around my soft head has stars bursting behind my eye lids, making me need to tense my thighs to stop myself cumming already. It might be weeks until we get her to loosen her inhibitions again, so I need to enjoy this for as long as possible. Taking me deeper into her mouth, her bound hands grip my base and balls, massaging as she builds up momentum. My tip slides into the back of her throat on long, deep movements and I fist my hand into her blonde locks, trying not rip the strands from her scalp. Cracking an eyelid, I see Axel's hand has dipped into her panties, circling her bud and biting on her neck.

Easing her mouth from my dick as carefully as I am able with my fingers digging into her underarms, I lift Avery to stand before me. Without any other choice since her arms are restricted, I rip the straps from her bra and watch it fall to the floor as she gasps. Her nipples are hard enough to cut glass as I take the first in my mouth, teasing it between my teeth and sucking painfully hard. Avery hisses and squirms, but doesn't tell me to stop. I hear Axel finish undressing as I take the other nipple and repeat the same process, Avery arching her back to push her breast further into me. Once Axel reappears behind her, I stand back and spin her to face him.

The phoenix on her back stares up at me, its fiery wings reminding me of the hell this girl has risen from and I'll be damned if I don't show her how our pain can be used for so many better things than dragging us down. Slipping my thumbs into the sides of her panties, I slip them down her silky, smooth legs and throw them onto the bed. Gesturing with my chin to the bathroom, a small smile grows across Axel's face and he leads her towards it. Dashing to my bedside table, I open the door and pull out the items I need before joining them.

Finding Avery's tied hands wrapped around Axel's dick as she pumps his length, I bite my lip and simply watch for a second. Axel pulls her in and kisses her without abandon, his fingers combing through her hair. Moving behind so my dick is nestled against her butt cheeks, I slide the blindfold over her head to cover her eyes. She jolts slightly so I push her hair over her left shoulder and talk directly into her ear while Axel is still kissing her.

"Let your senses guide you." I breathe, licking and kissing her neck in a move unnaturally sensual for me. Copying my move from earlier, Axel slips her arms over his head and I help him to lift her, holding her directly over his thick girth. Waiting for her to squirm with need, we share a smile and lower her onto him until she is fully impaled. Avery screams in shock, her lack of sight enhancing her other senses. Axel slides out as I hold her firmly in place, slamming back in with a clap of their flesh meeting. Avery's cries turn to moans as he repeats the move several times, her juices coating him as she adjusts to his length.

Once he's fully seated again, Axel leans against the bathroom counter and lifts himself onto it as I help to raise Avery. His back presses against the mirror with Avery straddling him, her shins firmly on the countertop allowing her to grind over him. It's Axel's turn the groan, his eyes rolling back in his skull as he grips her waist. Reaching for the lube, I squirt a generous amount of my rounded head and rub it down my length. Squeezing some more onto my index finger, I slip my hand between Avery's spread cheeks to massage her small puckered hole. She freezes immediately, glancing back in my direction despite the blindfold.

Axel glances at me nervously but I expected this, shifting forward to press my front against her back. "Just relax babe. If you don't like it, we'll stop." Her back sags against me slightly as I continue to circle her hole with my finger, dipping in slightly as Axel rolls his hips to massage her internally. Burying my face into her neck, I spread my legs to rub against Axel's thighs and line myself up with her back entrance. To her credit, she only tenses slightly as I begin to enter her in slow motion, inching in and then smoothing back out. Axel takes her mouth against his, swallowing her whimpers as the initial pain seeps into mind blowing pleasure.

Reaching around, I release Avery's wrists from their binds and her nails instantly find my thighs, digging deep enough to tear the skin. Sinking my teeth into her neck, I relish the feeling of her ripping me to shreds as I finally imbed myself fully into her. The tightness is unreal, Avery squeezing me tighter than a vice. Axel slowly starts to swivel his hips beneath her, the three of us moaning in unison at the feel of our cocks rubbing together inside of her. His balls rub against mine as he speeds up slightly, knowing any quicker will have us both coming undone in seconds.

Avery leans forward, feeling around before planting her hands on the mirror behind Axel as she pushes her chest into his face and starts to move herself. Any worries I had this would be too far for her evaporate as I watch the incredible woman in front of me take control of two guys at once. I follow her movements, keeping myself fully seated inside her as she winds her hips over Axel, his face the picture of how I feel. Avery's moans grow louder, the sounds filling the bathroom as she tips herself over the edge I'm barely clinging onto. The pulsing tightness that contracts around me is squeezing torturously, and I love every second. Sweat coats her slender body as she rides the waves of her orgasm, screaming 'Gaxel' as I knead her breasts in my strong hands. Tingling in my legs builds upwards, intensifying into an explosion as I pull myself free from Avery as slowly as I can manage and spill my cum into the nearby sink on a loud groan.

Judging by the screams to my right, I slid my dick out at just the right time and caused Avery a second orgasm. She's riding Axel's dick expertly, her cries softening as she starts to ease down. Judging by the look on Axel's face, he is seconds away from exploding so I quickly lift and cradle Avery in my arms. After relieving himself into the sink as well, Axel follows me into the room, an exhausted Avery slumped in my arms. Placing her onto the bed, I remove the blindfold and tuck her into my body.

"You're not escaping so fast this time," I say softly into her ear. Axel shifts in on the opposite side, caging her between us, although the limpness to her limbs says she's not in any state to stand unsupported anyway.

"I don't... stay after sex..." Avery breathes as she drifts off, no doubt being pulled under by the copious amounts of afternoon drinking. My eyes slide closed with a wide smile on my face, mentally high fiving myself for an excellent plan. Axel's hand finds mine over Avery's stomach, our fingers linking as sleep starts to take a hold of me too.

# Wyatt

Throwing the controller onto the carpeted floor, I slouch back into the gaming chair with a huff. I can't concentrate on any of the games I've tried to play, after seeking out a distraction from my fitful sleep. My mind won't switch off but that doesn't stop me from feeling fucking exhausted. My stinging eyes are begging to rest and I can't hold back the non-stop yawns leaving me.

It was so easy to buy into Ray's plot for vengeance while I was in his office, hearing the story of how his daughter was taken from him. I felt his hatred as if it were my own. But once I had retreated to my room last night, the internal war between my head and my heart started to rip me to shreds. Although I understand this daughter for daughter concept, a part of me wonders if I can go through with my side of the plan he has in mind.

Never mind the plan, the thought of seeing Avery again soon has me twisted into all kinds of knots. I've decided to leave her believing we are related, hoping she has the willpower to keep from getting to attached to me. 'Cause lord knows, I sure don't. Not that she will be a problem after Ray's had his way. Pushing down the guilt at that thought, I focus on the future I have waiting for me here. I'll be part of a family that wants me. No lies, no false promises.

"There you are," Rachel's voice leaks into the room, saving me from my thoughts. Rounding the chair in fluffy white slippers that make a scuffing sound with each step, she pushes a warm mug containing a pale liquid into my hands and orders me to drink it with a sweet smile. Returning it as best as I can manage right now, I sip the heated milk and hum slightly as it works its way down my throat. A sense of calms immediately seeps through me, relaxing my limbs to that blissful numb feeling.

Rachel perches on the low table opposite me, watching me keenly like I am the centre of her universe. Her hair is loose down her back and she is completely make-up free. A thick dressing gown covers her body, with 'R.P.' embroidered in gold on the left breast, which causes me to frown.

"Does everyone have to wear clothing stamped with Ray's initials when they join him?" I query. Following my eyeline, the brunette begins to giggle.

"No silly, those are my initials. Rachael Perelli. Ray is my husband." My eyes widen and I splutter on the drink like a complete idiot. Giggling more, Rachel leans over to take the mug from me while I wipe my face on the hem on my t-shirt. Mumbling an apology, she waves her hand through the air. "Don't worry about it, you weren't to know."

"So, Ray married his maid?" I immediately regret the rude question, but Rachel's smile doesn't even falter.

"I'm not a maid, I'm the lady of the house. But with Ray's line of work keeping him busy all the time, I prefer to occupy myself with cooking and cleaning my home. Truth be told, our marriage never fully recovered after Sydney's.... well, anyways, we prefer our own outlets but we still honour our vows, through sickness and health." Her smile has a sad edge now while I realise the extent of who she really is.

Her actions all make sense now. No wonder Rachel has been naturally mothering to me; I'm around the age Sydney was when she was killed. This incredibly kind and thoughtful woman has suffered at the hands of my so-called father and now my emotions are clicking firmly into place. Any doubt of the task I've been given has disappeared. I need to bring Rachel just-ice, and then I will look after her the way she's looked after me. I'll be the son she and Ray never had, since we're all swapping parents and children like candy these days.

Leaning forward, I stretch out my hand for her to take and speak softly. "I'm so sorry for what you've had to endure. I promise I will do everything I can to right the wrong that has been done to you."

∞∞∞

"Ahh, Wyatt." Ray rasps as I step into his office as re-quested, sounding croakier today than I've heard him before. "I'm sorry to have kept you waiting all day. Don't bother sitting down. Everything is in now place, it's time for you to prove your loyalty to this family. Just a technicality really, before we can allow you to leave." I hover inside the doorway, unsure what this technicality business is about but I'm happy to jump through his hoops so I can get onto the task at hand. For Rachel.

I shift my weight from foot to foot as Ray reaches for his phone. After placing a quick call and pocketing the iPhone again, two guards shove past me to assist Ray to his feet. Only now is his true fragility coming to light. Aiding him on either side, the old man grunts as he walks with the use of a long cane. But I'm still not fooled to think he couldn't have me executed with a simple word if he fancied it. Whoever Ray Perelli is, he has deep connections and more power than I could muster in my pinkie finger. That much is clear by the armed henchmen that run to his every whim and treat him with the upmost re-spect, despite his weakened state.

Edging out of the room, I follow the trio without being asked. I have to take tiny shuffles so as not to trip Ray up, which would be hilarious but I value my limbs. It takes us five times longer than necessary, but we eventually round the front of the house and find ourselves in the main hallway. Up ahead, I notice Rachel standing by a concealed door I hadn't noticed before, around the back on the staircase. As we approach, she opens the door wide and kisses Ray on the cheek as he passes, disappearing inside with his guards. I hesitate at the sight of darkened steps leading down but Rachel's chestnut eyes crinkle in encouragement.

The air feels different as I creep down the steps - cooler and laced with anticipation. As if the whole house is frozen, not a window flapping or floorboard creaking, waiting for whatever I'm going to find at the bottom of this staircase. The guard ahead has a torch for Ray, but it doesn't help me much. My foot hits the bottom level, the cold stone seeping through my socks and making me shudder. Glancing around in the darkness, the guards rush forward to switch on electric lanterns lining the long corridor.

"Joining us is a lifelong commitment, son. Once you've completed your task, you can live in the luxury you've tasted these last few days. Everything you've ever wanted will be yours. But first, you'll have to pass your initiation." Ray's voice bounces around the corridor and he grips onto my forearm with a surprising amount of strength.

Using my arm as support, Ray shuffles forward and drags me along with him to a doorway on the right. It looks straight from the medieval catalogue, thick wooden beams encased in steel. A small barred grate sits centrally, with an opened slidable sheet of metal for peering in. Inside is pitch black so I can't get a hint of what's on the other side, but I can hear scratching against the wall and a soft whimpering leaking through the grate.

My heart starts to pound in my chest, the easy feeling I've had since arriving here fleeing my body. The bigger of the two guards places the torch onto one of my hands and a weighted object in the other. After opening the door, he grips the back of my t-shirt and shoves me inside. The door slams shut and locks behind me as I scramble to locate the creature inside with the flashlight.

What I find is miles away from the vicious animal I was picturing in my mind. An emaciated woman, all skin and bone, is crumpled in the corner of the stoned cell, scraping her bloodied fingernails against the rock. Her matted dark hair covers her face and her pale skin is filthy. It's then the stench hits me. Raising the back on my hand to my nose, I remember I was handed something and on inspection, find a handgun clenched in my fist.

"This is your test, son. All of my men are required to exact their own revenge so they can understand the need for mine. This way, everyone is loyal to my cause and thankful for this chance I provided them." Ray's cracked voice sounds through the porthole. I stare at the feeble woman in confusion. She barely registers I've entered her cell.

"But I've never seen this woman before in my life. She's never done anything to me." I answer without taking my eyes from her, knowing I won't be able to do whatever it is they expect of me. Did Ray actually think I could waltz in and shoot this woman? Or is the real test to leave me locked in this cell with her until she inevitably tries to eat me like some cannibal psycho?

"Exactly," he chuckles darkly. "That is your birth mother, Wyatt. A druggie who sold you to the Hughes as a newborn babe. We've been able to track the records of Nixon's offshore bank accounts, he has been paying this woman monthly for the past 20 years to support her addiction and keep her quiet." To say a rush of emotions barrelled into me would be an understatement. Confusion, anger, misery, things I can't even explain pour into my being and consume my thoughts. My grip tightens around the semi-automatic, the flashlight's shine never wavering from her grotesque body.

"She abandoned you Wyatt. Now's the time to take your

revenge. Kill her." Ray's voice echoes around the walls, finally drawing a flinch from the horrendously skinny woman. Noticing me for the first time, she uses the wall to push herself up onto blistered feet. A slight hunch remains in her shoulders as she faces me, her thin hair falling aside to reveal matching clover green eyes staring back at me. My heart jolts as all hopes of this being a twisted joke vanish. It's really her. A mom I didn't know about until yesterday, looking upon me like a stranger. I have so many questions but the gormless look on her face tells me she's either high or her brain is too far past fried to respond. Does she remember having a child at all? Did she ever look for me? Or did she take the money and inject it all without a second thought?

"What are you waiting for? Do it!" Ray shouts from behind. Something metal hits the cell door causing a loud clang to assault my ears. Pulling the slide back on the pistol, like I've seen on movies, I raise it in line with her forehead. My hand quivers slightly as I swallow thickly. This isn't me, I've never shot a gun. I try desperately to muster some of the anger I felt a moment ago so I can blame the overriding emotion for shooting, but I can't get it back.

Looking into her blank eyes, all I feel now is misery. Misery for the life she's clearly led, for the chances she's missed out on, for whatever brought her to this makeshift dungeon in some mobster's house. But her misfortunes haven't been for nothing. Whether she remembers having me or not, she made the selfish or selfless choice to give me away, which has provided me with a life I wouldn't have known otherwise. I'd probably be addicted to heroin or dead if I'd remained with her.

Sighing, I shake my head and lower both of my arms. The second the flashlight leaves her frame, she shifts forward with a shriek that pains my ears and makes me jump. Knocking the flashlight from my hand, she tries to grab the gun with as much force as she can - which evidently isn't much. Pushing her away from me, she lunges over and over again like she possessed. I can't believe this – she would try to kill me after I spared her, despite whether she recognises me or not.

On another feeble attempt to knock the gun from my hand, my finger slips on the trigger. A bullet ricochets off a nearby wall loudly but not even that stops her attack. Continuing to scream, she claws and scratches my neck, biting down hard on my chest through the material of the shirt. Jerking in disgust, I shove her away from me forcefully.

I hear the scuffle of her fall but it's the immediate silence that follows which panics me. Shining the light across the floor, the addict is lying deathly still with her back at a twisted angle. A growing patch of dark red seeps from the back of her head to cover the stone around her. Rushing over and kneeling, I quickly check for a pulse but there's not so much as a flutter under my two fingers pressed to the side of her neck. No. She's dead, and it's all my fault. I've killed someone, regardless if it was an accident.

Metal sliding open sounds behind me as the door is unlocked and Ray steps inside, his cane tapping on the stone. One of the guards crosses the cell to retrieve the gun I'd dropped somewhere between shoving her and checking for signs of life. Ray's crinkled hand lands on my shoulder with a supportive squeeze.

"Well done my boy. Some say using a gun is the coward's way out. But you took your revenge with your bare hands, like a true killer. I knew you were the right fit for us, which is why I have such high hopes for you. Welcome to the family, son."

# Meg

The Range Rover flies over the rocky dirt path as I push my foot down on the accelerator. Glancing in the rear-view mirror, I see my mom and Nixon's shadows run from the house in the rising sunlight, no doubt shouting after me as I tear through the forest. Low hanging branches smack the rental with wet leaves as I uselessly try to duck them from inside the vehicle. I feel the tyres resist against the rough terrain but I don't slow down, needing to put as much space between me and them as possible. I need space and time to think. My breathing is coming out in ragged pants, a tightness in my chest making it hard to concentrate on the barely visible road.

Splashes of fat rain drops hit the windscreen, the weather apparently sensing my mood since I have a full-on shit storm happening inside. Before long, the rain grows so heavy my view is obscured amidst the rapid back and forth of the wipers. Catching a glimpse of a side road, I quickly twist the steering wheel and immediately regret it. The back end of the vehicle skids out as I lose control, frantically spinning the wheel in the opposite direction in an attempt to regain control. Slamming my foot on the brake, I lurch forward as the Range Rover stops and stalls.

"Come on, come on," I beg for the engine to turn over so I can get the fuck out of here. The headlights brighten outside as a rumbling rolls through my fingertips, although I can barely see where to go. Figuring I'll crawl the car through the dense woodland until I come to a main road, I push my foot down on the accelerator. I hear the engine rev and the wheels turning but I remain stationary. After a few more failed attempts, I open the door and lean out to see the back wheel firmly stuck in a muddy ditch of my own making. Fuck it.

Slamming the door closed to shield me from the now horrendous downpour outside, I throw myself over the steering wheel. My whole world has been spun on its axis and I can't stay here a second longer. But stealing the keys from my mom's purse and running out into yet another incoming storm probably wasn't the smartest move. I can feel my heartbeat pulse through my entire body and I know it's not because of my near crash. Information I don't fully understand is flooding my system, the only piece I can hold onto is that my mom lied to me.

*"Meg," Nixon's harsh eyes relax as they gaze upon me and an unnaturally kind smile takes position on his face. "Let's go inside, we need to talk." My mom fiddles with the rope belt to her dressing gown and refuses to meet my eye, a rogue tear glistening in the moonlight as it rolls down her cheek.*

*Following her inside, I see Nixon has taken his place at the head of the dining room table with his hands clasped on the glass surface. Busying herself making three mugs of coffee, my mom purposely keeps her back to me, which unnerves me the most about this whole situation. Sliding into a seat two down from Nixon, a mug is placed in front of me before mom sits opposite me.*

*"There's a lot you don't know Megan-"*

*"It's just Meg, always has been." I interrupt irritably, the clench in his stubbled jaw tells me he did not like that. Sipping my heavenly cup of caffeine, I wait for him to recompose himself and continue.*

*"Well actually, we named you Megan. Although, I'm aware this is not how you've been raised." His blue eyes flick across to my mom, an accusation held in their depths. Quirking my brow, I remain silent waiting for him to continue. "I need you to know that every-*

thing we have done, has been for your safety and happiness. I hope you will be able to see that."

"We?" I query, my eyes glancing between Nixon and my mom. Her throat bobs with a nervous swallow, her brown eyes filled with misery as they finally look up at me. Growing bored of being kept in the dark, I lift my hands and slap them loudly onto my outer thighs. "Oh, for goodness sake, will one of you just spit it out already?"

"Fine." Nixon takes control of the conversation, leaning forward on his forearms. "I found Elena 20 years ago at an infertility support group, after discovering Cathy was pregnant with twins. Both babies were girls, which wasn't the blessing it should have been. For reasons you won't understand, we had to hide the girls in plain sight and take in a boy instead – that boy being Wyatt. Unfortunately, the woman who promised to care for Avery went against our deal and fled. We lost track of her for years-"

"Wait, no. Stop. Avery is your daughter, like actual biological daughter?" I hold both of my palms up to halt the story, trying to keep up. Nixon rarely speaks more than a few sentences at a time but I've had to interrupt him twice now. His nostrils flare in irritation as he replies through gritted teeth.

"Yes, Avery is my daughter – as are you, Megan." The following silence continues for so long, a ringing starts up in my ears. The room around us starts to tilt and sway around the woman that suddenly feels like a stranger, opposite me. Centring myself on her face, I stare at my mom, confused above all other things.

"Explain to me the 'reasons I won't understand'," I mock his voice with air quoting my fingers, not fully believing him but judging by my mom's rigid posture, I'm going to want to hear what he has to say. Nixon sighs, hanging his head forward. The man who raises his head is not the same one that sat there a moment ago. Distressed lines are etched around his eyes, his usually tense jaw slack for once.

"There was a young girl, Sydney Perelli. Her father was, still is, the most notorious mob boss in Chicago. He is the head of the city's biggest drug cartel and infamous for making people disappear *without a trace. He has his hands deep in so many pockets, including the police force, that there's never a shred of evidence that can be used against him. Until Sydney." Mom leans over to place her hand on his arm, that one small gesture speaking volumes of their connection. Scrubbing a hand down his face, Nixon sips his coffee before continuing.*

*"She ran away, fled on a bus hoping to leave her father's expectations behind and start a new life. But he wouldn't allow it. He sent armed men after her with the instruction to use any amount of force to bring her back, and that's how she ended up in my car. I worked in New York as a stockbroker back then, before we came to Atlanta. I found Sydney hiding beside my car as I was leaving the office one day and I stupidly took her home. I didn't know who she was, where she came from – I had just wanted to help."*

*I can see by the shift in Nixon's demeanour every word he is speaking is the truth, and he hasn't told this story in a very long time. His eyes are closed, the heel of his palm supporting his head. Mom keeps glancing at me nervously, but we can deal with our shit later. I need to hear the end of the story to fully understand.*

*"Once we realised the danger she was in, Cathy and I made the joint decision to help her escape for good. We managed to get her some travel documents and a passport under a new name so we were at the boating dock when her father's thugs found us. Maybe I shouldn't have gotten involved but it was too late by then, so as they dragged her from the boat at gun point, I fought back. They kept coming out of nowhere, but I punched and kicked anyone who got close enough. Somehow, I managed to get the upper hand when a handgun fell to the floor. I crouched to pick it up when hands landed on my back so I turned and shot. I didn't... it was an accident, but it was Sydney who lay on the ground dying. I tried to stop the blood flow, I sat pushing my hands over the bullet hole long after she stopped breathing. But it was too late – so when I heard the police sirens, I fled.*

*It wasn't long after, Cathy discovered she was pregnant and that's when the threats started. 'A daughter for a daughter.' So, we came up with a new plan – find women who are desperate to be mothers, adopt a boy that needs a better life and watch our daughters grow from a distance. Which was the ideal solution until Avery..."* His voice trails off as he looks at the moon beyond the window. *"After we finally found her again and discovered the life she was living, we had to bring her home. Elena agreed to be her therapist so we could finally bring you both together again, in the mansion where you should have always been."*

The passenger door opening startles me, forcing me to focus on the man who is apparently my biological father as he shakes the rain from his umbrella and slides into the seat. Closing the door, he turns to face me in his pricey trench coat. Now I'm looking for it, I do see the resemblance. His pale blue eyes, Cathy's brown hair. The truth seems so clear now I wonder why I never saw it before, but I had no reason to question it. My mom may have kept this huge secret, but she raised me with more love and compassion than I needed. So, for that reason, I can't stay angry with her. We may not share the same genetics, but that doesn't erase every bedtime story, kissed grazed knee, and cheering lacrosse games in the rain.

"So, what now?" I dare ask already knowing the answer since my getaway vehicle has failed me. "You're going to make me stay here, aren't you?" I don't need Nixon's answer as the sympathetic tilt to his brow says it all.

"Perelli is more determined than ever to have his revenge. After Cathy's ceremony, there was a note pinned to her closed casket. It said, 'Your girls are next.' That's why I had to leave. I thought they might follow me thinking I was going to collect the other twin. Or at least if I weren't around to witness it, they were less likely to hurt Avery. I thought she'd be safer without me, but I was wrong."

Nixon's words have drowned out, the word 'twin' sticking as the world fades away. Holy shit. I'd been so distracted with the story and bombarding him with questions afterwards, the truth has barely had time to sink in. Avery is my twin! My anguish starts to drown beneath the bubbling of excitement rising within. My hands grip the leather of the steering wheel tightly while I process the tide taking over, a smile spreading across my face that I'm sure makes me look clinically insane. It's so obvious now. Our connection is instinctual, our bond created long before we even realised.

Nixon is looking at me with worry so I quickly slacken my features. The rain outside has started to ease, the sun poking through the overhanging forest canopy. Watching droplets roll down the windscreen in wavy patterns, I start to put all of the blatant facts together. Nixon owns the beach house, in the middle of nowhere, with a panic room. I've been staying in a safe house this entire time and if this threat is as real as Nixon says it is, Avery should be here too. Besides, more than ever, I need to see her. I need to be reunited with my twin now I understand why I've felt like my soul has been floundering without her.

"You believe this mob guy is going to hurt Avery?" I need to know the danger she is in, completely unaware. He nods slowly, his eyes filling with worry. "Then we need to bring her here ASAP." I demand, leaving no room for argument.

# Avery

Beginning to rouse from a sleep so deep, I wonder if I died briefly in the night. Painfully heavy weights are crushing my body. Finding myself completely immobile, I start to panic I have been buried alive as I crack my eyelid in the dark. Agony slices through my right eye at the movement and blooms around my skull, feeling like I've been hit with a sledgehammer. Unable to stifle my groan, the weights on me suddenly shift so I can take a full inhale. Where the fuck am I? Strobe lights flash beneath my eyelids making me wince, the thump of music pounding around my head as I remember the nightclub in my studio, and the alcohol. The image of green in a shot glass has me shooting up and covering my mouth, nausea flipping my stomach over and I swear I can still taste the overly sweet liquid coating my throat. My mouth feels like a sewer and I know I'm minutes away from hugging the toilet.

Glancing around in the shadows, long silhouettes stretch either side of me, the faint outline of their naked bodies bringing me back to reality. Running my hands over their heads, I find Garrett snoring softly on my left by his silky hair and the shaved scalp of Axel on my right, flinching every so often. Well, that happened. I can't deny I was wound tighter than a corkscrew so hopefully when this hell-sent hangover subsides, I'll be much more relaxed. Shifting down the mattress, a dark smudge on the floor has me sliding from the bed to retrieve it. Garrett's shirt, which smells of his musky cologne, is gripped in my hand. Shrugging, knowing I wouldn't have had the energy to squeeze into my tight dress anyway, I slip the material over my arms and button up the centre, the hem falling to my thighs.

Creeping across the soft carpet on my tiptoes, I crack the door and peer out. All is silent and still, so I step out and close the door behind me with a slight click. Not wanting to be caught on my walk of shame, I move quickly along the corridor, squinting through my half-open eyelids. Rounding the staircase, my door is in sight when I hear a sound further up ahead. Throwing myself against the wall and remaining statue still, although I'm as obvious as a pork sausage in the vegan aisle, Dax stumbles slightly as he leaves his room. His afro bounces with each step, his hand holding his forehead as he pads past on heavy feet. Exhaling and sagging my shoulders once he's passed, I start to inch along the wall.

"You can walk normally, you know." His voice reaches me as he starts to descend the staircase, the deep sound jolting me. Shit. Hunching forward in defeat, I slump the rest of the way to my bedroom door which isn't half as fun as playing invisible ninja was.

Dragging my feet across the floor with each step, I enter my room and head straight for the top drawer of my vanity, pulling out a foil packet of Advil. Covering a wide yawn and scratching my scalp, I retrieve a glass of water from the bathroom and take the medication before slipping beneath my covers on the bed. The mattress welcomes me, its padding hugging my shape as I snuggle further down. Pushing my head under my pillows, the heaviness of the memory foam weighs on my brain to give it a minuscule amount of relief from the constant pounding within. Taking a mental inventory of my aching bones, the sensitive flesh between my legs, nausea coiling around my organs and the mother of all headaches, I pray the morning brings me solace as I drift back into the waiting darkness.

∞∞∞

"Rise and shine!" I flinch violently at the shouting, my body protesting with stabs of pins and needles. Lifting the pillow, I glare at Garrett while yawning.

"What the fuck is wrong with you?" My throat is desert dry and my voice croaky. His wide smile, damp hair and lack of dark bags beneath his eyes seriously piss me off. Pushing a glass of water towards me in his hand and producing more pain relief tablets in the other, I begrudgingly sit upright and curse the sun for shining so damn bright. Taking the items from Garrett, he sits on the edge of my bed as I pop the tablets into my mouth and down the drink. Half choking, I spray the clear liquid all over the bed as vodka burns my throat. "What the fuck is wrong with you?!" I repeat in a shriek, coughing and spluttering but his stupid smile doesn't falter.

"Best way not to have a hangover is to never stop drinking." He shrugs and takes the glass from my grip before I smash it in my palm. In a pathetic attempt to shove him from my bed, my limbs not fully responding to the ass-kicking he's receiving in my head, Garrett chuckles and pulls me into his lap for a hug. I resist initially but it's so much harder to push him away when he holds me like this and smells so damn good from a recent shower. After nuzzling in my neck, he lifts me and carries me into my bathroom where I find the tub filled with bubbly water.

"It's not filled with acid, is it?" I ask, although all venom has gone from my tone as he sets me down. It's impossible to stay mad at him and I'd pay for the entertainment of watching anyone try. Unbuttoning the shirt I'd forgotten I was wearing; Garrett smooths his hands down my arms as he takes it from my body.

"Not this time, I just wanted my shirt back," he winks and saunters from the room. Smirking and rolling my eyes, I wonder how boring my life would be right now without these insanely hot guys living in my house. Slipping into the perfectly warm water, I wish Meg were here to enjoy their shenanigans with me.

After a well-needed long soak, my bones easing in the heat and my headache starting to shift, I wash the leftover hairspray from my hair and rise from the tub. Wrapping my body in a fluffy, white towel, I re-enter my bedroom a new woman to find a plate of breakfast, a tall glass of orange juice and my phone lying on a silver tray on my bed. My smile grows as I immediately know this wasn't Garrett, this has Dax's name written all over it. Grabbing some velvet tracksuit pants in a deep grey and purple tank top, I dress and twist my hair up into a towel turban before settling down to eat against my pillows. The scent of bacon makes my mouth water, the rashers nestled between hash browns and slightly salted scrambled eggs, the way he knows I like them.

Lifting the fork, I eat with one hand whilst scrolling through my fully charged phone with the other. Opening my photos app, dozens of images from yesterday fill my screen. The selfie I took, the four of us beaming at the camera in our smart outfits before we turned into messy drunks, followed by a mountain of photos Garrett clearly took whilst I was living my best life. Amongst the blurred and shaky images my terrible cameraman took, there's a few gems - Dax with his arms around me while we gaze into each other's eyes, Axel and I head banging with our tongues out and gun signs blazing which makes me giggle to myself.

My bathroom door opens, Huxley appearing with his chocolate eyes in full puppy dog mode. His hair is tied into a top knot and he's wearing his basketball jersey and navy tracksuit bottoms. My mouth drops open quickly at the sight of him more dressed than I've seen in weeks and a glimpse that maybe my tough love has been for the best. Patting the space beside me, he enters and takes a seat, his shoulder brushing against mine. I switch off my phone and push it under my thigh, not wanting to ruin his progress with images of us having fun without him - despite it being his choice to miss out.

"You okay?" I ask when he doesn't speak. Instead of replying, he shuffles down to place his head on my shoulder. I suppose my question was silly considering everything he's going through, and although I may not know the extent of it all, I will still be here for him regardless. Not because I'm the reason he got injured but because I care about him, about all of them really. Even Wyatt, the stubborn, non-existent jackass he's being.

Stabbing some scrambled egg with my fork, I lift it to Huxley's lips and hold it there until he finally takes it between his teeth and eats. Flicking on the TV and leaving it on whatever channel is on, we spend the rest of the morning relaxing together as I force Huxley to share half of my breakfast. By the time the third episode of some new show I like the look of ends, I dare to break our silence.

"Did you want to go outside? We could take the playing cards out for a little bit, have a few games in the sunshine?" His head nods against my shoulder, unnerving me that he's not speaking but I'm happy he's actually up and moving around. Rising from the bed, Huxley lifts my tray and carries it downstairs for me, taking it into the kitchen while I grab a deck of cards. Reconvening on the brown wicker chairs in the garden with a matching table separating us, I inhale the freshest breath to have filled my lungs in a long time. The sun is beaming down on Huxley's blonde waves, his brown eyes a shade lighter as they adjust to the light. He's not smiling but his features are relaxed as he spreads his legs wide and settles into the seat. Repetitive splashing sounds from Axel swimming lengths in the pool, laughter floating on the light breeze from Dax and Garrett playing basketball in the distance. Shuffling the cards, I deal while explaining the rules to my own take on a game I like to call

'Skinny Joker'.

The day drifts into afternoon and I've almost managed to get Huxley to crack a smile. The others are hovering around for a glimpse at the old Hux, watching our games from a safe distance so as not to spook him. Even though we are treating him like a timid little mouse, in my mind Huxley is more like a cornered lion – his reactions are unpredictable since none of us understand what's going on inside his mind and he won't open up no matter how much I've tried. So, I'm going with distraction.

There are two cards left in my hand, one is the 10 he needs to make his final pair and the other is the Skinny Joker he definitely doesn't want to choose. Huxley reaches over, holding his hand over each card to try and gauge my reactions, little does he know I have a mean poker face. His fingers clasp into the 10 of spades and I lift my mouth ever so slight to trick him into thinking it's the joker. As predicted, even though we've now been playing this for well over an hour, he changes to snatch the joker from my hold and I burst into a fit of giggles. It's his turn to hold his two cards, his eyes keep glancing back to the left one. With a smirk, I pluck the right card and place my last pair of tens onto the table.

"Okay, I'm done." Huxley speaks his first words to me as he throws the card onto the stack playfully, the corner of his mouth tilting upwards. Doing a victory dance in my seat, my phone starts to vibrate in my pocket. A blocked number appears on the screen as I pull it from my pants' pocket, so I excuse myself. Huxley has already disappeared back inside by the time I've rounded the pool, striding across the lawn to accept Meg's call in private.

"Hey, I was wondering when I'd hear from you again." I joke, my heart lifting with hope she has good news - like 'get some ice cream in, I'm on my way home.'

"Hello Avery," a crackled voice rasps through the

speaker, halting my steps. It takes me a second to place the tone since I was expected one much more feminine.

"Nixon?" My mind starts whirling with so many un-answered questions. What are the odds he is calling me from a blocked number? Where's he been and when is he coming home? But his voice comes in a rush, not giving me a chance to speak.

"There isn't much time. Your life in danger. I need you and Wyatt to pack and meet me somewhere safe. I'm going to send you an encrypted email with directions to me. The pass-word is our special place. It's imperative you drive here, no air-ports. Only tell Wyatt where you are going, avoid public places and hotels. You can't trust anyone." I've never heard him sound so worried which only panics me more.

"I don't understand, what's the problem? Everything is fine and Wyatt isn't actually here right now..." His scoff travels to me, his disappointment clear.

"Where the fuck- never mind. I'll get in contact with Wyatt if you call for Jenson to drive you. I can't explain any-thing over the phone, but the threat you received a couple of weeks ago is still very real. I expect you to leave immediately, I'll see you soon." The line goes dead, leaving me standing in the middle of the grass, alone and confused. Running back towards the house, I call for everyone to meet me in the living room be-cause I know two things for certain. I can trust these guys with my life and there's no way I'm calling Jenson.

# Huxley

Slinging my duffle bag and backpack into the back seat, I slip into my Nissan and inhale deeply. I'd forgotten the raw leathery smell and the squishy comfort of the seat I'm sinking into. Despite my decision to follow wherever Avery goes being instinctual, I had been rather apprehensive when she told us we needed to leave. I've created my own save haven on the second floor of the mansion I'm staring at through the driver's window. But this is not my home and Avery still needs me, whether she accepts that or not.

However, now my arm is slung over the wheel and my feet are hovering over the pedals, a feeling of calm is settling over me that I didn't realise has been missing. Through the windscreen, I watch Dax rush around the white Bentley to help Avery lift the mountain of bags into the trunk. Her legs are being hugged in a pair of purple cropped leggings that clash with an orange hoodie I'm sure isn't hers judging by the excess of material around her petit body. Her hair is trapped under a curved neck cushion as she turns to smile at me sweetly and wave.

I lift my hand from the wheel but can't return her smile, knowing she's about to spend all day with Gare's rubbish jokes and Axel's lingering touches. To be fair, the pair had offered to ride with me but I had wanted to reunite with Rhonda (my burnt-orange beauty I've barely had time to enjoy). Doesn't mean my gut clenches any less at the sight of Axel opening the door and sliding in after her. Garrett appears on cue, his arms wrapped around multiple tote bags stuffed full with snacks and drinks that will probably only last him today. Ever the trustworthy one, Dax locks up before skipping down the porch steps and striding towards me.

"You sure you're good driving so far? Avery won't mind squeezing in the middle if you'd rather join us." He offers once I've rolled the window down but I shake my head.

"The open road is the best kinda medicine." I reply, settling down further and spreading my legs comfortably. After telling me to suit myself, Dax returns to the vehicle in front and disappears into the driver's seat. The Bentley grumbles loudly, Avery glances back at me through the back window as it speeds down the drive and out of sight. Craning my neck side to side, I gently roll my Nissan along the gravelled driveway to make sure the others are out of sight as I emerge from the open gates, turning the opposite direction on the street.

Dax visited me in my room last night, talking game plans for our 3-day mission to California. I listened to appease him but had planned on taking my own route, refusing to trail him like a lost sheep. The motel we've agreed on is programmed into the built-in sat nav on the dashboard, I'll just arrive a few hours after them. Pulling up at a red light amongst the busy streets, a pair of college girls, all legs in tiny shorts, wolf whistle at me through my open window. Smirking, I throw them a wink as the lights change and I zoom over the crossroad. Good to know I've still got it.

Meandering through the town, I start to realise how much I've been missing out on these past few weeks. Nothing extravagant, but the simple things like popping out for a walk and returning with an iced caramel macchiato seem like a distant dream. The shooting wasn't even that traumatic, it's the nightmares and worry that's been crippling me. Yet the tighter I tried to hold onto Avery, the more I seem to push her away. I could sense the arguments brewing between us but I couldn't stop myself. She stopped sleeping in my bed almost a week ago which is around the same time my self-loathing took a nosedive to Drown Town, as I like to call it. The place inside where all rational thought and slithers of happiness go to drown in the gloopy, black depths of my misery.

The town sinks into a speck in my rear-view mirror as I leave it far behind, my excitement starting to build. Merging onto the interstate, the wind begins to whip through my blonde waves as I finally pick up speed. Resting my left hand in my lap, I steer with my right as I weave from lane to lane, speeding around vehicles going much too slow for my liking. Pushing my foot further down on the accelerator, car honks filling the air behind me. A genuine smile spreads across my face and damn does it feel good.

Ignoring the speed limit signs, I continue to push the car to new limits now there are less vehicles around. Adrenaline courses through my bones, reminding me of why I chose the Nissan GT-R over all those fancy Porsches. Creeping over 100mph, I lean towards the open window and whoop in excitement, the wind beating against my face and my tongue lolling to the side. It's good to give the exhaust a proper clean out once in a while, I muse. Brake lights up ahead have me slowing down as fast as I can without giving myself whiplash, returning to the speed limit as I pass a cop car. Saluting the officers as they eye me curiously, I behave myself now – the intended effect of lifting my spirits a thorough success.

That taste of freedom tingles on my tongue, many vehicles including the cops taking an exit so the open road stretches before me with so many possibilities. Who says I need to go to this safe house? It doesn't seem like I'm needed anyway, I just sit in bed staring at the blank wall wondering what's happened to me. Maybe it's time I found a piece of myself I still actually like and cling onto it, find people who would appreciate the sacrifices I'm willing to make for those I care about.

A sign up ahead shows the turning for Tennessee on the

opposite side of the lanes. My heart starts to pound, the thought I could change course and slip through the state to put me on track for Waversea College. Our house on campus is the closest place I have to a real home, even though my boys wouldn't be there. I could actually enjoy the rest of my summer break, my badass new scar acting as a magnet to draw ladies into my bed. By the time my brethren return for the autumn semester, the old me will be back. No, scratch that, a new and improved me that doesn't look out for anyone except himself.

The turn off ahead becomes visible, my fingers twitching on the wheel with indecision. Torn between my head and my heart, I push the pedal to the floor and spin the steering wheel left. A shitty Toyota sounds its horn behind as I cut straight in front, crossing the three lanes and just making the turn in. A shudder runs through me, my arms tingling with trepidation. The image of a blue eyed, blonde hair temptress flairs to life in my mind, a heavy pressure pushing down on my chest with anxiety.

For a fleeting moment, freedom had seemed so close. But somehow Avery has managed to pull me back into the darkened cage where the worst version of me lives and I don't know whether to love or hate her for it. Coming to an intersection at the top of the ramp, I take the exit directly opposite and re-emerge onto the interstate with a sigh. I was stupid to think I could leave her behind so easily. Whether Avery wants it or not, I'm invested in her safety and I won't be able to live with myself if I let her down.

The sky is a murky purple by the time I pull into the motel's tiny parking lot. The shabby, run down building has stepped straight out of a serial killer's catalogue. Only a handful of curtains have a dim orange glow behind them, the rest of the two storeys are in complete darkness. I understand Nixon Hughes wants us to keep a low profile, but we are some of the country's richest offspring – surely a small hotel with in-room coffee machines wouldn't have been a huge stretch. My mother would have a heart attack if she saw me walk into a place like this. Actually, that doesn't sound like a bad idea, maybe I'll FaceTime her as I bathe amongst the inevitable filth and cockroaches.

Switching off the engine, Dax appears in the entrance of a room on the lower level. His afro touches each side of the doorframe and he's only wearing a pair of low-slung pyjama pants.

"Hey, was starting to get worried. We stopped at an all-you-can-eat down the road, Garrett almost cleared them out but I got you a doggy bag," Dax shouts over, turning to head back inside.

"Don't worry about it, I already ate," I lie. "I'll grab something from there if I need to." I point at the vending machine a few rooms down, the flickering light inside making me certain it would take my money and switch off. The door beside Dax's flies open and Garrett's head pops out like a squirrel on the hunt for nuts.

"He didn't want it, did he?" He asks excitedly, bobbing on his heels. Dax shakes his head on a sigh and Garrett woops loudly, shoving past Dax and disappearing in his room. Axel appears in the doorway Garrett has just vacated, a white towel fastened around his waist and water droplets still clinging to his body. The three of us stand in a triangle of awkwardness, animalistic sounds and sensual moaning escaping Dax's room. I don't think I've ever enjoyed anything the way Garrett enjoys food.

"Where's Avery?" I start to wonder as she doesn't present herself, anxiety nipping at my heels like a vicious chihuahua. Dax signals to the door on his other side with his thumb.

"She's sleeping, there were only 3 rooms left so we agreed she should have her own. You're sharing with me," he smirks although I'm not in the mood to return it. I ought to be rooming with Avery, keeping watch while she rests. Glancing around the chipped paint covered walls and derelict reception area, I fail to see how there were only three rooms - it's like a ghost town here. Garrett reappears to hurry back into his and Axel's room clutching a napkin in his hands, no doubt concealing cake of some description.

"I'm gonna hang out here for a while, stretch my legs and that." I say, glad Dax buys it and leaves me be. Once the door clicks closed behind him, I slump against the car bonnet and cross my arms. I didn't drive all day to play sleepovers, I came to watch over Avery and that's exactly what I'm going to do. For as long as Nixon believes this threat on her life is real, so will I. Strolling back to my open window, I lean inside and pull out the pack of cigarettes I found in the side pocket earlier - no doubt left in there from the many times Dax has taken my car. I've noticed he hasn't been smoking half as much since we arrived at the mansion and had started to think he'd kicked the habit, but the small box in my hand says otherwise.

Flicking open the lid, I find 7 sticks and a yellow lighter inside. Should be enough to get me through the night since there's no coffee machine in sight. Leaning against the car door, I pop a cigarette in between my lips and light it. The bitter taste is akin to acid but I'm going to need something to keep me going tonight. The thought of digesting actual food has been making me feel nauseous lately, so I've resolved to eating scraps here and there. For Avery. Pulling drags from the stick until only the butt remains between my fingers, I flick it across the concrete and throw myself back into my Nissan.

In the glow of a streetlamp, I shift my eyes from window to window across the two floors, checking for curtain twitchers. A brass number '7' hangs on Avery's door with a paper 'Do Not Disturb' sign swaying slightly around the handle. There's several cars in the car park, most of them old bangers so our Nissan and Bentley stick out like real diamonds in a pawnbrokers. Another good reason for me to play guard out here, otherwise the vehicles would more than likely be missing by morning.

My eye-lids begin to feel heavy so I give my head a fierce shake, my hair whipping around my cheeks. Pulling another cigarette from the pack, I tease my tongue piercing between my teeth at the thought of the offending tar-like taste filling my mouth again. But what choice do I have? Avery needs protecting and if that means I lose her in the process, so be it.

A door slamming jolts me awake, my head flicking up to see Avery strolling from her room fresh as a daisy. Her golden hair rivals the sun's waking rays, her wide smile putting the crisp morning to shame. Although that smile isn't directed at me, it's solely focused on Garrett who is also leaving her room with her overnight bag in his hands. Rage slams into me, pissed at myself for falling asleep but also at the slimy weasel who managed to worm his way in when I stayed away so she could sleep peacefully. Taking my eyes off the pair, I run a hand down my face and glance around the inside of the Nissan. A perfectly rounded hole is burnt into the edge of my leather seat, the offending cigarette butt lying by my foot on the floor. Fuck no.

This day just went from irritating to full on hell. I hear my name being called as the pair notice me, so I turn the key for the engine to come to life and back out of the car park. Garrett's arms flail as I turn onto the main road and speed off, deciding to meet them at the next motel check point after a day of brooding. There's only two things that can soothe me right now, and as Avery has given up on her vow to help me heal since my pain is no longer external, the open road will have to do it.

# Wyatt

A pitch-black moonless sky looms through the windows, but I can't close my eyes whilst knowing what's waiting for me there. Rubbing a hand down my face roughly, I pace in a circle at the foot of my bed. An old-fashioned clock on the chest of drawers irritates me with its insistent ticking, telling me I shouldn't be awake. Tick. Tick. Tick. Growling, I stride for the door since I can't stay in here another minute without smashing that fricking clock in a million pieces. Wrenching my door open, I go in hunt for some of those vitamins Rachel always has. Those little tablets must be herbal or some shit 'cause they work wonders for my stress levels.

Reaching the top of the blackened staircase, I freeze at the sight of a body collapsed by the bottom step. A shiver rolls through my spine, a slight tremble shifting into my fingers. There she is again. Her thinning hair fanned out across the floor, thickening as blood seeps from her skull. From this distance, I can merely see a shadow that's growing darker by the second but in my mind's eye, I can see every tiny detail. Especially her glassy green eyes which I see every time I look in the mirror.

"It's not real, it's not real," I whisper to myself as I creep slowly down the stairs, stepping widely to avoid the imaginary figure. As soon as my feet slap against the cold flooring, I turn right and half-run for the kitchen at the back of the house. The terrace outside the glass doors is swallowed by the night, casting everything around me in darkness. There isn't another soul about, just me and the visions that refuse to leave me be.

Walking through the kitchen doorway, an eerie outline by the fridge spins around quickly as I enter and makes me flinch. Her head is twitching side to side like a bird, the emerald orbs in her face never wavering from mine. Gritting my teeth, I stride past and yank the fridge door open, the woman disappearing in the bright light that glows from within. Pulling out the other half of the meatball sub I couldn't stomach earlier, I close the door and lean against the counter. Glancing around, I seem to be alone as I stuff the food into my mouth, suddenly realising how hungry I am.

Cooking is another one of Rachel's fantastic traits, along with keeping this huge house spotless. I don't know how or even why she does it, surely Rachel could spend the rest of her life relaxing by the pool being waited on if she wanted to. My only guess is she has learnt to distract herself from the missing presence of her daughter, a space I'm happy to fill for a while. She reminds me of the mom I had growing up, before they reclaimed their real child and turned their backs on me. I suppose in a way, I'm using Rachel as much as she's using me.

Devouring the sub in record time, I turn to rinse off the plate when I see the woman's ghost pressed against the window. Jumping enough to drop the plate, which smashes loudly onto the floor, I lose my shit.

"Leave me the fuck alone!" I yell, spinning away only to find a bloody shape sprawled across the floor. Her legs are twisted unnaturally, a look of horror on her pale face. Gripping the sides of my head tight enough to crack my skull in two, I clench my eyes shut and slide down the cupboard to hunch on the floor. Voices spring to life in my mind, swirling and shouting. They grow louder and louder, blurring into a whirlwind but one voice stands out amongst the rest. Ray's crackled tone full of conviction. "Kill her!"

I didn't mean to do it. Granted, I didn't give a shit about some crackhead I'd just met, but I've never wished death on anyone. And now she'll never breathe another breath, see another sunset or have another chance to get clean and sort her life out. All because of me. I was the one to shove too hard and end her life which makes me a cold-blooded murderer. The thought makes me sick to my stomach, no matter how many times Ray praises me.

Something clutches my shoulder, my hand shooting out to catch the wrist in a tight grip. Rachel's whimper forces me to open my eyes and shoot to my feet. I slide up her sleeve to check for a mark, despite it being too dark to see properly but needing to check she's okay anyway.

"Oh my god, Rachel I'm so sorry." I babble and fuss over her forearm but instead she takes my hands in hers gently and smiles.

"Don't worry, I'm fine. I shouldn't have snuck up on you." The worry etched into her face for my wellbeing brings tears to my eyes because I have finally found someone who cares about me the way I need. As soon as the first tear escapes, they all begin to pour out, some invisible dam inside me being breached. Rachel pulls me into her shoulder and holds me while I cry like an infant with a grazed knee, running her hands over my back and stroking my hair. Her sweet scent envelopes me, the fluffy material of her dressing gown brushing against my cheek.

"I keep seeing her everywhere." I whisper as my warring emotions start to ease in her presence. "She won't let me sleep." Rachel pulls me upright to look into her brown eyes, complete understanding shining in them. She doesn't need an explanation, nor does she tell me to man up. Just lifts my hand to kiss the back of it and pulls me across the kitchen to a cupboard in the far corner.

Pulling a key from her large front pocket, she pushes it into a tiny lock in the cupboard I hadn't noticed before, wedged into the corner. Rising to her tiptoes, she pulls a long box from the middle shelf. The box is split into seven sections, each one with the initial for the day of the week. Flicking open the 'W', Rachel picks out two of the small pink vitamins and places them into my palm. As I chuck them into my mouth without hesitating, Rachel reaches up to cup my cheek lovingly, the warmth radiating from her palm allowing my body to finally relax.

"Let's get you some warm milk and back to bed. Everything will seem better in the morning, I promise." Mimicking her smile and nod, I can't help but believe her. Watching her rounded frame potter around the kitchen, not a single shadowed illusion tries to find me. Soon enough, she is escorting me back to my room with a steaming mug nestled between my hands.

As I slide beneath my covers, my phone lights brightly on the bedside table. Huffing, I lean over to see yet another WhatsApp from a very persistent Dax asking me to call him urgently. Switching off the screen, I throw the device into the drawer and lean back against the trio of fluffy pillows. Rachel rounds my bed and pulls the phone from the drawer I've just slammed closed, frowning at the screen.

"Why haven't you answered any of these messages?" she asks, settling onto the mattress beside me. I shrug, sipping my drink and reclining back into the plush pillows. I don't know why I even bother keeping the damn thing charged since I have no idea what to say if I actually answered any of their constant phone calls. *'Hey guys, I'm great. Just chilling with hallucinations of a dead mom I just found out about and then accidently killed. How's life screwing my sister who's not really my sister?'* No, it's definitely easier to let them think I'm passed out in a ditch somewhere.

"Wyatt," Rachel's soft voice brings me back from my thoughts. "I don't get involved in Ray's plans, but from what I understand, you will be going back home soon. You should reach out to your friends, act natural. That will be the easiest way for you to ease back in to complete your task and come back quicker. I look forward to having you here with us permanently." Her lips lift in a sad smile, knowing I can't replace what she's lost but I'll be close enough. I'm determined to be enough.

After leaving the phone by my side and patting me gently on the shoulder, Rachel rises to leave and bids me goodnight. The door clicks shut behind her and I immediately tense, expecting a creepy figure to jump out at me. But the room is still, nothing stirring. Even the clock seems to be ticking softer, the repetitive sound making my eyes heavy. Placing the mug onto the table, I slump onto my side and pull the covers up to my chin.

Sleep starts to pull me in, a peaceful draw on my conscious thoughts to sink and rest for a while. Images faintly appear in my mind; my brothers lifting me high in the air after scoring the winning point of a basketball match, the insane after parties we would throw where I couldn't stop laughing. Life was so much simpler when it was just me and them, nothing and no one could come between us. But I've seen how protective they are of Avery, it's like my parents all over again except this time the rejection hurts so much more. I'm an outsider once again, which is why Ray's proposition sounds so alluring.

Vibrations by my face jolt me with a snore from the doze I'd drifted into. My phone buzzes repeatedly while I peek through my eyelids and wipe the saliva that had escaped my mouth, creating a wet patch on the pillow. The number is withheld but I can imagine one of the guys is on the other end, trying a different tactic to get me to answer. Now is as good a time as any I suppose, sighing as I answer the call and hold it to my ear.

"Hello?"

"Where the fuck have you been?! I've been trying to call you for two days." I shoot upright, my father's voice waking me completely like a bucket of ice water has been thrown over my head. "I know you're not watching Avery as I'd asked. Seriously Wyatt, one simple task. Her life is in danger and you can only think about yourself like usual." I'm stunned silent for a second, before my eyebrows crease and the anger seeps back in.

"You care so much about her, you watch her. I'm not a fucking babysitter." I seethe, wanting to call him out for all the lies so badly but needing to hold my cards close to my chest if I'm going to draw him and Avery here. He sighs loudly, his tone relaxing slightly.

"I've told Avery to leave Brookhaven, it's not safe for her there. She's already left to meet me at a safe house, so you'll have to make your own way here." Swinging my legs onto the floor, I hunch forward wondering why he cares what I do.

"Why would I need to go, I'm not in any danger."

"I'm not so sure. You have no idea what we are up against, anyone could be a target. I'll send you one of those password encrypted emails with the location. Tell no one where you are going, you hear?" My eyebrows shoot up as I realise how perfectly this is planning itself out. I have been wondering how to get my father and Avery together, but it seems like that's happening for me. I can't wait to tell Ray. "Wyatt! Do you understand the severity of what I'm saying?" His voice shouts at me down the phone making me scowl.

"Yeah, yeah I get it. Send me the address, I'm on my way."

# *Avery*

"Absolutely not."

"Oh, come on Avery, you have to! It's truth or dare, not truth or if you feel like it." Garrett whines from the passenger seat, turned all the way round to face me. I cross my arms defiantly and shake my head.

"There's no way I'm gonna sit here butt naked for the entire journey. I'll take a forfeit." Garrett's eyes darken and I gulp loudly, wondering if I should have just done the damn dare. Axel whistles low from the driver's seat, apparently reading my mind.

"Alright. Flash the next vehicle," he smirks, pointing at my window. Rolling my eyes, figuring it's not as bad as it could have been, I shift up onto my knees and lift my top, pushing my breasts against the cold glass. A truck passes, the driver's eyes popping out of his skull as he hollers and beeps his horn. Cheers fill the Bentley, the boy's loud whooping drowning out my giggle as I readjust myself into my bra and settle back into the leather seat.

"Your turn Garrett. Truth or dare." He replies dare without hesitation, practically bouncing in his seat. Looking around the moving car and across the backseat to Dax, who shrugs uselessly at me, I see a Cheeto roll out from under the seat in front. Garrett was sitting here yesterday so it must be one he dropped in between handfuls. Lifting to inspect the orange cheesy stick, there's hair and fluff stuck around, which makes it perfect. "Eat this," I lean forward to hand to him.

Without a second's hesitation, he throws the chip into his mouth and swallows, making us all gag. "Ew!" I squeal, suddenly very aware I've had my tongue in that mouth multiple times and I don't know what he's had in there. He smiles widely over to a shuddering Axel, possibly thinking the same, and winks back at me. It's Dax's turn to play next apparently, to which he chooses truth.

"Pussy," Garrett mutters. "Okay then. What's your biggest regret in life?" Dax turns his head to stare out the window, staying silent for so long I don't think he'll answer.

"Seeing the most important woman in my life in harm's way, and there's nothing I can do about it." He finally says in a tiny voice, Axel's concerned gaze catching mine in the mirror. Reaching over to grip Dax's bicep, I pull him over to rest his head in my lap. Bending over, I kiss his forehead and half squish him under my boobs but I'm sure he doesn't mind. I know a little of Dax's past, the way his father raised him with his fists but I'm not aware of the current situation on that front. My heart sinks to think of a woman stuck at home with such a man while Dax is here protecting me.

Stroking his afro through my fingers, we drive in silence for a while until Garrett reaches over to turn up the radio. Dax's eyes have fluttered shut, giving me a chance to study him close up. His square shaped jaw chiselled from granite, the thick eyelashes fanning his cheeks that any girl would kill for, his skin is a smooth shade of mocha. I don't drink coffee but I'd take the biggest cup of Dax to go any day of the week. Refocusing on the landscape outside, trying not to picture how gorgeous our babies would be, I find we've entered a small town.

Each building is a different colour, signs hanging from each doorway to show a particular trade. There's a handful of people on each sidewalk and not many cars on the road, making our Bentley stick out like a nun in a brothel. Heads turn as we pass, children staring at us like aliens.

Pulling into a deserted gas station, Axel hops out to fill us up. A girl around our age gapes at him through the glass window of the small shop next door, not that I can blame her. Axel's driving attire consists of no top, his broad chest and washboard abs looking lickable in the sun's rays, his thick thighs are poking out from his sports shorts and well-defined calves flexing with each movement. The well-rounded attendant that appears from the garage notices too, straightening his posture whilst speaking with Axel in an attempt to look taller. After paying, Axel turns to slide back into the driver's seat as the man's beady eyes roam over our vehicle and land on me, rubbing his greasy hands on a dirty rag and licking his lips in a way that makes me cringe.

"Matey says there's a diner and the motel we're looking for on the other side of this town, about 15 minutes' drive." Axel says as he restarts the car.

"Is it wise staying somewhere like this? I mean, we're a bit noticeable." I say in a low voice, knowing without looking the attendant's eyes are following me as we pull back onto the main street. I've been trying to supress my worries from Nixon's phone call but I can't shake the feeling I'm being watched and everyone outside of this car is suddenly a suspect.

"We can take turns driving if you'd prefer not to stop somewhere tonight," Axel replies sensing my concerns. But that's not fair on any of them and I'm sure it's all in my head.

"No, no, it's fine. This is where we agreed to meet Huxley. Besides, I can hear Garrett's stomach grumbling from here." I half-laugh, shoving my doubts away for when I can ask Nixon what is actually going on. Driving further down the surprisingly even tarmac road, I slide lower into my seat to avoid the attention we are drawing. Dax begins to stir on my thighs, his afro tickling below my denim shorts.

"Hey," I whisper as his blue eyes open, arresting me in a cerulean prison I would gladly receive a life sentence for. A smile takes his face hostage, those full lips close enough to make me blush. The Bentley pulls to a stop, breaking the moment between us as we both sit up to see Huxley resting against his Nissan.

The motel looms behind him, just as welcoming looking as the last. There're only six rooms on each level with metallic steps leading to the second floor. The walls probably were a fresh cream when originally painted in the 60s, but now the only hint of colour is of the brick peeking through the peeling, murky exterior. The windows are too dirty too see through and those feelings of trepidation have come back with a vengeance.

"Already got our keys," Huxley states as we step out of the car, throwing Garrett and Dax a pair each. Moving to pop the trunk, Huxley removes only my bag and slings it over his shoulder. Dropping his meaty arm around my neck, he begins to pull me away from the others and towards a room tucked away in the corner. "You're with me."

Skidding my feet to a halt, I elbow him in the side and take my bag from him hands forcefully. I may not want to be alone in a place like this, but no one plays a power move like that on me. I belong to nobody and I'll be damned if any of these guys think they can click their fingers and I'll come running. Whoever I room with will be my choice, and right now I choose myself.

Throwing my bag back into the open trunk as Garrett is trying to remove his, I stomp across the car park towards the diner sitting opposite. The elongated building looks like a crumpled tin box dropped from an unfortunate height. I'm 90% sure the windows are Perspex and the bushes planted around the entrance are plastic. A red flashing sign hangs above the doorway, the capital letters reading 'Mal's'.

Gripping the swirly metal handle, I yank the door open and cross the black and white checked flooring to a red booth in the corner. My butt has barely touched the leather when a heavily afroed shadow slides in across from me. Lifting a menu, I hide my face knowing I've acted like a brat and probably sent Huxley back into his shell again.

"Don't be too hard on Huxley. He's never cared about a single thing in his life, and now he cares for you and doesn't know how to handle it." Dax's voice travels across the table, using his fingers to lower the laminated card. There's only understanding in his eyes, a small smile playing around his lips. Garrett lands beside me, knocking me sideways as Axel slides in gently beside Dax.

"Have you seen the size of the milkshakes they do here?! I've ordered us all one, extra cream and marshmallows." Garrett beams. I can feel the excitement radiating through his bloodstream from here, he's practically vibrating. Staring out of the window, I watch Huxley pace around the car park, lost in thought. Pulling out my phone, I open the messages and start typing.

**Avery:** *If you ask me nicely, I will consider your proposal to share a room.*

I see him halt and pull out his phone, gazing at the screen for a while. Apprehension fills me, wondering if he'll play along or shut me down.

**Huxley:** *I don't beg for women to spend a night with me.*

**Avery:** *First time for everything. Humour me.*

The three dots appear and vanish on my screen multiple as he retypes his reply.

**Huxley:** *Oh, fair maiden, will thee shareth my bed chamber on this night?*

My giggle has Garrett looking over my shoulder and tutting.

**Avery:** *That wasn't so hard, was it? I can't talk like that but sure, sounds good to me.*

**Huxley:** *Neither can I, had to Google a Shakespearean translator. Figured that's how everyone speaks in the UK.*

My heart lifts and a grin spreads across my face, hopeful our friendship is on the road to recovery. I've hated staying away from him but I can't help someone who won't help themselves. Axel raises the key to unlock the Bentley through the window as Huxley rounds the vehicle and removes my bag once again, this time successfully making it into his room with my belongings. Our milkshakes arrive in tall sundae glasses, each one a different flavour. Garrett snatched the chocolate one with extra sprinkles, which I'm sure isn't a coincidence, as I reach over for the banana one.

The sun has set by the time we leave the diner, Garrett having sampled one of everything they have to offer. The waitress nearly died at his generous tip though (no innuendo intended), so I'm sure they didn't mind too much. Clutching a Styrofoam container for Huxley, I knock on the door to his room. Appearing in the doorway, he looks haggard with dark creases beneath his brown eyes. His lips hook up in a lame attempt at a smile, stepping aside the let me enter.

"When's the last time you slept?" I ask, although the question goes unanswered. Pushing the container into his hands, Huxley flips open the lip to glance at the club sandwich and chips inside. Sitting on the edge of the double bed in the centre of the room, I stare at him expectantly until he lowers himself into a metal chair at the matching table and begins to peck at it. I wait a whole ten minutes before moving to join him, eating the other half of the sandwich he's started pushing around the box. Baby steps are better than nothing. Huxley fails to suppress a yawn so I point for him to go to bed. Standing, he removes his t-shirt and tracksuit pants to place them in a nearly folded pile on the chair he's vacated. I have to force myself to keep chewing, saliva filling my mouth for a whole different reason.

Huxley has lost quite a few pounds lately, but that's hasn't diminished his ripped abs and firm chest. The rounded pink scar above his heart is visible in the room's overly orange lighting, the Samurai scene tattooed against his back standing out boldly as he turns. The piece has jumped straight out of a cartoon strip, exaggerated clashing symbols surrounding a huge sword that the central character is holding. Stripping to my own underwear and crawling into the bed beside him, his furnace-like warmth seeps into me. Cuddling into his side with his chunky arm beneath my head, I breathe in Huxley's manly scent.

"I've missed this," I admit quietly. Huxley shifts onto his side and pulls me into his chest, his hands sprawling into my hair as he immediately drifts to sleep in our lovers embrace.

# Garrett

"There!" Axel shouts from the passenger seat, pointing out of his window. Slamming on the brakes, I lean forward and squint to see a wooden sign hanging on a tree's branch with the word 'Avalon' written in white script. The Nissan behind skids loudly, barely stopping before crashing into our bumper. Huxley waves his middle finger at me through his open window, causing me to smirk.

"How the fuck did you see that?" I mutter under my breath, turning the steering wheel into a dirt path hidden from view. "Are you sure this is the right place?" I ask, creeping the Bentley along the track being mindful of not scratching the paint job.

"That's what the directions on the email said." Avery small voice pipes up from the seat behind me, her eyes catching mine in the rear-view mirror. Those blue irises are filled with worry so I smile and act like everything is going to be fine, which I seriously hope it is. To be honest, we are all going into this blind, but one thing I know for sure after listening to Wyatt's rants for years is that Nixon Hughes loves his daughter. He wouldn't bring her on a three-day mission to put her straight back in harm's way.

The trees start to hang lower, scraping against the car roof as we inch along the bumpy track. It takes much longer than necessary but I dare not arrive at our destination with wing mirrors missing or punctured tyres. A deer darts in front of the vehicle, my foot smashing against the brake and jolting us all forward. Luckily, I was going slowly enough that everyone and the deer are unharmed, only our jitters affected.

Continuing, I feel each person's trepidation building as I force my hands to keep steady on the wheel. Winding around yet another bend, the dense forest opens to reveal a three-story beach house. Powdered blue walls stretch around a much larger structure than I was expecting, a wooden porch visible on the side. I spot yellow sand and a shimmering sea beyond the building, my chest suddenly bursting with excitement.

"Beach!" I yell, my previous anxiety disappearing as I jump from the car with the engine still running. Meg bursts from the house, hurtling towards Avery so I have to dodge her in my haste. Ignoring Axel's shouts behind me, I push my legs at top speed toward the shore while tugging my vest over my head. Pulling my phone and Air Pods from my pocket, I chuck them into the sand for someone else to pick up and charge into the water. The cool water splashes around the heavy pound of my sneakers, my shorts sticking to my thighs as I dive into the water.

Swimming against a strong current, I breach the surface to see a huge wave crashing down onto my head. Being pulled down forcefully, I tumble and roll, fighting to find the way up. The tide steals my shoe from my foot causing me to shout underwater and lose previous air bubbles. Finally breaking free of the undercurrent, I gulp in a large breath and wipe the water from my eyes to look for my missing sneaker when another wave plummets onto me. Forcing my legs to kick powerfully in time with my arms, I push myself further into the sea until there's no longer the sounds of crashing overhead.

Bopping up, the house is tiny in the distance as I safety float far enough away from the waves, my sneaker is well and truly lost. I bet some fucker finds it washed ashore and has a field day at the custom made hightop I probably should have laced tighter. Bending to pull the left one off, I launch it as far as I can into the vast ocean. Hopefully, the son of a bitch can find the other to have a matching pair.

My limbs are already aching from merely getting to this point of calm beyond the turbulent waves. Not wanting to waste my efforts, I take my time swimming lengths back and forth from the house to a fence I find down the coast. Irritation at my own stupidity begins to ease, the burn of exertion filling me like my own brand of adrenaline. I love everything about the sea, mainly the freedom it holds beneath its surface. A whole world is hidden from view down there - mountains and volcanos, sunken shipwrecks, stunning displays of coral.

Axel's whistle carries to me on the wind, a speck of his figure waving to me from the beach so I turn back. A sea turtle drifts by, lazing contently under the sun's rays. A marbled effect covers his brown shell which is smooth beneath my fingertips as I stroke it. Watching the creature pass, barely having to move its limbs, I smile to myself. That's the life - no stress or commitments, just floating along enjoying the peace each day brings until a bull shark jumps up to eat you. Deciding turtles are my new spirit animal, I start to head towards my... whatever he is, just Axel.

Nearing the beach, the waves begin to pick up again, helping to push me the rest of the way now I'm not resisting. Realizing I can stand on the seabed, I rise to my full height and walk the rest of the way with water slapping across my back as I go. Emerging onto the beach in my soggy socks, Axel's amber eyes assess with a hint of amusement and slight disgust. Closing the gap between us, I throw myself into his body and squeeze him tight, ignoring the sounds of disgust. Forcing his hands between us to push me away, I smirk at his now see-through white t-shirt sticking to his muscled torso.

"What happened to your shoes?" he questions.

"Sea stole 'em. Waves are a bit choppy today," I grin as he

shakes his head at me.

"That's what I was trying to tell you. Here, take these back and go fight over a room like the oversized man-child you are." Axel hands me my phone and Air Pods with a roll of his eyes.

"You mean our room," I run my tongue up his cheek and flash my dimples in the way I know he loves. I mean, likes. Ugh whatever. He's right, I've been wasting precious time to throw someone out of the room with the best sea view. Looking up at the house, I've already picked out which one I'm taking and run towards the house.

Slipping my socks off and leaving them on the porch railing, I locate our bags in a heap on the living room floor. Shouldering mine and Axel's, I nod a greeting to Nixon, who's sitting on the sofa glaring at me, and stride upstairs. He's not my dad and Avery asked me to come, so his issues with me are not my problem. I don't put on a false front or change my mannerisms for anyone.

Opening the door of my selected room, I frown at the floral blue suitcase upon the bed surrounded by stacks of folded clothes. Well, shit. I can't kick a female from her room, I may be a dick but even I have my limits. Avery's therapist walks in from the bathroom, jumping and gripping her chest in fright at the six-foot, topless man filling her doorway. A floaty peach skirt with a high-slit sits at her waist, a tightly fitted white vest on top with brown waves lying on her shoulders. Wondering why she would be here, it takes me a second to remember she is Meg's mom.

"Holy broccoli stems, you scared me!" My eyebrows raise and I snort as she collects her and straightens. "It's Garrett, right? I've just met your friends; I didn't realise Avery was bringing all of you." I shrug with one shoulder, starting to turn away when I notice she has her toothbrush and paste clutched in her hand.

"Are you leaving?" I ask, trying not to sound too hopeful. She smiles sadly, opening the suitcase to pack the items spread across the mattress with expert organisation.

"I'm afraid so. Nixon thinks it's best that I return to keep up appearances - act normal."

"I have no idea what you're talking about, but I call dibs on your room." I saunter inside, setting the black duffel bags by the bay window. Axel is still out on the beach, having cleverly removed his shoes and socks to wander along the water's edge. He repeatedly runs a hand over his head, meaning he is deep in thought, worrying or both. I'll beckon him up here shortly and help him forget about any concerns that might be troubling him.

"Ahh," the therapist says beside me, making it my turn to flinch. Sneaky little devil. "I know that look. How long have you two been a couple?" I choke on my own inhale, spluttering and spinning around to face away from the delicious view.

"I don't do monogamy." I state gruffly, helping fill the rest of her clothes into the bag haphazardly to move this conversation swiftly along.

"And why is that?"

"The notion to be trapped with one person for the entirety of life is ridiculous to me. People are constantly changing, whoever I may or may *not* fall in love with now won't be the same person in five, ten years. No one will stick with me for that long anyway." Zipping her suitcase closed, I place it onto the wooden floor.

"Does being with Axel make you feel trapped?" Her brown eyes pierce my skull, reading my thoughts.

"Well, no but he's... ahh, I see what you're doing here. You can save your therapist voodoo for paying clients. I'm content with every aspect of my life." Kicking the wheeled bag towards her, it halts at her feet, my intentions clear that she has overstayed her welcome. I'm not a gentleman by any stretch of imagination but I can't stand people trying to worm their way into my head.

"Mmmm. Because being content is the goal." She mumbles, looking back out of the window. A defensive part of me wants to whip the curtains closed, blocking her view of him in fear she can psychoanalyse him from here. Fuck my own, Axel's issues are sacred. I'm the only one who can help him, I'm the only one he needs. If there was going to be one special person in the world I could see myself being... romantic with, it would be Axel. But that's not who I am, and he knows that. Right?

Shouting sounds from downstairs, dragging my attention to the doorway. Leaving the therapist in the room, I take the stairs two at a time to see what the fuss is about. Nixon orders Avery and Meg to go upstairs, their sulky faces pushing past me as I hop from the bottom step. "What's going on?" I ask no one in particular.

"A car has pulled up outside." Huxley answers for me, everyone is standing around the living room poised for some kind of attack. Sweat lines Nixon's brow as he flexes his hands beneath the cuffs of his cream shirt to match the black suit trousers and dress shoes that are at complete odds with our humid surroundings. Huxley and Dax are hanging back by the staircase, but if this is a real threat then I need to get to Axel.

Shooting through the kitchen, a shadow on the other side of the blinds follows me. My heart begins to beat wildly, emotions I can't pay attention to rising and guiding my actions. Pausing with my palm hovering over the back-door's handle, the figure steps in line with me, their face obscured by a black hood. From behind, Nixon shouts for me to move out of the way but there's no way I can leave Axel out there now. Grabbing the handle, I twist and throw the door open, bracing myself for a fight. Green eyes widen at the sight of my raised fists, Wyatt's eyebrows cocking in surprise.

"Well, hello to you too."

# Wyatt

A heavy weight collides with me from behind, sending me fly-ing into Garrett. Initially thinking I've been attacked; I elbow and squirm until I recognise Axel's fingers pushing in my hair and forcing my hood down. Garrett pulls us into his tight em-brace, my bones threatening to crack under the pressure. It only hits me now how much I've truly missed my boys, a feeling that was much easier to suppress when they weren't around. Releas-ing me so I can breathe again, I find Dax approaching to clasp my hand.

"Welcome back, I hope you're staying?" His piercing gaze watches me closely as I slap on the relaxed smile I've been prac-ticing the whole way here from the driver's seat of Ray's navy Sedan. Not having the words to lie to him, I nod and move into the modern kitchen, removing my backpack and placing it on the glass dining table. Blonde waves catch my attention, the saddest brown eyes I've ever seen glancing across the room but he makes no move to greet me. Crossing the kitchen, I initiate the hug this time, having known seeing Huxley would be the hardest part of this whole charade.

"Hey Hux." Gripping him tightly, he buries his face into my neck and squeezes me with the same vigour.

"Why didn't you return any of my calls?" His voice is muffled against my skin, moisture pooling in my collar-bone telling me a few tears have escaped him. I swallow down my guilt, forcing myself to remember the real reason I came here.

"I've really needed you." He whispers, clearly not wanting the others to hear.

"I know, I'm sorry man. I'm here now." I pat him on the back, my heart breaking as I say the words knowing they're not the truth. Needing to distance myself, I step back and my eyes land on my father standing uselessly in the living area. His hair has more grey in the temples than he's ever allowed, disappointment etched into his pale blue eyes. Stubble lines his tense jaw that seems at odds with his overly smart attire.

"We need to talk." There's no fondness in his tone as he walks towards a staircase, clearly expecting me to follow. Hatred begins to seep back in, making it much easier to focus on my plan. Find the other twin and contact Ray when I somehow manage to get them all together under the same roof - most likely back in Atlanta.

Not in any rush to obey orders, I take in my surroundings. A charcoal grey sofa large enough to sit five people faces an impressive fireplace with two matching armchairs parallel. A dark coffee table divides the seats with a similarly coloured sideboard by the window, and absolutely nothing else. No TV or games consoles, no entertainment in the slightest. Wow, I can feel the boredom settling into my veins already.

Without anything else to do, I can feel four pairs of eyes following my movements as I march around the banister and take the stairs two at a time. My father is waiting impatiently, tapping his foot and checking his watch for added effect before disappearing into a room on the right. I stride onward purposefully, ready to get this over with as quick as possible.

"You look like crap," my father says as I enter a study, handing me a glass of whiskey. I look down at my black hoodie, dark jeans and Timberlands thinking I look smarter than usual. "Not your clothes, you. Your eyes are bloodshot to shit and you've lost weight, are you on drugs?" Scoffing and refusing to answer such a stupid question, I throw myself into a deep red armchair beneath a huge bookcase. Tipping the whiskey into my mouth and swallowing, I hold the glass out for a refill. He huffs and rolls his eyes, but pours me another good measure anyway.

"Why are we here?" I ask instead. Closing the door and pulling a matching armchair around to sit in front of me, he sits with an ankle resting over the opposite knee. For a moment, he doesn't speak. In the bright overhead light, shadows of creases pull at his eyes and mouth showing how much he has aged in the past month since I last saw him.

"There's so much I need to tell you but I'm afraid I can't stay long. An extremely dangerous man is after Avery so I need to keep moving, throwing him off her trail." Staring at him for a while, I think carefully on how to respond – not wanting to say anything I shouldn't know or give myself away. It's imperative I keep them together but if I've learnt any of Nixon's bad habits, it's his stubbornness.

"Surely Avery is easy enough to track if someone really wanted to. You might as well stay close by if you're so worried." A loud sigh leaves him as he leans forward, resting his elbows on his knees to be closer to me.

"It's not just Avery. Wyatt, I need you to hear every word I'm about to say." He focuses on me with every ounce of his attention, something he hasn't gifted me with for an exceptionally long time. I nod for him to continue. "Your mom and I adopted you at four days old to cover up the fact we had twin girls. It's a long story I don't have time to dive into, but you need to know this. You are our son and we've loved you in a way your biological mother never could. All three of you are our children, please never forget this." Acting confused, I glance at the floor and draw my eyebrows together.

"I don't understand. My eyes..."

"Are the exact reason we chose you. They were a perfect match to Cathy's even as an infant, but none of that matters now. I can't survive losing anyone else." *Exactly*, I smirk to myself on the inside. A small part of me knows I should feel remorseful at the mention of my mom, but nothing penetrates the numb sensation that has taken up residence in my body.

My father hangs his head, giving me a chance to look around the room we are in. An empty fireplace sits on the wall across from me, the lack of carbon residue tells me is has never been used. A desk is pushed against the huge window, giving a perfect sea view. The sun has begun its descent, thick rolling clouds turning orange on an autumn coloured sky.

"So, who's the other girl? Presumably they are both in danger." I finally ask when I figure it's been long enough, trying to slow my pounding heart. My head pulls forward on its own accord, my ears pricked. Keeping his head low, avoiding my eye contact, his answer travels to me on a low breath.

"Meg." My eyes widen, that one syllable setting off an explosion of emotions within. She's been there all along, right in front of me. In my house, sharing my food. In one way, I feel relieved this mystery girl isn't countries away or impossible to find, but another part of me spirals deeper into my self-loathing. This is another stab of betrayal proving I wasn't good enough for the pair I've called mom and dad my entire life. They needed her close by, secretly completing their perfect family circle behind my back.

Standing, I move over to the window, unable to be close to him any longer. I've been used as a façade my whole life, a smokescreen to hide the fact the man behind me killed Sydney. Struggling to remember to breathe, my body shakes with treachery. The throbbing vein in my temple I haven't felt for weeks starts pulsing again, adding extra irritation to my already foul mood. The glass clasped in my hand starts to splinter so I drop it onto the carpet. In my mind, I'm shouting every curse word I know and throwing the desk through the window. Shuffling behind me reminds me I'm not alone, and that I need to keep up this act for a little longer.

"Wyatt," his hand falls onto my shoulder, every part of me screaming to remove it. "I believe Avery's identify has been discovered, but Meg is still safe hidden in plain sight. Promise me you'll help to keep her safe. We'll have time to sort out our issues one day soon, but I really need you to do this for me right now."

"Don't worry, I will handle everything." I manage to grind out evenly, his hand patting me before he moves away. An evil sneer takes up residence on my face, the image of dragging Avery and Meg into the Perelli household by their hair filling my head. I can practically feel the silky strands wrapped tightly in my clenched fists and hear their screams. The handle twisting snaps me out of my daydream.

"Wait, what's the plan then? Are we just going to wait here for you to return or shall I bring Avery back to Brookhaven when you deem it safe?" I spin around as he steps from the room, jogging to stay hot of his heels. Further down the corridor, my father opens the door at the far end. A black suitcase is sitting by the bed, seemingly ready to leave right now. Lifting his bag, I stand firmly in the way with my arms crossed so he can't pass without answering me.

"I don't have those answers yet, Wyatt. There's no signal at the safehouse but the closest town is 40 miles away, drive down every few days to check your emails. I'll update you when I have more information." He barges past me, obviously finished with this conversation but I'm not. I can't stay in a house in the middle of nowhere with my enemy for god knows how long.

"What about College? Or my birthday, am I meant to just sit here-"

"This isn't about you Wyatt!" He turns to shout in my face, despite having to look up slightly. No, nothing ever is. Letting him leave, I scowl at his back with the anger I've been hiding. A few days or weeks here will be nothing compared to the warm welcome I'll receive in Chicago once Ray's retribution has been delivered to him. Nixon, Avery and even Meg will pay for the mockery they've made of my life, only then can I reinvent myself surrounded by people who appreciate me. Want me.

Trotting down the staircase, the open front door gives me a view of my father slamming the trunk of his Rolls Royce shut and sliding into the driver's seat. A brunette is sitting in the passenger seat although I can't get a good enough look to see who it is as the engine roars to life. Leaning against the sofa, footsteps on the stairs distract me from thoughts of how Ray's revenge is interlinked with my own. Looking over my shoulder, my blood turns to ice in my veins.

I'd anticipated seeing Avery for the first time being difficult, but nothing could have prepared me for this. My stomach plummets and my heart stops beating in my chest as I gape at the pair standing on the bottom step. Two sets of blue eyes land on me, varying in shade beneath perfectly arched eyebrows. Their button noses smeared with light freckles above full lips they are both biting subconsciously. Wearing matching hoodies and leggings, only the colours differing like the long hair upon their oval shaped heads, the truth of their genetics is so clear I can't believe I've never seen it before.

My eyes zero in on Meg, confusion at her presence fogging my brain. "What the fuck are you doing here?" I half-shout, looking between the two of them and the car driving into the forest, out of view. Shit.

# Meg

Leaning my head on Avery's shoulder, I watch the vehicle carrying my mom be swallowed by the forest, the backlights fading as night falls. We've spent more quality time together these past few days than we have in years, rebuilding our relationship in light of the truth. Snuggled under a blanket in front of the living room fireplace, swimming in the sea, endless hours of board games. Even though I hadn't known of the lurking secrets, I feel more connected to her than ever. A part of me thinks I lucked out, having a parent who was always around to give me her full time and attention. My mom raised me with more love than the Hughes' money could ever buy.

Avery and I have sat on my bed all day, sifting through the information we held to piece our lives back together. A part of me still can't believe I have a twin but being with her feels too natural to deny it. Tears filled her eyes as I repeated every detail of our origin story I could recall, whether from grief for Sydney or the realisation someone is in fact trying to kill her, I'm not sure. By the time Nixon had come to see us both, she flung herself into his arms and cried, finally reunited with her father.

Avery kisses my forehead, jarring me from staring into the distance and refocusing on the room. Wyatt's rigid posture stomps towards the kitchen, retrieving his backpack and reappearing in front of us. A vein is protruding from his temple, his jaw clenched tight enough to crack a tooth. The pure hatred swirling in his green eyes are directed solely at me for once. Leaning close, he comes nose to nose with me, despite being a step lower, speaking through his teeth. "You'd better watch your back."

I don't know what he was expecting, maybe a curtsey or for me to scurry away in floods of tears, but the shock in his face says it definitely wasn't the full powered shove to his chest making him take a step back. Even Avery gasps in shock and grabs my arms, knowing I'd take a swing if I felt like it. I understand his world has been flipped upside down and he's no longer sitting above on his titanium pedestal, but I'm not meek and it's best he realises that from the start. He can't intimidate me.

Dax materialises between us, holding Wyatt at bay as he tries to advance on me again. He rams his shoulder into his friend, those haunted irises glued to me the whole time. Something has changed with him. He's always been a moody shitbag but physical violence has never been one of his spoilt brat traits. A hand wraps around my wrist, Axel's arm gently tugging me out of the way. Wyatt growls like an animal, practically frothing at the mouth as I allow myself to be removed from his firing line, taking Avery by the hand and pulling her with me. As soon as we are clear, Wyatt twists to throw his fist into the nearest wall before shoving past Dax and storming upstairs on thunderous feet.

"I can see he is going to be a barrel of laughs," I deadpan. Realising Axel is still holding my wrist, I shake out of his grip and eye them all suspiciously. Huxley is standing in the threshold between the two rooms, his hands clasped in front of him like a warden overseeing his prisoners. His pale cheeks are surprisingly hollow, no hint of the smile he wore permanently when I saw him previously.

Garrett, however, is the polar opposite, swinging his legs back and forth whilst sitting on the kitchen counter. A huge grin reaches from ear to ear, his hazel eyes sparkling with excitement. Beside him, brown paper bags cover every other surface in the kitchen, my heart leaping at the thought of food. Real food that doesn't come in a tin and have years left on the expiry date. My stomach grumbles loudly, Avery laughs by my side and drags me over to the counter. Riffling through the bags, I find heaps of sugary snacks and fizzy drinks.

"Oh, sorry Nutmeg, those are my provisions." Garrett hops down, drawing over half of the bags into his arms and skipping from the room before I have a chance to tell him that nickname won't be sticking. There's only three bags left, making me frown as Avery starts to empty them. Once finished, we both stand staring at the fruit and veg while I resign myself to becoming vegan. Dax appears at Avery's side with a duffle bag in his hand, bumping her playfully with his shoulder.

"I snuck out last night to stock up. If we hide it all in the fridge behind the veg, he shouldn't find them there." I don't miss the lingering gaze and smile they share, tucking it away to ask Avery later just how close she's been getting to these guys. Placing the bag on the dining table and unzipping it, the three of us rush to fill the fridge and freezer, tucking blocks of cheese and packs of ham behind broccoli and cauliflower florets like we are stashing gold bars. I am starving by the time we've finished, my hands starting to shake.

"Here," Avery hands me a banana and ushers me into the living room. "Keep Huxley company while we make dinner for everyone." I only now notice him sitting on the long sofa since he is unnervingly still, staring at the opposite wall. Crossing the room, I take the armchair on the far side so I can watch Avery and Dax's dynamic. Looking over to my companion for the next half an hour, he doesn't acknowledge me until I clear my throat.

"Rough couple of weeks, huh?" is all I can think to say. His head turns slowly, like one of those creepy dolls in a horror movie, his eyes as equally vacant. Fidgeting under his stare, I continue talking like an idiot. "It's been so boring here-"

"Did you get shot?" My eyes widen and mind goes blank. "I didn't think so." He returns to facing forward, playing with his tongue piercing between his teeth. Sitting back against the cushions, I unpeel my banana and turn my attention to Avery instead. She is currently washing a lettuce while Dax's hugely overgrown afro wobbles in time with his vigorous cheese grating. He flicks a strand of cheese at her, landing in her hair as she giggles and flicks water onto his face.

A topless Axel hops down the stairs, following the smell emanating from a large frying pan only to find himself in the middle of a food fight. Grabbing her around the waist from behind, Avery squeals as Axel spins her in time for a handful of coriander to hit his bare back. Arming himself with a chopping board as a shield and a spatula as a sword, Axel advances on Dax who fails to dodge the spatula spank he receives on his backside. Huffing at the sound of Avery's giggles, Huxley pushes himself to his feet and leaves swiftly.

"It was nice talking to you," I call after him, unable to resist. He doesn't glance back like I expected, opening the front door and slamming it shut behind himself. "Well, fuck me I guess." I mutter. Garrett jumps over the back of the sofa to land on his side, his hand beneath his head as he watches me take a bite of my banana.

"If you insist," he winks. I try not to smile back but the guy is an enigma I can't figure out. Usually, he's the type I'd steer clear off, my rational mind telling me he's a self-centred jackoff. But for some reason, I like him. The others in the kitchen have returned to preparing a meal, the smell of onion wafting over making me groan. In record time, they are transferring plates to the dining table so I move over to the same chair I sat in when Nixon first arrived.

A stack of wraps takes pride of place in the centre, surrounded by chopped lettuce, cucumber and peppers. Large serving bowls hold seasoned chicken strips and onion beside grated cheese mountains and a range of sauces. All of the men present take a seat like me while Avery remains standing, preparing a fajita and carrying it outside. Following her with my eyes, I watch her walk around the outside porch through the windows and hand the plate to Huxley who is now on the wooden swinging seat.

Even though my fingers are inching to dive in, the guys wait for Avery to return so I fist my hands in my lap. Finally, her butt touches the chair opposite me and I feel guilt-free about taking the first wrap, filling it with a bit of everything. No one moves until I'm on my third bite which is when I realise I'm moaning and stuffing my face like an animal. Garrett looks impressed and Avery smirks, starting to build their own fajitas with much more restraint.

"It's a lovely surprise to have you here with us, Meg. Avery's been so lost without you." Dax smiles kindly from beside me just as I take the biggest bite yet. He glances across the table to Avery, clearing his throat uncomfortably. "But why exactly are you here?" Avery and I both start laughing at the same time, realising they haven't got a clue what is going on around here. Just lost lambs following their blonde Bo Peep across the country for a vacation.

"It's super complicated but you'll find out soon enough anyway. Wyatt was adopted by Nixon and Cathy, Meg and I are their biological twins." Dax and Axel have matching looks of surprise, flicking their eyes back and forth between us looking for similarities. Garrett shrugs and keeps eating, not seeming bothered in the slightest by Avery's revelation. The rest of the meal passes in a comfortable silence, everyone slowly computing the news in their own way.

By the time I'm stuffed and lean back contentedly, Dax and Axel are already on their feet to wash up after having to pry a plate from Garrett's fingers as he insists on licking it clean. I can definitely see the appeal for Avery, having lived with these three the past few weeks. No doubt each day was filled with fun and laughter, despite the other two being a mild inconvenience.

Glancing at my watch, its nearing 10pm but I'm not tired in the slightest. Too much has happened today for my mind to rest anyway.

"There's a cupboard in the back of my room full of old boxes and board games. Shall I grab one?" I offer, Avery's bright eyes lighting up. Taking that as a yes, I smile and rise from my chair, thankful I'm wearing a baggy sweatshirt to cover my bloated belly. Walking up the first staircase and turning to take the second to my private floor at the top of the house, a smash beyond the door at the end makes me flinch. I'd grown so accustomed to only having my mom around I had forgotten Wyatt was up here. Another crash follows down the hall as I tiptoe up the steps.

Shaking off a shudder and rounding my room, I open the cupboard and sift through the board games boxes for one I haven't played yet. Selecting one from the bottom, naturally, I wiggle the cardboard box free and return to the others downstairs. The table has been fully cleared, Avery and the boys are sitting around waiting for me. Garrett's head is lying on Axel's shoulder, who's twiddling the brown strands between his fingers.

"Whatcha got?" Avery asks, perking up to get a glimpse at the box.

"Trivial Pursuit," I beam, ready to play against opponents I may be able to beat – unlike my mom who is ruthless in every game on earth. Laying the board out, I automatically pass Avery the purple counter knowing it's her favourite colour and keep the green for myself. Placing our chosen counters in the middle, we take turns to roll the dice for the highest number to go first. I end up with a six so I shift my empty pie holder onto a yellow space. Garrett flicks a question card from the holder and pretends to read it.

"Megaroni, what's your favourite flavour of ice cream?" I scrunch my nose up and point to the card he's teasing in and out of his fingers.

"That's not the question, yellow is history." Avery glances to him in confusion, which makes two of us.

"Yeah but I figured since we will be living together for the foreseeable future, we should know a bit more about you." I quirk a brow, trying to sense if this is a trick but he seems sincere for once.

"Fine. Quick fire your questions and then we can play properly." His lips slide up into a smile as we begin a back and forth of bio on me.

"Favourite ice cream?"

"Salted caramel."

"Colour?"

"Maroon."

"Who the fuck has maroon as their favourite colour?!" He scoffs. "Dream Job?"

"High school sports coach."

"Sexual position?"

"I'm not answering that."

"Worst fear?"

"Slightly claustrophobic, especially in the dark." His lips remained sealed, so I push my tongue into my cheek, his eyes tracking the movement. "You finished?" Garrett nods like an excited puppy, throwing me a yellow piece of pie and moving on with the game at last. The fridge closing behind me makes me turn to see Wyatt exiting the room, my eyes watching his back leave curiously. Shaking my head, I remind myself I should keep my guard up around him and the demons he's failing to hide.

# Dax

Stretching my arms above my head, I twist my torso in a delicious stretch. I needed that sleep, not being cramped in the back seat of a car or in a stiff motel bed. Stuffing my hand beneath the pillow, I pull out my phone to see it's just gone six and curse my body clock. Rolling onto my front, I bury my face into the pillow intending to drift back off when I hear a soft bang downstairs. Remaining still, my ears perk up and catch faint mumbling around outside. Too curious to go back to sleep now, I creep over to the window in just my boxer shorts and peer out of the blackout curtain.

Day has just broken, a golden semi-circle peering over the sea. The sky's palette ranges from the palest yellows to the deepest reds, the porch and bushes below still hidden in darkness. Two figures walk across the beach in full Lycra with messy buns fixed upon their heads and their arms linked. Finding a level spot, Avery begins to lead the yoga routine I've seen her do multiple times at the mansion, Meg mimicking her actions. Stretching their arms in full circles, the pair push their palms together and bow towards the sea. From this distance, the two of them look identical, their hair colours masked by the shadows that cling to their backs, but I can tell which one is Avery from miles away.

Her stance is straighter, radiating the type of confidence one can only get from walking through the flames of hell and back again. I've been catching feelings for a while now but in this moment, I yearn to hold her gently. To stroke away any doubts that she is unlovable and give her the future she thinks she doesn't want. I should move away from the window to stop spying on her like a crazed stalker, but I know the second my foot moves I'll be out that door and pushing her beneath me in the sand. So, instead, I stand frozen in this spot, watching them stretch and balance, becoming more and more torn between my heart expanding with Avery's inner strength and my mouth watering at her flexibility.

By the time the pair turn to bow to each other, the sun is much higher and the sky has lightened to its usual pale blue. My eyelids start to feel heavy, my feet dragging as I slump back onto bed. Sleep comes for me quickly this time, knowing I have smooth creamy curves and silky blonde hair to dream about.

A weight settles onto me, straddling my hips and stroking my chest with featherlight touches. A lazy smile grows on my face, my body squirming slightly as the fingertips graze my sides. Through my closed eyelids, the dream I'd been having continues while my hair is being stroked. Avery and I huddle beneath thick blankets in some weird igloo structure, but I'm not complaining, sharing our body heat and sweet kisses. Lips brush mine and a stubbled jaw scrapes across my cheek towards my ear. Wait, Avery doesn't have-

"Wakey wakey, eggs and bakey." Garrett half-shouts directly into my ear drum. Jolting my hips sideways and shoving his chest hard, he falls to the floor laughing like a maniac. Rearranging my unwelcome erection into my waistband, I grab my phone and stomp into the bathroom, locking the door behind me. Switching on my workout playlist, I place the device beside the sink, reminding myself I need to get back to exercising regularly soon or I'll struggle when returning to the basketball court. At least it's past ten now so I don't feel as rough as before, switching the shower onto cold and shedding my boxers.

Without giving myself time to back out, I dive into the spray. An involuntary noise escapes me, the water skating over my body. My abs start to cramp from being tensed so I squirt a heavy dose of shower gel directly onto my chest and rush to rub it all over. Leaving my hair for another time, I turn the dial and hop from the cubicle.

Securing a towel around my waist, I stand watching the horizon through a massive window whilst brushing my teeth. After running a comb through my hair as much as I can, I sneak a look out of the door to see my room is empty. Exhaling, my shoulders relax as I pad over to the chest of drawers I tucked my clothes into. Dressing in comfy tracksuit pants and a white tee, I leave my room in hunt of food. Trotting down the stairs, I find the odd view of Avery hunched over a plate of food on the dining table.

"No, no, no, no!" She shouts at Garrett who is advancing on her.

"Come on, please! I'm so hungry! He clearly isn't coming." Cocking my eyebrow, I lean against the sofa to watch Avery attempt to keep food away from Garrett – even if it is my meal in question, it'll be hilarious.

"You've already had two servings!" She squeals as he dives for her, moving to stand between him and the table with her arms firmly crossed.

"But that one smells so good," he sulks like a child, stamping his foot. Spotting me, Avery points to the chair and orders me to eat in her best stern voice, which is completely adorable. The plate of waffles has been topped with a colourful range of berries, the way she would have known I liked it. Leaving me to enter the sitting room, Avery sits between Meg and Axel, who look gloomy on the large sofa. Garrett hovers in the threshold while I eat, waiting to see if I leave any scraps. Not one to pass up such a golden opportunity, I plunge the fork into the fruit mountain as I wrap my lips around the mouthful with sensual slowness.

"Okay, that's it. I can't stand here for another second. Let's do something," Garrett says loudly, drawing everyone's attention to his jittery body.

"Go have a swim in the sea," I say around my food.

"I already did that," he whines. "Besides, they all look as bored as I feel." Glancing over at the trio, I have to admit he's right. Placing the cutlery onto my now empty plate, I carry it over to the sink, mentally promising to return and wash it up later.

"Oh, I know!" Garrett starts jumping up and down excitedly. "Hide and seek." His smile shifts into one much more menacing, his hazel eyes drifting to Avery's widened ones. "One..."

We all scramble in opposite directions, his counting sounding from behind. Realising too late I didn't put sneakers on, I rush out of the back door and circle the building. Checking through the front window, Garrett has turned to hide his face in the corner of the room. I smile to myself, picturing a tall pointed dunce hat upon his head and dash into the forest. Heading for the first tree with a thick trunk and low enough branch to reach, I launch my body into the air and grab a hold. Pulling myself up, I continue to dodge and climb until I'm high into the greenery near the top.

I can see far into the distance if I pop my head through the canopy, even if all there is to see are miles of foliage in one direction and the stretching sea in the other. The overhead sun shines down on me, all clouds having rolled on by to leave it completely exposed. Birds swoop and twirl in a dance of flight, singing loudly as they pass by. Resting in the arch of a branch, I lean back and relax, knowing I'll be here a while. When it comes to being the competitive one in our group, I'll proudly take the crown.

A short while later, although nowhere near as long as I thought, the front door bashes open. "Come out, come out wherever you are!" Garrett's shout travels to me from below. Peering down, I see him pass with his lapdog by his side, Axel prowling like a lion on the hunt. The pair move deeper into the woodlands, so I start descending quickly and quietly. Pausing near the last few branches, I bend low to search for them. Once satisfied they aren't too close by, I drop from the tree and land on silent feet. Coach had made me practice jumping and landing without a sound as a part of a gruelling detention once, although it's come in handy now.

Racing forward the second I'm back on firm ground, I pump my arms and push my calves to carry me back onto the porch. Ducking low, I creep around the corner to see Huxley on the wooden swing, absentmindedly staring towards the sea as he rocks back and forth. Noticing me, I raise my index finger to my lips to keep him quiet, not that I thought he'd rat me out anyway. Slipping inside the kitchen door, I dive straight into the tight cupboard that holds the pantry. Surrounded by shelves on all sides, my biceps are cramped to my sides as I'm plunged into darkness. Stepping backwards, I tread on something soft and squishy.

"Ow, my foot!" Avery whisper-shouts, making me spin around and reach out to feel for her shoulders.

"How did he not find you in here? I'm surprised he didn't use the game as a ruse to get us all out the way so he could eat everything we have left." Avery giggles, her breath fanning my neck.

"I moved, like you apparently." My initial smile drops from my face, realising her body is pushed up against mine in our tiny confines. Running the backs of my fingers down her arms, her sharp inhale tells me she feels the shift in the air too. Energy crackles between us, lust thickening the oxygen as my heart starts to pound heavily. Her hands slip beneath my t-shirt, running them over my muscles and across my chest. Our lack of sight heightens every other sense, each touch bringing goose bumps to the surface as her sweet scent envelopes me. Lowering my head, I catch her cheek with my lips before she shifts to connect her mouth with mine.

The first press of our kiss breaks an invisible barrier between us. Suddenly needing to be closer, I pull her into me and push my tongue into her mouth. Breathy moans escape her between the attack of our kisses, tongues crashing and teeth nibbling bottom lips. Pressing a hand against her lower back, I hold her firmly in place while I grind my hard on against her. I want her in so many ways, my dick overruling my head currently. Clearly eager for the same, her hand slips beneath my waistband, her nails scraping gently across my tip. My eyes roll back in my head, a groan I can't hold in leaving my throat.

The door flies open, the light temporarily burning my eyes. Reluctantly withdrawing from her hold, a large figure with dark hair blocks the exit. Thickly muscled shoulders tense at the sight he's just found, but it's not Garrett as I expected - it's Wyatt. His top lip rears back in disgust, his emerald eyes surrounded by dark patches. I reckon he is much paler than usual but it could be a trick of my adjusting eyesight.

"What the fuck is wrong with your own rooms?! You have to taint our food supply too?" Slamming the door in my face, I readjust myself for the second time today before reopening it and stepping into the kitchen. Garrett, Axel and Meg are leaning against the counters, their faces filled with amusement. Ignoring their bobbing eyebrows and smirks, I step aside to allow Avery to exit. Her full lips are swollen and a darker shade of pink as she smooths down her hair and returns their grins.

"Guess it's my turn," she giggles. "One…"

# Wyatt

Slamming the door shut, I slump against the back of it and fall to the floor. Pushing the heels of my palms into my eyes, I try to erase the image I just saw from my mind. This is never going to work if I can't get myself out under control. I wish I could disappear, leave and start fresh somewhere else. But I already know ignoring my issues wouldn't work, only the knowledge I've helped Rachel will.

I miss her. She makes me feel like a young child desperate for the end of the school day to run into his mom's arms. Something I never had since a nanny would be waiting for me at the gates each day. I thought we'd still be able to call and speak regularly so she could keep me centred, but the lack of signal around here prevents that – another one of my father's tricks to ruin my life. Instead I feel completely isolated without her to anchor me, each night I drift further away.

The group downstairs were everything to me up to two months ago, but so much has changed since then. I'm not the same person I was, and I have no idea how to open up to them. They wouldn't accept me this way even if I were able to, not after the things I've done. After Avery and Meg have been delivered to Ray, I'll be a distant memory, hiding away in Ray's mansion to live out my days in peace. That's the best I can hope for anymore.

My anger has fizzled marginally, so I stretch my legs out and place the back of my head against the wood. Drifting my eyes closed, I inhale and exhale deeply the way a normal person might to relax. Although, I'm so far removed from normal it's laughable I'd even try. Knocking sounds on the door behind, jolting me forward. Taking another moment to compose myself, I push up onto my feet and twist the handle. Axel is standing on the other side, his amber eyes trailing over my jeans and blue polo top. The concern in his expression has me ready to close the door again. I don't need his pity.

"Hey, I thought I should check on you." He fists his hands, no doubt trying to refrain from pulling me into a hug. Behind him, I see Avery chasing Garrett through the hallway and disappear downstairs as a part of their stupid game, laughter echoing around the corridor. Stepping aside, I allow Axel to enter so I can shut their happiness out. He halts suddenly a few steps inside, so I turn to see my room through his eyes.

The blackout curtains are still drawn, the sun desperately striving to light the space within from around the edges. Clothes are strewn across the floor, my bed a mess of twisted covers. Evidence of a mini meltdown I had yesterday lies heaped in the corner, broken wooden shelves and a fan that got in my way. I'm just thankful the bathroom door is closed so he can't see the state of the oval mirror, or now lack thereof. Axel's eyes narrow on the long pill box Rachel gave me sitting on the pine chest of drawers, todays already popped open and empty. Not wanting to explain, I spin him by the shoulders and give him the damn hug he'd wanted.

Embracing me tightly, he rests his cheek on my shoulder. After resisting at first, I ease into the support he's offering, the rest of the world briefly fading away. My life has been flipped upside down, tossed side to side and back again since the last time we spent time together like this. But for a split second, I wonder if Axel might be able to help dust me off when I eventually stop falling and crash into the ground.

"How did you do it?" I ask softly into his ear, his short

hair scraping my neck gently.

"Do what?"

"Find yourself again after..." A part of me feels terrible comparing my situation to his. Axel's been through things I can't even imagine, but maybe he could offer some advice on how he rebuilt and moved on. He doesn't answer for a long while, the cogs turning in his mind. Stepping back for his amber eyes to assess me, I'm stunned by the resentment held within.

"What makes you think I've found myself? Look at me Wyatt, I'm a man that can't survive without affection, who relies on everyone else's moods to get by. I live through others to avoid the pain that still plagues me. I'm as fucked up as I was almost 7 years ago, you just can't tell as easily." Axel steps away from me and leaves the room in a swift movement.

My eyes focus on the spot he had been standing in long after, trying to understand how to turn his words into something I can use. I don't know what answer I had been hoping for, one that will magically give me a light to strive for. But instead, all I heard was *'you're never coming back from this.'* Throwing my foot against the edge of my bed with a cry of rage, the wood splinters and the end of the mattress dips slightly. If all I was destined to be was a rich couple's decoy, then I wish I'd never been born at all.

High pitched laughter beyond my door drags me back from the brink of self-destruction to remember the only reason I came here. Since I can't easily contact Ray or convince them to return home without Nixon's say so, I'll have to do something to assuage my anger for now. Those girls need to pay for the mistreatment I've received. My very existence has been used to protect them their whole lives, which will make it all the sweeter when I'm the one to deliver them to their bitter end.

Crossing my room with powerful stomps, I swing the door open to see Avery and Meg huddled together at the far end of the hall, looking around for whoever is hunting them. I may not be the one they were expecting but, no more games, here I am. Their eyes widen as I bare my teeth at them, feeling every bit the animal I probably look. My clenched fists hang by my sides, no clear plan in mind other than to strap them into chairs and scream in their faces - "why?!" What makes them so special my life had to be used to defend theirs.

As I begin to advance, the girls rush forward in hopes they can reach their second staircase before I can. Without needing to sprint, I near the stairs first, smirking at the look of horror on their faces when they realise they won't make it. Relishing in the panic in their faces, I stretch my neck side to side in anticipation of an evening of torment. At the last moment, Meg forcefully shoves Avery into the study and closes the door with a loud bang.

Grinding my teeth together, I stride along the corridor with my chest heaving. In a futile attempt to escape, they've cornered themselves anyway. Prickling races through my body with every step closer which I'll guess is excitement. Coming level with the door, I kick it open with enough force for the handle to snap off. Stepping over the pieces of splintered wood now decorating the floor, I enter the room to find it empty.

I freeze momentarily, not enjoying the sinking feeling I've been tricked. Needing to be sure, I check behind the door and beneath the table but they've both vanished. Bookcases line the left wall and the fake fireplace on the right leaving nowhere to hide. There must be another way out of here but no matter how long I spend looking for a false floorboard or hidden exit, there's nothing. Growling in frustration, I run a hand through my hair roughly and leave. Next time, I won't give them the chance to run.

Deciding against returning to the boredom awaiting in my room, I head downstairs and exit the house through the back door. Huxley is rising from the porch swing, pausing when he sees me. Apparently, I don't look approachable since he continues to push past, leaving me alone in the descending dusk. Figuring it's probably for the best, since I don't need to hide my scowl for a while, I remove my socks and cross the timber terrace.

Hopping down wooden steps, I walk across the sand until reaching the ideal spot to set myself down, a few feet from the water's edge. Waves roll lazily, not having the energy to break properly in the setting sunlight. Once in a while, a light breeze carrying mist passes over me, the saltiness filling my senses. Pushing my fingers into the soft sand, I draw the figure of eight on either side of my legs over and over. I also slide my toes into the fluffy white sand in an attempt to feel grounded, not that it works.

A small, curved shell of brown with white specks moves towards my hand, the murky green legs of a hermit crab poking out from underneath. Lifting the decapod, it shrinks back into its shell slightly as I examine it closely. Long red antennas sit beneath beady eyes and hairy legs have bright blue bands around the tips. The bigger claw tries to pinch me wildly so I set it back down, watching the crustacean scurry away as fast as he can move. Even the birds overhead seem to be avoiding me, spinning and flying in the opposite direction when I look up.

Turning my attention back towards the sea, I catch the last speck of sun peering over the horizon, just as it sinks out of sight. The sky has already gone dark, only a strip of red visible in the distance mourning the loss of light. At least now my surroundings resonate with how I'm feeling and I can wallow in peace, shrouded by the shadows. Shuffling out of my jeans, I toss them aside and walk into the water in my boxers. Icey coldness seeps into my feet, numbness creeping up my legs with every long stride.

Walking further into the inky depths, the water level rises over my thighs, stealing all sensation on its way. Only stopping once my chest is fully submerged, the material of my top floating around my torso, a sense of calm finally settles over me. My heartbeat slows, the low temperature surrounding me biting at my skin. I stand there for a long while, the numb feeling I was enjoying starting to merge into a sharp sting. The notion of staying right here is almost too tempting, allowing the sea to draw the life from my pores and carry me away. I wonder who would mourn for me, but on second thought – why do I even care?

Only Rachel's face in my mind's eye pulls me back to the beach, my polo top sticking to me like a second skin as I collect my jeans. My skin is starting to burn and my eyes feel itchy, begging for a better sleep tonight if my emotions will allow it. Sometimes I dream of an alternative universe where Avery is hanging off my arm, all smiles and laughter. Other times, I'm standing over her limp body in the same position my birth mom was when I left the cell on that god-awful day. I can't decide which fantasy I would prefer, not that it matters. Ray decided Avery's fate long before I knew him, and the only chance I have at a new start is to help him. All I need to do is be patient enough for it all to come together.

Soon I'll have a family. Soon I'll belong.

# Avery

Watching multiple rooms at once via the laptop screen, Meg lifts the landline to call Elena. The panic room she told me about isn't as high tech and futuristic as I had imagined, but it's still pretty cool. The best part was seeing Wyatt's face via a secret camera, completely dumbfounded as to where we had gone. I'm so glad Nixon hadn't told him about this place so Meg and I can have a private oasis when he's being a dick – which seems almost permanent as this point.

Glancing over at the bunk beds, I wonder if Nixon created this room with us in mind for the inevitable day his past caught up with him. There's enough bottled water and preserved food in the cupboards to last us around a week if we ration, which is a slightly scary thought. Hopefully the only reason we will need to venture in here is to wind up the moody Myrtle that's now left the house.

Pulling my attention back to the screen, I see Dax in his room running through some drills with the bed pushed aside. Currently doing push ups, his biceps are bulging and shoulder blades shifting beneath a vest. Biting my lip, I flick my eyes onto the next window to see Garrett and Axel making out on their bed. Hands are roaming freely on top of their clothes. Heat rushes to my neck and cheeks, not knowing which camera to focus on so I minimize them both.

"Love you too mom, speak soon." Meg returns the receiver to its chunky white base and gestures towards the screen.

"So, are you going to tell me what's going on with you and them?" She crosses the room to sit on the edge of the bottom bunk, giving me her undivided and very much unwanted attention.

"What do you mean?" I avoid her gaze, hoping my face will pale to its usual alabaster colour if I ignore her probing questions. The quirk of her eyebrow tells me she won't drop the conversation until I spill. "Okay fine. I may have slept with Garrett and Axel... twice. Dax is-" I demonstrate my mind blowing up with my hands and added sound effects, "but we haven't gone further than kissing, and touching." Throwing my head into my hands, I groan at how bad it sounds out loud.

"Both Garrett and Axel, twice? What, are they keeping score?"

"No, I mean together. They are kinda a package deal." She sniggers at the word package and I roll my eyes. Moving to sit beside her, I lean my head onto her shoulder and sigh loudly.

"Fair play. I get the other two but I am surprised about Garrett to be honest. You usually avoid the loud, self-absorbed guys like him." She's not wrong; at frat parties I would steer well clear of the jocks. Their booming laughs and hoards of woman hanging off their every word. I had pegged Garrett as the same originally, but he's become a vital part of my life lately, bringing a smile to my face every time he enters a room.

"Trust me, I know he's not the easiest to live with sometimes, but at least with Garrett, I know exactly where I stand. There's no bullshit or expectations. He and Axel help me escape when the stress builds up too much, that's all." Nodding against my hair, Meg places a kiss on my head and tells me to be careful, which I understand to be on a medical and emotional front. Not that she has to worry about either, I have the implant and whilst I may care for each of the guys downstairs, my heart isn't something I could ever offer. It's barely glued back together enough to beat properly, never mind to present to another willingly.

Deciding the coast is clear, we exit the hidden room and push the door back to click into place. After agreeing to meet Meg downstairs shortly to help prepare dinner, I stride for the second staircase towards our room to grab a hoodie.

Passing the middle door along the corridor, a low groan barely registers with my ears. Freezing in place, I wait for any other sounds but only silence follows. Yet a niggling within tells me something is wrong. Slowly twisting the rounded handle, I crack the door open a tiny bit to peer inside. Everything is dark, only a tiny slither of the moon's light allowing me to see the perfectly made bed and tidy space inside. Huxley's denim jacket lies over the back of a wooden chair, his white and blue Air Jordans tucked beneath the matching desk. Pushing my head further into the room, I notice a shine bleeding out from beneath the bathroom door.

Tiptoeing across the space, I press my ear against the timber separating us. Everything inside is silent. Knocking softly, I wait a second before entering the room. Huxley's head is leaning back against the bathtub, his damp blonde hair falling over the rim. Each of his legs are hanging loosely over each side, giving me a full view of his junk. Edging closer when he doesn't open his eyes, I realise his skin is a bright shade of red and sweat is covering his face.

"Huxley?" I whisper, giving his arm a nudge. The limb falls lifelessly into the water with a splash, panic seizing me. Grabbing his face in my hands, I shout his name and give him a rough shake. His eyelids crack open ever so slightly, but his brown eyes remain unfocussed. "Fuck. Huxley, have you taken anything?" I ask but his only response is a twitch of his lips. Glancing around, I don't find evidence of empty pill bottles or anything suspicious so I'm going to hazard a guess that he's dehydrated. Whipping the plug out, I leave the bath to drain while I run back into his room. After turning the fan on and directing it towards the bed, I return to the bathroom and fill a cup on the side of the sink with cold water.

"Drink," I order, lifting Huxley's head forward and pushing the cup against his lips. He flinches as the cold-water splashes over his chin and chest, the moment rousing him enough to take a few sips. He groans as his head lolls back so I place the cup on the back of the toilet and grab a towel from the overhead shelf. Now the water has fully drained from the tub, I throw the towel over his mid-section to cover his modesty. Leaning over him, I pull his meaty arm over my shoulders and wiggle my hands beneath his bulky body.

"Huxley, I need you to help me here." I say whilst giving him a rough shove. He gasps and mumbles incoherently, but his hand grips my back which is enough for me. After counting down 3, 2, 1 – mostly for myself, I heave with all my strength to lift him slightly. His body rises enough to greet mine and his head flops onto my shoulder, his wet hair soaking through my t-shirt. Huxley starts to shake his head with a small whine, but I refuse to let go of him now.

Gripping his other arm and throwing it around my waist, I urge him to hold on and I heave upwards again. Rising to his knees, I feel him start to slip back into unconsciousness, so I give the back of his head a smack. "Stay with me, you heavy sack of shit," I grumble into his ear. Using my shoulder in his chest, I push him upright with all my might until he is semi upright. The towel becomes trapped between us as he leans onto me. "Okay, one foot," I say, pulling him forward so his left leg flops out of the bath. Stepping back with him, Huxley's other leg starts to lift over the rim and eventually slaps onto the cream mat on the floor.

His weight is crippling but I force us to move across the room, his body trembling with each step. Nearing the door, I feel the second Huxley zones out again just before his legs give out from beneath him. A scream escapes me as he topples down, his weight doubling over my shoulders. Dragging us both at a snail's pace, I make it to the open door and push our way into his bedroom. My own knees are beginning to buckle but I persevere, half throwing his floppy frame onto the mattress as I reach the foot of the bed.

His top half lands safely, his legs hanging widely over the edge. After rearranging the towel and tucking it either side of his waist, I move the fan onto him and retrieve the cup of water. After a few attempts to rouse him, I change tactic and move across the bed. Peeling his head and shoulders up, I use my body to stop him from sagging back down and force him to drink at least half of the water I'm pushing against his lips from behind. After I'm satisfied he's beginning to cool down, his face returning to its usual beige colour, I leave him to rest against my front.

Combing his hair back with my fingers, droplets fly over my top but I don't care. I had thought if I pulled away from Huxley, he might start to take care of himself a little more but clearly, that's not true. I can't be with him all the time to monitor him, and not just because I'm torn between being with Meg or worrying about Wyatt. For my own sanity, I can't help him in the way he needs. Huxley's lost to a turbulent sea of his own making, only he can build a raft and find his way back. Stirring, his head shifts as he glances around the darkened room while I continue to stroke his hair. He groans as he pushes himself upright so I use my hands against his back to help him.

"You can run off and tell everyone how messed up I am now." His voice reaches me in a harsh tone. Passing his lack of appreciation off as embarrassment, I shuffle forward and hook my legs around his waist. Leaning my face against his back, I slip my hands around to hold his biceps.

"It's not my business to tell." I state, remaining in place to support him. Gradually, Huxley's frame starts to relax and he shifts further up the bed. Crawling across the sheets with him, we sit together in the dark, propped up by his pillows. I miss the pig-headed guy that claimed my bathroom the day he arrived in my life, who threw me in the pool and took me on my first ever date. The mischievous light to his eyes and cheeky smile are a distant memory these days.

But there's nothing else I can do or say, recovering has to be his choice. He needs to find a reason to rise from the darkness he's trapped himself in and it can't be me. On the outside, I may appear carefree and confident, but internally I have my own shit to deal with every damn day. In fact, everyone in this house does.

"Are you going to start eating again now?" I ask softly, feeling like I'm about to poke the beast. Huxley doesn't react, just sits beside me statue still.

"I can't enjoy anything anymore, food included. I just feel numb inside. Nothing's the same as it was." His voice is barely a whisper, his shoulders tensing like that confession caused him physical pain. I chance a look up at his face, his strong jaw is clenched and chocolate eyes glazed over.

"Allow time to find yourself again. One day you'll wake up and the sun will seem a little brighter or juice will taste a little sweeter. But in the meantime, promise me you'll try to eat properly."

"For you, I will try." His chest rises and falls on a large breath, his fingers moving to link with mine.

"No, not for me. I won't always be around. You need to do this for you or it won't work. You're special and funny, you light up every room and the guys out there love you like a brother. That's the Huxley you need to hold onto."

# *Meg*

Two large saucepans of spaghetti begin to boil as I endlessly rotate meatballs until cooked through, removing them and starting on the next batch. Cooking for seven wasn't what I had envisioned this evening but Avery must had got held up shaving Axel's hair or something. The back-door crashes open, a dripping wet Wyatt trudging through with his jeans in his hand leaving a soggy line behind him like a snail. His polo shirt is clinging to his body, indenting around each muscle. My eyes drift to his rounded thighs, rippling with each step beneath tight black boxers which are bunched up higher than usual.

"The water's meant to stay in the sea," I put on my best bitchy tone, dragging my eyes from his body to the puddles on the kitchen floor. He doesn't break his stride, crossing the living room.

"And my organs need to stay inside my body, so I won't be eating any of your cooking." He shouts back from the stairs. My spaghetti starts to bubble violently, water escaping over the lip of the pan while the blackening meatballs spit at me with venom. Touché.

"Woah, here let me help." Axel runs up behind me, his hand brushing mine as he takes the tongs from my grip. Leaning over my shoulder, I stand for a second too long in the warmth of his body. Risking a look up, his sharp jaw and high cheekbones are slack, his unique amber eyes completely focused on rescuing the dinner. He is stunning, his shaved head adding a powerful edge to his beauty. Extracting myself, I find Garrett leaning against the fridge with an amused look on his face. "Like what you see, Megster?"

"I did before I turned around," I jest, pushing him back a step so I can retrieve the hidden cheese from the fridge. His booming laughter fills the space as he shifts behind me, trapping me between his body and the appliance. Dipping his head to my ear, he runs his tongue up my lobe and around the curved shell causing me to shudder. I should shove him away or elbow him or something, but all I can focus on is how hard my nipples are growing from a mix of lust and the refrigerator's cool air.

"If you want a piece of Axel, you get a slice of me as well." Grinding against my ass for good measure, he reaches over to pluck the cheese from my grip and steps away. If it weren't for the frigid temperature levelling me out, I'd have been panting like a dog in heat. Garrett has moved to grate beside his lover, the picture of calm while I collect my dignity and force my jelly legs to walk straight to find a mop. It's definitely been too long since I last got laid, I've never been so easy to fluster.

Avery appears as I finish cleaning up Wyatt's mess, which I can see becoming a common chore. I can't believe I had a crush on that guy, why do I always choose the bad ones? She skids a little on the drying floor, using me as a pillar to right herself. "I'm so sorry, I got a bit caught up with something."

"Or someone," I murmur without a shred of judgement. I mean seriously, who can blame her? Her confidence has come along wonders recently. Besides, once this is all over and they go back to college, she'll be home schooled alone again. Let the girl live a little.

Dax arrives in time to help serve dinner, my eyebrows bopping as I put two and two together. Sliding onto the black leather padding of a dining chair, Avery sits beside me for us to be waited on. Axel's managed to save my bolognese and magically produce rows of garlic baguettes, the strong smell making my mouth water. Setting the plates in front of us, I dig straight in while the guys carry theirs over. Garrett's is a cheese covered mountain which he attacks like a caveman. I don't want to watch the meatball massacre, but I struggle to look away.

"How are you not morbidly obese?" I have to ask, he's basically an anomaly who should be studied by scientists. They could make a whole TV series tracking his everyday habits.

"I train in basketball six hours a day, thirty-three weeks a year," he muffles though a wall of spaghetti hanging from his mouth. Sucking them up and swallowing, he grins at me. "So, during the holidays, I let myself pig out. But looks like you have quite the appetite too, Megatron." Rolling my eyes at his wink, I glance over to check if Axel isn't bothered by his flirty comments. Fully invested in his meal, he doesn't seem to even be listening.

"So much for lady and the tramp, I wonder which ones which." I gesture to the two of them with my fork, Avery laughing behind her hand. Shrugging, Garrett shoves another meatball into his mouth.

"Some people go on dates and share strands of spaghetti; we host parties and share women." His cheeks bulge like a hamster hoarding food as he smiles, nudging Axel with his elbow to agree.

"Hah! We all know dating and sharing will never be your speciality. Too much effort." Axel chuckles, missing the way Garrett's eyebrows crease slightly at the comment. Movement on the stairs halts any further banter about their strange dynamic, Huxley appearing on the edge of the kitchen. Avery jumps up to dish him a small plate and summons him to take a seat next to her. Crossing the room cautiously, his skin looks red and blotchy with bags so dark under his eyes, it looks like he has two black eyes.

The rest of the meal is spent in silence, everyone seeming on edge with Huxley's presence. Opposite, Dax's afro shifts comically with his chewing, providing me with a secret entertainment. I finish first, pushing my chair back and taking Avery's plate as soon as she's speared the last meatball. Placing them on the counter, Dax sweeps in from behind to fill the sink with steaming hot water. Smirking at me, he takes the crockery and proceeds to wash up.

"Let's head to bed, I'm exhausted," Avery reaches for my hand and pulls me away. On cue, a yawn grips me, my mouth stretching into a large O. Leading me up the two flights of stairs to the room we share on the top level, I kick the door closed and hunt for a baggy t-shirt to sleep in. Avery disappears into the bathroom, returning a minute later in her teal silky vest and shorts. Throwing her hair into a messy bun, she slides into the bed from the left as if we were back at the mansion. Having donned a thin t-shirt, I peel my jeans off and slip in next to her.

The mattress welcomes me back into its memory foam embrace, the dent of my body starting to take hold. Pushing my arm under the pillow, Avery snuggles in closer and links her fingers with my free hand. "Nightie, nightie," she breathes, sleep already pulling her consciousness away from me.

"Pyjama, pyjama Aves."

∞∞∞

"What shall we do?" I moan, torrential rain hammering on the windows and trapping us inside. Crossing my legs on the bed, I watch Avery pace around in dark grey yoga pants and a loose workout vest, tapping her finger on her chin. It's not like we had many more options even if the sun was shining, but the gloomy clouds covering the sky are depressing the shit out of me.

Throwing myself back onto the mattress, I moan loudly

trying to block out the images out what I could be doing right now if I were back home. A gentle stroll past Starbucks on my way to lacrosse practice, or some window shopping with Avery. I'd kill for some fast food and wine.

Avery's sharp intake of breath has me pushing up to my elbows to stare at her with a question mark etched into my eyebrows. "I've got an idea! Hang on," she beams, darting into the bathroom. Sitting upright, I watch her return holding a bottle of talcum powder like a trophy. "Follow me."

A short while later, we are sitting on the living room sofa with the biggest grins that could fit on our faces. My hair is dripping, a sprinkled pattern of raindrops covering my college sweatshirt, but it was totally worth it. The wait is almost agonising, my foot twitching impatiently until there's finally footsteps thumping down the stairs.

"Hey pretty ladies. What are you both up to?" Garrett strides past the back of the sofa, heading for the kitchen. Axel throws himself down next to Avery, who is fully composed as she pulls out a deck of cards and asks who would like the play blackjack. After shuffling the pack, she deals for each of us and sinks down to sit in front of the wooden coffee table. Axel and I also shift onto the soft carpet, although I keep my eyes firmly on the kitchen.

Opening the fridge, Garrett grabs a bottle of water from inside the door before joining us. The game begins, Avery still keeping her stone-like poker face while I'm bubbling up inside. Not wanting to make it obvious, I stare at my cards and squash the smile trying to grow as Garrett unscrews his bottle's cap in my peripheral vision. Lifting the plastic container to his lips, I flick my eyes up in time to watch the twisting of his features as if it were in slow motion.

Spitting the water back out in a prolonged spray that covers us all, Garrett scrapes his tongue with his nails, making choked noises from his throat. "What the fuck is that?!" he croaks and retches. Avery and I lose ourselves to a fit of cackling hysterics, rolling onto our backs.

"Sea water," I manage to rasp from my position on the floor. A stitch pulls at my side as tears stream from my eyes, not having laughed this hard in so long. Risking a glance at Garrett, his hazel eyes lock onto mine, a menacing smile appearing across the lower half of his face.

"It seems like someone thought they could prank me and get away with it. What do you say we show them how wrong they are, Axel?" My laughter dies as Axel smirks and nods his head slowly, his full attention on Avery. Without having a chance to warn her, the pair lunge for us. I have time to shoot away, barely planting my feet beneath me to rush around the sofa and make a run for the stairs.

A strong arm snags around my front, yanking me backwards. Before I have the chance to fight my way out, my back lands on the sofa and Garrett's bulky frame pins me down. Holding me in place with his knees on my forearms at my sides, he starts to hunt for my tickle spot. Squirming and resisting, he struggles to find one around my upper body so reaches behind to grasp my thighs in his large hands. Digging in his nails and squeezing, I can't hide my howls of laughter. His eyes brighten with glee at finding my weakness, relentlessly attacking my thighs. A similar sound is emanating from Avery, Axel hovering over her body not having to work as hard since she's ticklish everywhere.

"Please stop," I beg through my unladylike chortles. A snort escapes me, Garrett finally releasing me to laugh himself. Leaning low, my heaving chest brushes against his as those full lips come threateningly close to my mouth. Excitement of a different kind blooms to life in my lower abdomen.

"Next time, I won't stop until you're screaming beneath me." My eyes widen, suddenly thinking of any and every way I could mess with his food to ensure that happens. Lifting off me, my body instantly missing the heat, Garrett offers me a hand up. Avery is lying on the floor, the skin around her upper arms and chest a flushed pink as she collects herself. Axel had returned to his previous spot, waiting for us to continue with our game as if nothing happened.

Resuming as dealer, Avery has a queen of spades facing up and her other card face down as she waits for us to play our hands. Garrett sits opposite me, glancing at his pair and rightfully decides to stay with his nine and seven. Axel also has high numbers, a ten and an eight so he stays too. Scrunching my nose up at my double sixes and feeling reckless, I tell Avery to hit me. Flipping over a nine, I cheer for myself and wiggle my shoulders side to side. Avery turns her face down card, a fricking ace. "House wins," she giggles, mocking my shoulder victory dance and stealing the smile from my face.

We play on until the rain has stopped, a slither of sunlight harpooning through the clouds into the sea below. Stretching my arms above my head, a bellow sounds from the floor above. Freezing with my arms raised, Avery's head whips around to gasp at me in shock. "Oh my god, I completely forgot about-"

Stamping down the stairs, Dax emerges with his shoulders bunching and posture stiff. Garrett and Axel point and scream jeers at the white powder covering his face and hair from the talc we poured into his hairdryer. His features are hidden from view, every strand of his hair coated in the chalky residue. I try so hard not to laugh, my eyes watering as I bite down on my lip, but when he glares at me like a grumpy clown, I just can't help myself.

# Wyatt

Cracking my eyelids, the shadowed figure I was expecting to see in the corner of the room is there, like every morning. Dark scruffy hair and pale skin sticking to protruding bones. She transfers from my nightmares into real life freely to the point where I'm not even surprised anymore. In a weird way, it's like having a companion who follows me around and plays dead once in a while.

Needing the bathroom, I swing my feet onto the hardwood floor and cross the room. She doesn't notice me, continuing to scratch the walls with her jagged fingernails as I walk past. Taking my time to relieve myself, a trick of my mind can hear the scratching sound through the door. She'll remain until I take my vitamins, only then can she be at peace the way I hoped she'd be when I killed her. Hunching over, I use the only remaining section of mirror to get a look at my haunted green eyes, veiled in a sea of red. Running a hand through my chestnut coloured hair, I smooth it back as much as my bed head will allow.

Taking a deep breath, I leave the safety of the bathroom and edge around to the chest of drawers, keeping my back to where the hallucination is. Popping Saturday's section of the pill box open, I chuck back the small pink tablets and sag forward onto my forearms. How is it the weekend again? I should be ruling our frat house like a goddamn king, running rings around the basketball court and throwing the greatest parties with the hottest women in attendance. Instead I'm stuck in the middle of nowhere, isolated and scared of a fucking shadow.

Squeezing my eyes shut tightly, I brace myself to see if she's gone yet or not. The scratching has stopped, but that could be because I'm about to witness her death for the millionth time. Peering over my shoulder, the corner is empty, as is the rest of the room. Relief washes through me, knowing I'll have a least a few hours of peace from the heinous incident that haunts me. Straightening my back and squaring my shoulders, I stride through the wooden door in just my black pyjama pants. I can hear raised voices before I've even reached the staircase, which makes me want to turn and head back to the solace I find being alone, but my grumbling stomach says otherwise.

"You fucking idiot, you're eating away at our entire food supply!" Huxley shouts as I descend the stairs and round the banister. His anger is directed at the back of Garrett's head, who's sitting at the dining table with his version of a normal breakfast. A plate heaped with rashes of bacon and heaps of sausages, scrambled egg, beans, fries and toast. He doesn't pause his munching to shrug and reply.

"What's it matter to you, you're barely eating away." Huxley's face is growing redder by the second as I stride past, grabbing an apple from the fruit bowl. Gare holds up his hand to halt Huxley from speaking again. "Besides, I'm doing us all a favour."

"How'd you figure that?" Hux seethes. I head for the fridge, plucking a bottle of water from the top shelf and turn to leave.

"The quicker the food runs out, the quicker we have an excuse to leave." At this I stop moving, suddenly interested. If I can hitch a ride to the closet town, I can try to contact Ray and get some advice on what the fuck to do. Huxley makes a choked noise in his throat, his fists clenched by his sides.

"The girl's lives are in danger, you stupid asshole! We can't go grocery shopping just because you said so, we have to wait for word from Nixon and who knows when that'll be." His tone is getting louder but no one comes running to see what the issue is, like I expected they would.

"Psh, I don't buy it. He left Avery in the mansion for weeks, no one came. There's no threat or mob, this is a sick power move a bored rich guy can make against his kids." The word 'kids' has my own anger bubbling beneath the surface since I'm no longer included in that category. Placing the items in my hands onto the counter, I cross my arms to see how this unfolds.

"Wow. You're even stupider than I thought." Huxley has barely finished the sentence when Garrett shoots from his seat, grabbing him by the neck and throwing him down onto his back on the lino floor. Hux's shaggy blonde waves are scattered around him, a vision of blood seeping into the strands messing with my head.

"Call me stupid one more time." Garrett says in a low tone through his teeth. Hux doesn't try to fight back, just lies there with a mask of rage in place. His eyes slip to mine, probably wondering if I'll save him, but how can I? I'm too distracted by the dark patch oozing from his skull, his hollow cheeks and the glaze ascending over his eyes that's becoming too similar to the figure of my nightmares. Panic freezes my bone while pure fury boils my blood, a toxic combination I can't control.

"Leave him alone!" I yell, slamming my shoulder into Garrett's side, rugby tackling him across the floor. Throwing my fists into his stomach, he twists and knees me in the chest. Black spots hover around my vision, removing me from the modern kitchen and tossing me into a cell inside my head. The walls are gloomy, the stoned floor damp but I relish having a place to vent my emotions and a living target to take them out on.

Forcing myself on top of my faceless opponent, I punch wildly at his chest since raised forearms are blocking me from a clear shot at his head. Bucking violently, he tosses me aside and kicks his foot into my gut, pushing me away. Catching his foot, I drag him back down and clamber up his muscled frame. Taking his head in my hands, I smash my forehead into his nose with a vicious crack.

Another body collides with me, knocking me onto my back. Various hands pin me to the floor while I growl, bucking and kicking. My heel connects with a thigh before it is also restrained, words I can't understand being hollered at me. I'm surrounded by my demons now, trying to drag me under but I refuse to go without a fight. Twisting my right wrist free and swinging, my fist connects with a jaw. A sharp blow is delivered to my temple, halting any further attempts to defend myself. Agony soaks into my pores, absorbed into the fire running through my blood stream. Acting like kindling, the fire roars and consumes me in the process as darkness takes over.

Waking for the second time today, my head throbs and I gasp with the onslaught of pain that barrels into me. An ice pack being placed on my forehead makes me flinch and hiss. Opening one eye, Axel stands over me, blocking the glare from the window with his large frame. A purple mark is blooming along his clenched jawbone, his eyes a mix of irritation and pity. The visions in my mind start to ebb away until the truth of what I've done becomes clear.

"What the fuck is wrong with you?" Garrett grumbles from the other side of the kitchen, holding his nose. That's the real question, isn't it? One I don't have the answer to. Sitting upright on the dining table, ignoring the discomfort it causes my head, I grip the ice pack tightly.

"I'm sick to death of your petty squabbles, that's all." I lie, needing a reason to hide behind. Hopping down from the glass surface, I leave the room before any of my four former brothers can respond. Reaching the first floor, Avery and Meg appear in my way. Creamy skin and curves I can't ignore catch my attention, bathing suits barely covering their assets as I fake a grimace. Whether due to my scowl or aura, they both jump out of my way as I attempt to barge past and lock myself in my room once again.

I try not to care, but all I can think about is how they are most likely pawing all over the guys downstairs. Tending to their battle wounds with light touches and soft kisses, praising them for the heroes they are. Meanwhile, I'm the monster lurking behind the door at the end of the hall, plotting to deliver them to their final destination. The back-door slamming closed has me tossing the ice pack onto the chest of drawers and creeping towards my closed curtains, shifting the heavy material to peer out.

Flicking rolled towels into the air, Avery and Meg place their cotton mats side by side onto the yellow sand. Meg has donned a huge black hat, hiding her face from my view. The pair lay on their stomachs facing the house, opening a book each and smiling easily in the sunshine. I can't wait to wipe those smiles from their lips and steal the laughter from their lungs. Before long, they will feel how I have felt every day for the past seven years, how my parent's rejection has festered inside and distorted my soul. All because of them.

Hollering, Garrett runs from the house with Axel and Dax on his tail. Winding his arms around Meg, he hoists her up while Dax rushes to save the book from her hands. Ignoring her protests, Gare throws her over his shoulder and skips like a schoolgirl until he's knee-deep in the sea. Only after removing her hat and placing it on his own head does he launch her six feet into the air. Landing in the sea with an almighty splash, she shoots to her feet and attempts to tackle Garrett the same way I did, except she's no match for him.

Rushing to save her friend, I mean... fuck, her twin, Avery jumps onto Garrett's back. Gripping her thighs to hold her in place, Gare runs and dives into the water, taking Avery beneath the surface with him. Coming up for air, Meg has to throw herself into an oncoming wave to rescue her hat while the pair laugh together. Avery's arms are still around Gare's neck, her face stroking against his for a moment too long. Soon Axel and Dax have joined them in the water and even Hux has ventured far enough from the house to sit on the towels and watch.

Their playfulness turns my stomach. If only they knew how close real danger was, maybe they wouldn't be so fucking happy all of the time. Or maybe it's time I showed them. Meg exits the water, dragging her dripping wet hat with her. Her toned legs allow her to cross the sand without any effort, her hips swaying with each step. Grabbing her towel and wrapping it around herself, she disappears from my view as she enters the house. My heart starts to pound, the thought of cornering her alone filling me with an excitement I haven't felt as long as I can remember.

Glancing at the group splashing in the sea one last time, I shove on a pair of black shorts and t-shirt from a pile on the floor and sneak around my double bed to unlock the door silently. Pushing my ear against the wood, I wait for the creak on the second staircase to sound before exiting and creeping after her. Edging up the steps, I peer through the crack in her door just in time to see her pull the black swimming costume down her legs. Stepping out of the sodden spandex, she returns to her full height to reveal perfectly rounded breasts, ideal for a handful. Her darkened nipples are hard as pebbles, causing my mouth to go dry. The junction between her thighs is completely bald, capturing my attention like a pervert as she walks past.

Returning into sight a few moments later, she has thankfully put on a robe so I can focus on the reason I've been spying on her. Show them who's in charge, make them suffer. Shaking off the lasting effects of the trance her body trapped me in, I look past her to see an open cupboard. Shelves line the inside, supporting hoards of boxes and board games. Narrowing my eyes on the floor space, I reckon there is just enough space for someone to fit in with the door closed and an idea forms in my mind. Didn't she say something about closed, dark spaces?

Smiling to myself, I wait for the moment her back is turned. Bolting from my spot on the top stair, I shove the door open with my shoulder and race up behind her, covering her sudden scream with my hand. Pushing her forward, I desperately try to ignore the bulge growing in my pants against the curve of her ass as she resists me. Telling myself I get off on her anguish, I shove her into the cupboard and slam the door shut before she can spin around. Conveniently finding a key on the other side, I twist the lock and step away.

She's shrieking and hammering on the door like a caged animal, begging me to let her out. The grin is so wide on my face now, my cheeks might split. This is what I needed to pick me up, the sounds of her completely at my mercy, suffering as I am. Stepping away slowly, I watch the door judder from her persistent attack and wonder if she might actually be able to break through. Slipping into the hallway, I shut her bedroom door and slink back to my own.

Lying on my bed, I push my arms beneath my head and sigh contently. I feel so much better now. The sounds of her screaming are still faintly filtering through the floorboards, soothing me inside out. Soon they will both be out of my life for good and I can feel like this all the time, with Rachel giving me a reason to wake up each day. Thoughts of her and the mansion fill my mind as I start to drift off, the promise of a better life to come lifting my spirits.

The back-door banging closed barely registers through my daze, footsteps pounding on the floorboards as someone runs to the top of the house. Meg's screams quieten, giving way for floods of hysterical crying which resonate with me just as much. She may be free for now, but that was only a taster for what's to come. Both of them will soon be screaming my name, begging for mercy and I won't give an inch of it.

# Avery

Closing our bedroom door as quietly as I can, a soft click sounds and I exhale in relief. Meg has finally drifted off for an afternoon nap, after the violent shakes raking her body had eased enough to allow it. There's not many things that can rattle Meg, but a dark enclosed space will do it every time.

A part of me wants to peg Wyatt's actions as his childish response to the overload of information we've recently been handed, although I'm not so sure. He's always been a cock-womble, but now there is an anger in him that scares me – not that I'll be admitting the fact out loud. If only he'd open his damn eyes to see nothing has actually changed, we could avoid all of this. I don't care if I'm legitimately a Hughes' child or not, my cards have been dealt and I want to keep moving forward.

Tiptoeing down the stairs, I hear murmurs coming from the bottom floor. Peeking around the wall, three figures are filing out of the door in jackets and sneakers. Garrett and Axel are holding Wyatt by each arm, practically shoving him out and closing the front door behind them. The distinctive roar of the Bentley's engine sounds, tyres crunching over the rocky path as I strain my ears. Looking around me, the rest of the house is utterly silent. Backtracking, I pause outside a slightly open door on the right-hand side and knock softly.

"Come in," Dax calls, so I step inside. His room is identical to all the others on this floor, exposed wood leaking from the walls and into the furniture. An incredible view of the sea lies beyond his bay window, despite the heavy clouds beginning to roll over the horizon.

"I was wondering where-" my words dry up along with all my saliva as my eyes land on Dax. Lounging on his back on the mattress in only a pair of shorts, he quickly folds the corner of the page he was reading and places the book down onto his chest. A river of rippling muscles peek from beneath the paperback, leading down to a sexy V that appears sharp enough to cut glass. Pushing himself up onto his elbows, my eyes are drawn to his thick biceps and the network of protruding veins trailing along his arms. Rolling my tongue between my teeth, Dax clears his throat to grab my attention.

"Where... the others had gone?" He asks, his smirk and quirked eyebrow showing he knows my mind is in the gutter. Managing a nod, a shudder rolls down my back I'm unable to hide. Removing the book and setting it on the floor, he shifts onto his side and uses a finger to beckon me over. Like a puppet on a string, I push the door closed with my foot and walk over, unable to resist. Lying alongside him, suddenly remembering I'm only in a vest and pyjama pants, I force myself to keep my eyes on his.

"They left for the nearest town, wanting to restock our food and give Wyatt some space to... re-evaluate." His fingers stroke a line from my wrist to shoulder, leaving a blazing trail of fire in their wake. Smoothing his hand around the back of my neck, he leans in closer. "They'll be gone for the rest of the day," he whispers. My lips part with an excuse that dies on my tongue, desire pooling in my core as his blue eyes darken. My head pulls forward on its own accord, keen for another taste of him, this time uninterrupted.

Moving close enough for our breaths to mingle, I run the edge of my tongue along his bottom lip and push it into his mouth. The second our tongues meet, his hands fly into my hair as he drags me into his firm body. Gripping his pecs, our mouths crash against each other in time to our bodies grinding urgently. Pushing my hand against his shoulder, I attempt to force him onto his back but he doesn't budge an inch. Hooking my leg over his waist instead, Dax presses his groin against the molten heat between my thighs. Breaking our kiss to glide his lips along my jaw, his body weight starts to push down onto me slowly. A flurry of panic washes through me, dread dousing my mood and sends me bolting from the bed.

Dax's eyes widen with concern, rising to sit on the edge of the mattress and hold his hands out for mine. There's no judgement or annoyance in his expression, just patience I wasn't prepared for. Gradually, I step forward and place my palms in his. "I'm sorry, I don't do missionary. It's too… close for my liking." My eyes slide to the floor, letting him think I mean in physical terms. His large hands travel to my hips, pulling me gently into his lap and burying his face into the crook of my neck.

"Firstly, don't ever apologise for not feeling comfortable again. To anyone." He places a kiss on my collar bone. "And secondly, this doesn't have to happen." Spinning my face to his, the sincerity in his gaze is a direct contrast to the bulging erection straining against my thigh.

"I want this to happen, trust me I can't handle holding back from you any longer." His lips curve into a smile, his blue eyes twinkling against his mocha skin.

"Then I'm all yours, take all the control you need. But if the day ever comes you would like to rewrite history, I'll be more than willing to do that for you." My eyebrows dip briefly as I stare at the opposite wall, Dax still kissing my shoulders sensually. The notion I could scratch over and replace bad memories with new ones has never occurred to me. But then again, I've never met anyone like Dax. He's compassionate and protective, but never overbearing. Subtly thoughtful, which he rarely takes credit for, understanding without needing explanations. And above all else, he makes me feel something I haven't felt for as long as I can remember – safe.

Leaving his loose hold, I round the bed and steadily lower myself until I'm flat on my back. Leaning over me with his arms fully extended so he isn't too close, his eyes search mine. "Avery, you don't have to-" I shoot my hand up to push my fingertips against his lips. All of a sudden, I need to do this, and for reasons my heart is keeping under lock and key, it has to be with him. Gripping the back of his head, his blonde curls tickling my fingers, I pull him down onto me. Our lips move much slower this time, the incredible softness of his kiss captivating me.

His forearm beside my head keeps him from fully lying on top of my body, his free hand cupping my cheek and thumb making small circles along my jaw. Ending our kiss, his head drops to my ear so he can whisper to me softly. "You can leave at any time." If I'd had any doubts up to this point, they just evaporated and I now know for a fact, I'm not going anywhere. Slipping my arms between us, I lift the hem of my vest and slide it over my head. Chucking it onto the floor, Dax rears up to help me remove my pyjama pants before standing to dispose of his shorts. My mouth falls open at the sight of his vast girth, a smooth pink head bulging at the top.

Kneeling between my legs, he nudges me to spread wider. Cool air meets my centre as I lie exposed beneath his heated gaze whilst chewing on his lip in a way that's driving me crazy. Running the pad of his thumb up my already slick seam, he finds my small bud instantly and applies delicious pressure. A flush bursts to life across my neck, searing heat burning me from inside with anticipation.

"So beautiful," he murmurs, bending to take my nipple in his mouth before I can respond. Keeping one hand between my legs, the other massages my breast as he sucks and licks. Repeating the sensual assault on my other nipple, his long index finger slides into me, stroking my inner channel expertly. I arch and squirm, torn between wanting this delightful torture to last for hours and to have all of him right now.

Withdrawing his finger, he pushes it into his mouth and sucks my juices clean. "Mmmm, next time," he promises, lining his bulbous head at my entrance. I briefly wonder if he'll be able to fit as he pushes in on a prolonged thrust. Crying out, my nails scrape his thighs as I adjust to his length. I've never felt so full. Feeling like he's still holding back, I grip his hair in my hand and pull him down onto me. His weight presses me into the mattress and I wait for the anxiety in kick in, but it never comes.

Sliding all the way out, he plunges back into me causing my back to arch. Gripping his shoulders, he continues his pounding while I spread my legs as far as I can to accommodate him. Dax pushes his face into my neck, his hair tickling my face as he lifts my hips to spear even deeper into my core. Each time, I moan and cry in shock, his cock caressing my G-spot, coaxing the orgasm from me. My toes curl and my teeth sink into his shoulder, muffling the scream as I come apart on the next thrust.

Light bursts behind my closed eyelids, an earthquake of pleasure tearing my body in two. Waves pulse around his thick rod, holding him firmly inside while I ride those glorious currents. The energy thrumming in my veins dissipates, leaving me to sag back contently. Grinding himself within me, I jolt in shock and open my eyes to find Dax staring down like I'm the most precious jewel he's ever seen. A darkening mark on his shoulder is surrounded by the imprint of my teeth though he doesn't seem to mind.

Working up to another steady rhythm, Dax hooks my leg up onto his bicep. His eyes stay linked with mine, emotion passing between us. With one hand supporting my ass, the other reaches up to caress my cheek as he lowers his head. Capturing my lips in his, something shifts within my chest that I don't have time to understand, my next climax already building.

Sweat slicks our bodies, our movements building to a crescendo of the sweetest music.

His stamina is relentless, never wavering from the powerful stride he's built up. My walls start to clamp down, this time taking him with me. His dick swells as cum explodes into me, causing both of us to shout out. My core throbs in time with him as the intensity eases, our chests heaving together in unison. His smile drops, a hint of panic in his piercing blue eyes.

"Should have... used a... condom," he rasps out between heavy breaths. I reach over limply to tap my upper arm, drawing his attention to the implant beneath the surface of my skin. Seeming satisfied, he kisses my forehead and pulls out of me. Disappearing into the bathroom, he returns quickly with a wet cloth to clean me delicately. I know it's ridiculous, but the intimate act is the first time I've felt self-conscious since walking in here.

Dax rolls onto the bed, his arm sliding around my middle as I try to rise from the bed and pulls me into his body. It goes against my personal rules to stick around after sex, but I can't deny how right his body warmth feels joined with mine. If there was ever a person I could envision myself being with long time, it would be the strikingly beautiful, dark skinned man beside me. But that's not possible for me. I'm better off alone, only committed to myself. That way, no one will be given the power to hurt me. In theory anyway.

# Wyatt

Breaking through the tree line of the forest that's been passing by the Bentley's windows for well over two hours, the road suddenly changes to tarmac beneath the wheels. Sitting upright in the back seat, I peer around Axel in the driver's seat to see a small town in view. Every building looks the same, exposed red brick and black tiled roofs. A large clock tower stands directly in front at the end of the single street that makes up the 'town', showing its already late afternoon.

Rolling down my window, I hang out on my forearm slightly. The scent of gasoline and smoke fill my nose as we drive past a group of bearded men in leather jackets, hanging outside a bar. Lines of motorcycles are parked along the pavement, bulky saddle bags on the backs suggesting they are just passing through like we are. Within 5 minutes, Axel has driven us from one side of the town to the other, parking the vehicle in the shade of a huge sycamore tree.

Neither Garrett nor Axel have spoken a single word to me, since dragging me from my bed with unnecessary force. I was more than willing to come along for this ride, having my own agenda. It was a unanimous decision to take me away from the house once they'd all heard Meg's over-exaggerated cries. I don't see what the big deal is, I was helping her face her fears – she should be thanking me. Never mind the fact Garrett would have found that shit hilarious and even joined in a few months ago, but people change. I sure have.

"You can stay in the car." Gare grumbles, slipping out and slamming the door. Axel looks back at me in the rear-view window, concern in his amber eyes.

"Just... make sure no one steals the Bentley. I don't fancy walking back. We won't be long." Running after Garrett like the lost puppy he is when alone, Axel disappears from view and I finally relax. Not wanting to waste any time, I pull my phone from my pocket to see the full signal bar in the top right corner. Opening my contacts, my thumb hovers over Ray's name but at the last second, I press Rachel's. The dial tone is music to my ears, my heart lifting with optimism.

"Wyatt?" Her sweet voice sails through the speaker with a hint of shock.

"Rachel!" I half shout, grinning ear to ear like a schoolboy. For the next ten minutes, she fawns over me, asking if I'm okay and telling me about her days lately. I notice how she completely avoids any questions around Avery or my task, her sole concern focused on my wellbeing.

"The house isn't the same without you. I've been practising a new jambalaya recipe I want you to try when you get back, it's a dish I've always struggled to perfect." My heart starts to ache, longing to return to her. Thinking of which, I need to speak with Ray before Tweedle-Dum and Tweedled-Dee return with the groceries.

"Sounds perfect, I can't wait. I have to call Ray, but I promise I'll be home soon." I say the words without realising, but once they are out there – they feel so right. Rachel makes me feel at home with her, accepted just the way I am. Bidding me goodbye, she hangs up the phone so I can move onto the real call I need to make.

"Ahh, Wyatt my boy. I was wondering when I might hear from you," Ray's crackled voice sounds equally as happy to speak with me. "I hope you're calling with good news for me."

"I am, actually. I know who the other twin is, and even better, both of them are staying in the safe house with me." Ray gasps in delight, shifting around on the other end to give me his full attention.

"Do tell, who is she?" I can practically see him sitting forward in his office chair, clinging onto the information I'm about to impart.

"Meg Connors. Her mom is Avery's therapist and the girls have been best friends for years."

"Well blow me down, I know of this Meg. We have case files on all the staff and known associates of the Hughes' household. But I never thought the one we've been searching for would be so close by. Nixon is a crafty one, I'll give him that." I grimace at the mention of my father's name, a bitter taste filling my mouth.

"He's not here unfortunately so I can't get them all to you-"

"No need, dear boy. Change of plans. We can't pass up the opportunity to have them both before Nixon thinks to separate them. Send me your location, I'll have men come to collect all three of you." My eyes widen, knowing with how protective the guys have become which means this won't be a simple task.

"I'll email you directions, but can I make one request? The guys I used to roll with are here, at the safe house. Promise me none of them will get hurt, again." There's a pause of silence, causing me to doubt if I'm in a position to make requests.

"I'm only interested in the girls. My men will be instructed to stay under the radar so there shouldn't be any more unnecessary casualties." The line goes dead so I start to type out the quick email, trying not to think on how that wasn't exactly a guarantee. I just have to hope we can sneak the girls out before anyone notices we've gone. Pressing send, I slump back and look out of the window.

Only from this angle can I now see a small church hidden behind the street, more like a converted house than an image of worship. White planks lay horizontally around the structure, with a grey roof and gothic style windows. The rounded window at the top has been replaced with stained glass, a cross sitting amongst patterns of red and green. Wooden crosses have also been fixed above the front and side porches. A small notice-board sits on the manicured lawn, black letters standing out against a white background. 'God Expects Spiritual Fruit, Not Religious Nuts. '

Noticing my body feels stiff, I exit the car to straighten my legs for a minute. Raising my arms above my head in a stretch, the faint sound of a ball bouncing drifts to me on a gentle wind. Shifting my head side to side like a meerkat, I locate a shabby court around the back of a barber shop on the corner. Closing the car door, my feet start to take me towards the several players running up and down the stony patch surrounded by a metal fence. The hoop is just that; a hoop with no backboard and covered in rust.

Noticing me approaching, the group pause their game to judge my Air Jordan sneakers and Nike sports outfit with contempt. A short dude with a mess of black curls on top of his head and pale skin is holding the ball in the centre of tall, muscled guys that are a similar size to me. "You better turn around and walk away rich boy, your private coaching aint got nothing on us." I cringe at his double negative, biting my tongue from proving his point about my upbringing. But I'm not going to argue about his grammar, I want to play some ball.

"How about a wager then? Me against all of you. If you win, you can have my sneakers." His eyes trail down to my feet, smirking with over confidence.

"And what do you get?" he shouts back through the fence. My first instinct is to say 'fun', but I shake off the notion. I don't want to have fun; I want to crush their cocky attitudes in my fist and force them back into the cardboard box homes they crawled out of.

"Experience," I settle on, which seems to please them all. Entering the court, the one I've named Diddy, due to his small size, chest passes me the ball to start. Tossing its weight from hand to hand, I reacquaint myself with it like an old friend I didn't realise I've been missing. Bouncing it under my legs and back again, I crouch and brace myself to wipe the floor with seven untrained, street players. Quick as a flash, I dart to the side, pre-empting each of their lazy moves and dodging each rogue hand flailing for the ball. Seeing an opening between two oafs looking in opposite directions, I launch myself upwards and throw the ball easily into the net with a flick of my hand. Diddy catches the ball as it bounces his way, glaring at me.

"First one to five," he growls, dribbling the ball around the arc line rather than start in the centre like I did. His eyes flash to oaf number three behind me as he fakes a shot and throws the ball sideways. With my training, it's comical he thought I'd even fall for that lame trick shot as the ball lands right in my hands. With minimum effort, I toss the ball into the air and hear the satisfying 'oomph' of it sailing through the net. The men around me grumble, one of them stealing the ball and making a show of bouncing it around the court. Approaching me, he jumps to shoot so I reach up to block his way. Another player dives at me, throwing me forcefully to the ground. Glancing up, I see the ball be netted and hear the team cheer for themselves.

"That's a foul!" I shout, pushing up to my feet and dusting myself off.

"This is street ball, Moneybags. There are no rules," Diddy grins with either something yellow stuck in his teeth or never having owned a toothbrush. Shrugging, I now understand anything goes, so they'd better watch out.

∞∞∞∞

My heel connects with a shin at the same time as I swing my elbow into his cheek, allowing me to pluck the ball from his fingers and score my fourth basket. I can taste the blood from my split lip and will have a few bruises on my torso tomorrow, but I feel so much better. Our match has turned into a brawl which doesn't seem to have any limits, judging by the knee that almost caught me between the legs. Snatching the ball, I run around the court ducking out the way of punches. A crowd has gathered on the other side of the fence cheering for their home-boys, even though they are clearly losing.

There's only two oafs and Diddy left, the rest are sitting alongside the court nursing split heads or possible broken ribs. Looking down at the ball gripped in my hands, my knuckles are swollen with splatters of blood decorating them, none of which are mine and I briefly consider needing a shot. Who knows what I might contract from a bunch of gutter rats that smell like they haven't seen a shower before? Although, I'm starting to smell quite ripe myself, sweat pouring down my face and stinging my busted lip.

Diddy runs at me, his eyes blazing with a rage I under-stand all too well, but I spin and kick out his legs from beneath him anyway. A mountain of a man, who I reckon is deceivingly younger than he looks, tries to block my way. His movements are sluggish so a simple fake left is enough to fool him without the need for violence. Nearing the basket, I leap into the air for a slam dunk when the last player still in the game ploughs into me. The ball leaves my fingertips as his heavy weight throws me into the metal pole holding the hoop. My back makes an unnerving crack, his forehead slamming into the pole and knocking him clean out. The ball made it to the basket, my eyes tracking it spinning around the hoop. Looking like it's about to fall the wrong way, I shove my shoulder against the pole causing a judder that sees it slipping inside. Boos and jeers fill the air, but nothing can wipe the smile off my face for now, pushing sleeping beauty from my legs so I can stand. Diddy approaches me for a customary handshake, even in the slums.

"Good game," I snigger, clasping his hand. There's a hint of mirth in his eyes, his lips lifting at one corner. He hands me the game ball begrudgingly as would happen in a real playoff, not that I'll be keeping it.

"Yeah man, that was something alright. Come for a rematch one day, we won't hold back next time." I laugh as a loud whistle distracts me. Garrett is glaring at me through the dissipating crowd, his jaw clenched and hazel eyes furious. Axel is by his side, stroking his fingers along Garrett's inner arm to keep him calm. Telling him I'll be right out with a sigh, Diddy quickly snatches the ball roughly from my grip. A scowl of disgust contorts his features as he takes a step back like I'm suddenly contagious.

"Actually, don't come back here. We don't play with their kind." He gestures towards Garrett and Axel with his chin, his whole team practically snarling at them.

"Oh, I'm not-" the words die on my tongue, wondering why I care what this parasite thinks of me. My breathing grows heavy and my fingers curl into my palm, ready to show this asshole just want I think of his small-minded opinions. Garrett has the same reaction, his voice booming through the fence.

"What's that, small fry?" Straightening his shoulders, he makes a move to enter the court, but Axel stops him. After a few tense moments, Garrett allows himself to be pushed back a step. The crack of a whip echoes through my mind, the guy I knew having completely morphed into a pussy. The old Garrett never backed down from a fight, or cared about anyone else for that matter. "Get in the fucking car," he growls, spinning on his heel to stalk away. Axel reaches for him but he sidesteps, keeping his fists clenched by his sides.

"Hey," Diddy captures my attention again, resting a hand on my shoulder that I immediately shrug off. "You seem like a stand-up guy so let me offer you some advice. There's two kinds of people in this world, those who add to society and those who mock it. You're either with 'em or against 'em, what's it gonna be?" My mind registers this pinhead is trapped within the limitations of his tiny mind, but his words sink in on a personal level. Never mind Garrett and Axel, It's clear to anyone with eyes that I'm in neither of those categories, so what the fuck does that mean for me?

# *Axel*

"I'm out," I say, handing my remaining stack of coloured paper money over to a smug Meg. I'm the second one to have been made bankrupt by her red, plastic hotels filling the top and right edges of the Monopoly board. If Lacrosse doesn't lead to a career for her, Meg could definitely climb the ranks in real estate or find herself in a corner office with a city view on Wolf Street.

Trying to catch Garrett's eye, he continues to ignore me, as he has since leaving town. The entire journey back, he blasted his music so we didn't have to talk about what had happened. In my head, there's no issue. I don't give a shit what people say or think about me, it can't be worse than what I already think about myself.

Rising from my position on the hard floor to stretch my long legs, I leave Meg, Avery and Garrett playing in the living room while I head into the kitchen. Pulling a carton of juice from the fridge, I lean against the counter to watch Huxley push food around his plate with a fork at the dining table. I'm eager to comfort him, but I honestly don't know how to since he's been so easy to fly off the handle lately. Lifting his chocolate brown eyes and noticing me watching, Hux grumbles as he stands. The chair screeches in protest as he pushes it back and abruptly exits the room, leaving me to clear up after him.

Once I've disposed of his cold, untouched pasta and washed the plate, I leave it to dry and head upstairs myself. Stretching across the mattress in the room Garrett claimed for us, I unplug my phone from its charger and unlock the screen. There's not much I can do without any internet, but my old-school Tetris app still works. Losing myself in the game, I don't realise how long I play for until I hear the sounds of multiple bedroom doors in the house closing for the night.

Rolling from the bed, I decide to head for a shower since I'm not tired yet and I'd wait for Garrett to return anyway. The ensuite is almost as big as the bedroom, which makes sharing it much easier. There's an overly large tub in the centre of the space, facing towards the huge glass plane that is the far wall. The sea stretches across the horizon, thousands of glimmering stars covering the midnight blanket above. Being this far from the busy city life I'm used to gives me a break from glaring artificial lights and noisy crowds. A part of me would gladly stay here for good, no stress or pressures, no college work.

Even my nightmares have eased since arriving here, although I'm not sure if it has so much to do with the surroundings as it does with the man that's been sharing my bed permanently for the past few weeks. I'm trying to guard my heart, knowing Garrett isn't one for commitment and there's a very real chance I'll wake up one day and he'll be gone. But the way he looks at me sometimes steals the breath from my lungs. He knows me better than anyone else. What I need and what I want at all the right times.

After brushing my teeth in the sink, I switch on the shower and strip out of the knee-length shorts and polo top I wore for a beach stroll earlier. Entering the cubicle and closing the glass door behind me, I relish the cool spray of water raining down upon my shaved head. Taking the sea mineral body wash from the plastic shelf attached to the tiled wall, I squeeze the blue liquid down the centre of my chest before rubbing it across my body. Spreading the lather to the back of my neck, I try to conjure happy images in my mind before the impending horrors awaiting me in my dreams.

Every scenario I can imagine, from a basketball game to luscious green parks or five-star restaurants, Garrett is in each one with me. With his wide smile and adorable dimples, brown hair that doesn't have a favoured side to rest on, and the light hazel hue to his irises. But more than his looks, Garrett's humour brightens my days and his easy acceptance of my troubles make me feel comfortable to be with him. He doesn't judge or care about pasts; Garrett accepts everyone for who they are without a second thought.

Stepping out of the shower, I turn the dial to switch off the water. Pulling the top brown towel from the folded pile on a nearby shelf, I rub the rough material over my head and head to the mirror hanging on the far wall. The only part of me that could be deemed as slightly interesting would be my eyes, and I would change them in a heartbeat if I could. They are the sole reason I still hate to look at my refection as I always see that weak, 14-year old boy staring back.

Turning away when I can't bare to look at myself any longer, I pad back to the fluffy circular mat that sits beside the bathtub. After drying off the rest of my body, I secure the towel around my waist and exit the room. Garrett is waiting for me in our room, shifting nervously on the other side of the bed separating us. Clothes are laid out on the covers, which he gestures to before scratching a hand into his floppy brown hair.

"Don't over think this. I hate labels. Just get dressed and meet me on the porch," he says bluntly, shifting towards the foot of the bed to meet me halfway. Joining him in the middle of the room, I look around curiously.

"Is this a da-" Garrett's hand covers my mouth to stop me from talking.

"What did I just say?" He steps forward to stare into my eyes, with a dangerous edge to his hazel ones. He seems strangely on edge; his body language is rigid and breathing slightly laboured. Stepping back and lowering his hand, he holds up his palm with all fingers stretched out.

"Porch, 5 minutes." With that, he disappears through the doorway in a rush. I stare after him for a moment, then down to the clothes he's laid out on the bed. Nothing fancy, a pair of navy tracksuit shorts and plain grey t-shirt. Pulling the items on, I throw the damp towel into the laundry basket in the corner and sit on the edge of the bed to wait the full five minutes as requested.

I don't think I've ever seen Garrett flustered as he's usually the most confident of us all. He hides himself deep inside to stop others from seeing his vulnerable side, even I barely see it. Waiting an extra minute for good measure, I leave the room and head down the staircase. It's almost midnight so the rest of the house is silent, only the groan of the wood beneath my feet penetrating the air. Passing through the living room and kitchen, I emerge onto the back porch where a faint flickering light catches my attention.

Small lit candles trail the banister leading to the built-in porch swing. A thick blanket covers the seat with a bowl of popcorn placed in the centre. Garrett walks up the steps, a metre-long indent in the sand behind him tells me he's been pacing for a while. Avoiding my eye contact, he points to the swing for me to take a seat but I remain where I am. Holding my hand out for him, his eyes flick to mine with a nervous shine to them.

"We don't have to-"

"I want to," he says quickly. Taking my hand, we walk together to lift the blanket and settle ourselves beneath it. The bowl is resting in Garrett's lap where I would expect it to be as we face the landscape in silence. It's too dark to see the sea, but the sky looks like a monotone Jackson Pollock painting, flecks of light filling the space up above.

Gare's hands lift the bowl and move it into the middle of us, equally resting it between our touching thighs. Looking up at him in shock, noticing he will not take his eyes from a particular candle on the timber railing in front of us. To anyone else, this would seem like the lamest evening ever, but I realise what's happening here. Garrett doesn't willingly share food, nor does he do dates or commitment. And in one single move, he's offered me all three.

Without pausing any longer, fearing he may think I'm freaking out inside the way he clearly is, I snuggle down further to rest my head on his shoulder and take a cluster of popcorn. Popping it into my mouth, it crunches loudly between my teeth. Only after I've taken the fourth piece, does Gare's body start to soften and he joins me in his midnight snack. I dare not tell him I'm not a big fan of popcorn, nor am I hungry but I keep on eating, knowing this is about more than food.

"I don't do romance or flowers, and I rarely sleep with the same person more than once. I'm an asshole that pushes people away so I can never be hurt again. I don't like to count on others and I'll probably fuck this up too. Really soon. But you make me want to be better. I want to be with you, like all the time. As a proper..."

I've remained still this entire time, not wanting to give him any reason to stop talking but now I risk a glance upwards. His face is illuminated in an orange glow, his jaw tight. "Boyfriend?" I supply for him when I realise he's not going to say it. Without moving his eyeline, Garrett gives a single stiff nod which causes me to smile.

"Is this about what those assholes said?" I ask in a low voice.

"No, this is about me. It's time I re-evaluated certain aspects of my life, mainly the part with you in it." Sitting up, I take the bowl and lean forward to push it under the seat we are swinging gently on before turning back to face him. Taking his cheeks in my hands, I force him to face me despite the effort he puts into trying to resist. Pushing my lips against his, the connection of our mouths instantly allows him to relax beneath my touch. His dimples deepen under my fingertips as I pull back, his easy smile back in place.

"The day you can say I'm your boyfriend without it causing you such strain, I'll be right here waiting." I wink. A breathy laugh fans over my face as he leans his forehead against mine. We huddle under the blanket for the rest of the night, our limbs tangled as we force the night's cool air to stay out. By the time the sky lightens to a mix of mauve purple and rose pinks, Garrett's soft snore sounds above my head. Nudging him, we collect up the blanket and sneak back to our room before the rest of the household wakes up.

Garrett flops onto his side on the bed, allowing me to be the big spoon for once. Normally I'm the one to sleep the most, but I don't even feel tired right now. Thoughts from his mini pre-rehearsed speech last night keep floating around my mind. I've never suggested to Garrett that I want big romantic gestures or needed confirmation of what he is to me. Just knowing he is there for me to lean on and isn't ready to ditch me quite yet is more than enough.

I've never expected him to tie himself down and I know he will never be a one-partner kinda guy, but that's fine. He's here when I need him the most. He knows more about my past than anyone and still sees someone worth loving. And I suppose a secret part of me fell for him long ago, before I even came out. Those feelings have blossomed and grown at a rapid rate since we left Waversea, which is probably why I'm almost dreading going back. I don't want to lose everything we've built between us. The connection we have, the security and the compassion. Fuck, who am I even kidding? I'm in love with Garrett – and if he retreats back to his old ways when we return to college, it will crush me.

# Meg

Extending my arms into warrior pose, I feel the stretch in every part of my body. My shoulders, my core and my legs all hum with the delicious burn yoga provides. Avery's fingertips nudge mine in the same pose, a smirk on her face in the fading sunlight. "What, beach isn't big enough for you?" I joke, slapping the back of her hand with mine. The sand shifts beneath my toes, cool air descending after a scorching hot day.

Placing our feet together, we bend forward in unison to hold our ankles. We've done yoga together on the beach every day since Avery arrived, her presence being a god-send in an otherwise dull place. The sea laps gently near our feet, a white line of foam leading the water towards us. Standing upright, I make a prayer sign with my hands and raise my right leg, tucking my foot into my left thigh. Stretching up with my arms, I stand in the tree pose with the shifting sand testing my balance.

"Arrrgh, Captain MegLeg," Garrett's gruff voice sounds from behind me. Turning my head curiously, he has one eye closed and is pumping a fist across his front.

"Were you dropped on your head as an infant?" I ask, seriously worried for his future.

"More than likely," he replies normally, dropping his pirate act. It's only now I notice he isn't alone, Axel and Dax are crossing the beach behind him carrying a huge log between them. Avery has dropped her pose too, her eyebrows creasing inwards. "We're making a campfire, wanna help?" Avery and I gasp in excitement at the same time, offering to find driftwood from across the beach. Strolling along the water's edge, we chat and giggle together while filling our arms with wood that's washed ashore. Thankfully, the sun has ensured none of them are damp in the slightest. I take the larger pieces while Avery hunts for smaller ones, only turning back when we can't bend to collect anymore without dropping them all.

Returning to our original spot, Dax is arranging a circle of stones to form our fire pit. There're now two thick logs lying opposite each other on either side. Garrett has a paper bag in his hands as he emerges from the house, Axel carrying a large bucket of ice and beer bottles behind him. Placing our wood to the side of Dax, goose bumps start to line my arms as the sun dips behind the horizon.

"I'll fetch some blankets," I say, turning towards the house and pausing. Last time I went in alone, Wyatt snuck up on me and I'm not looking for a repeat. Glancing over at Avery, she's started to help Dax make a stick tepee for the middle of the fire. "Aves, would you like to help me?" I feel awful dragging her away from Dax when even a blind person could see the connection those two have, but there will be loads of time for them later. Especially when they're cuddled under a blanket.

Nodding without hesitating, she joins my side and walks with me into the house. Entering the kitchen door, we can see Huxley sitting on the sofa gazing at the plain wall again. He clearly wants to be involved, otherwise he wouldn't leave his room but the version of him I originally met is a distant memory. There's no cheeky grin or laughter lines on show, just blank stares and thinning muscle. Avery leaves me to go to him, sitting on the coffee table so he has to look at her.

"Come join us outside, we're having a campfire." Her tone is soft, like trying to coax a child out from behind their mother's skirt. His eyes soften as they shift to hers but that's the only change.

"I heard. I'm fine here," he mumbles, barely moving his lips.

"We spoke about this, remember. Please join us, I want you there." A ghost of a smile appears over his mouth, giving a single nod that has Avery beaming. She leans forward, her hands on his knees to plant a kiss on his cheek before following me up the stairs. Avery can lie to herself if she wants, but I see the truth. She cares for each of the men that have entered her life unexpectedly, and in doing so she's broken through titanium barriers she erected years ago without realizing.

Checking various cupboards along the hallway, we find one with hoards of blankets, bedding, spare duvets and pillows. Pulling out a whole pile of blankets, all thick with checked patterns, I push them into Avery's open arms. An aged cardboard box stuffed at the bottom catches my attention, seeming thoroughly out of place.

"No way," I breathe, bending down to pull the box free from its hiding space. Dust unsettles at the movement, kicking into the air around me so I wave my hand in front of my face. Pulling the item that grabbed my attention free, I twist to show Avery with the biggest smile on my face. A silver battery operated CD player with rounded edges that is surprisingly heavy. The box is stacked with old school CD's, our entertainment for the night sorted.

Avery squeals as if I'd found a pot of gold, not that I can blame her. Placing the player back into the box, I lift the whole thing to take downstairs. Pausing in the kitchen, I grab a pack of spare batteries from the drawer and take a second to switch them over, figuring the old ones are either long gone or have leaked by now. Securing the batteries in place, a shadow appears over my shoulder, making me jump.

Huxley dives his hands through the box on the counter, shifting through the plastic cases and selecting a handful of his choice. Flipping the 'on' switch, a small red light comes to life on the front of the player. Huxley takes the handle from my grip, silently carrying it out for me in a chivalrous/overbearing kind of way but I don't mind. Just seeing him up and getting involved is good enough. Following him, I step onto the porch to see the fire is now lit, flickering flames stretching towards the stars. Rounding the timber banister, I skip down the steps and walk by Huxley's side.

"Look what Meg found," his deep tone draws everyone's attention, holding the player above his head. The three other guys whoop and cheer, bounding over to us.

"Nice one, Meghead!" Garrett lifts me clean off my feet, my hair whipping as he spins me. Shrieking for him to put me down, he finally does so I can make my way over to Avery on the log. Giggling, she lifts her blanket for me to slide beneath and hugs me to her body. A full moon, surrounded by thousands of twinkling stars, is rising from the north-east to shine down on us all brightly. Dax passes us a pre-opened beer each, gesturing for the others to join with their own.

"To the Shadowed Souls," he cheers, all bottles clinking together except for mine. Watching the display, Avery pulls back her bottle from the centre and takes a long swig, as do the others.

"What is that? Sounds like a cult," I ask in jest, although genuinely curious. I remember Avery mentioning something like that back when the guys first arrived on her doorstop, but I'd been a bit distracted by the smoking hot figures passing through the house to listen properly. The way Avery toasted with them easily has intrigued me even more.

"No, nothing like that." Huxley grumbles from beside Dax, Garrett and Axel lost in their own hushed whispers and secret smiles. "Wyatt gave us that name when he formed our group. It just reminds us how far we've come to form this dysfunctional unit of fuck-ups."

"Oh gee, thanks. No one told me that when I joined," Avery giggles and winks at him. The crease between his eyebrows eases slightly, a ghost of a smirk crossing his lips. Sliding my eyes back to my twin, I remain silent and watch her interact with Dax as Huxley moves over to the CD player. I don't think she's realised how attached she's grown to this group, they've welcomed her into their fold and whether she will ever admit it to herself or not, she's let them in too.

Michael Jackson's 'Smooth Criminal' begins to play at a surprisingly loud volume, the rhythm filtering through my body to my tapping foot. Sharing a smile with Garrett, my head bobs as I feel the music in the depths of my being. Swaying our shoulders in time to each other, Avery and I sing along with the lyrics flawlessly. Each song blends into the next forming our fireside karaoke until 'Dirty Diana' plays and I drag Avery to our feet.

Keeping our fingers linked, we lip sync to one another and dance like we would at any of the house parties we usually attend most weekends. Axel places an open beer into our free hands, his fingers lingering on Avery's for a moment longer. The glow from the flames dance alongside us, an orange hue licking at our skin. Following Axel with my eyes, I watch him return to a spot on the log to join the audience we seem to have, every eye focused on our movements as if we are their entertainment.

The song comes to an end after we've made sure to give a good show, taking our seats to face the others. Beyond the fire, a darkened figure is standing in the doorway of the house. Noticing my diverted attention, everyone turns one by one to see Wyatt looming in the distance and beckon him over. Even Avery waves for him to join us to my surprise. After a moment's hesitation, he begins to casually stroll over without any sense of urgency and lowers himself onto the far end of our log, which is perfect for me as I don't have to look at him. I can be the most understanding person in the world at times, but in this instance – Wyatt can sit on a landmine for all I care right now. Okay maybe not, but I'm still pretty pissed with him.

Rustling in his paper bag, I concentrate on Garrett, curious as to what snacks he brought, probably only for himself. Producing a bag of marshmallows, he hands them to Axel who passes down to Dax. Next, he pulls out a packet of thin roasting sticks which Axel removes from the packaging to hand out to each of us. Holding it by the wooden handle, I wait for Dax to do the rounds with the marshmallows and push mine onto the metal prongs. Wyatt and Huxley get involved too, leaning towards the fire like the rest of us with their speared cube of sugary goodness.

"Did you plan all of this?" Avery asks, rotating her stick to get the perfect singe on all sides. Garrett and Axel share a sweet smile, dividing cubes of chocolate and graham crackers between them to pass around. Accepting mine with a thanks, I pull my sticky marshmallow from the fire and place it into my s'more sandwich. Nibbling at the edges, as not to burn my mouth, a feeling of calm washes over me.

I watch Garrett suspiciously as he pulls a blanket from the folded pile and drapes it over them both before making his own, expertly stacking the melted ball of goo and chocolate between the crackers. He's not being his normal annoying self, but instead calm and controlled as he acts like the group's leader for a change. Blowing on his s'more briefly, he twists to hold it up to Axel's mouth and waits patiently for him to take a bite. My mouth drops open, a dollop of marshmallow missing my lips and glopping down onto my t-shirt. I may not have spent much time with him, but I know rule number one well enough – Garrett doesn't share food.

Avery has also clocked onto the weirdly intimate behaviour happening across the campfire, her blue eyes transfixed on their actions. Nudging her, we swap a look of "Damn" and continue eating, simply enjoying the atmosphere. Only the fire is making noise, its crackling drowning out the seas gentle lapping. The air is so fresh, my stress ebbing from my body under the mass of stars.

Even my anger towards Wyatt is lessening, being at ease with the close proximity reminding me that recent discoveries will have affected him the most. Where Avery and I simply gained knowledge and nothing else has really changed, he's had his world flipped upside down. His parents aren't biologically his parents, not that I've had any issue with my mom on that front. Other than for medical history, DNA means nothing to me. I'd much rather have the life I've always known with love and nurturing than have lived my whole life like this, hidden from view and living in fear of a revenge-seeking psychopath.

Rising from beside me, Avery walks over to the CD tower Huxley has made in the sand since the MJ tracks finished a short while ago. Flashing a Madonna album at me with a huge smile, she slinks around the back of the guys to push the disc into the player and hit play. Giggling as the first track plays, Avery runs around to lift me to my feet this time. Spinning me in a circle, she pulls me into her body and sways me exaggeratedly, singing 'Everybody' into my ear.

"Get a room," Garrett hollers, halting our dance to face him. Axel's head is leaning on his shoulder in a similar way to how Avery rests her cheek onto mine. Bobbing my eyebrows, I push my tongue into my cheek and try to think of a witty reply.

"I'd offer to let you join but I seem to remember you come as a pair," I come out with, resisting to face palm myself with my fist. My cheeks heat as his eyes darken, the flickering flames crossing his face giving him a dangerously sexy look that has me biting my lip.

"You remember correctly, Meggles, but I'm sure it's nothing you couldn't handle. Avery managed, rather well in fact."

# *Avery*

"You fucked them?!" Huxley shoots to his feet and shouts accusingly, pointing his index figure at the pair huddled up under a blanket on the chunky log. My eyes widen, heat scorching my neck and face which have nothing to do with the campfire we've created. Wyatt's jaw goes slack briefly in the orange glow as his emerald eyes flick between the three of us. Clenching his teeth tight enough to produce a tic in his jaw, he stands and leaves without saying a word, although the rigidness of his posture speaks volumes.

"It's none of your business what or *who* I do." I say defensively, Meg mimics my stance by crossing her arms and standing shoulder to shoulder with me. Her eyes are blazing with anger that he would call me out so boldly. Noticing he's the only one left here with an issue, the crease in Huxley's eyebrows lifts and he pokes his tongue into his cheek.

"Huh, I figured you had more class than that." He shrugs, changing from outraged to a petty dickwad in seconds.

"What's that supposed to mean?" Garrett chimes in, rising to force Huxley to face him. I don't miss the way he steps in front of Axel defensively.

"Well, you'd fuck anything with a pulse and he probably cries when he cums. Not to mention the amount of STD's you two are probably swapping back and forth." At that, Axel shoots up from the log too, the promise of death fixed into his amber eyes. His shoulders are bunching in time with tight clenches of his fists, snarling through his teeth like a wild animal. I've never seen him react so impulsively before. Anyone who thinks Axel is weak due to his calm nature would find out the hard way how extremely wrong they are. If It weren't for Garrett blocking his way, Axel would be pummelling Huxley into the ground right now.

"Oh, you wanna go Chrome Dome?" Huxley taunts. "Bring it on." Stepping forward, he throws a sucker punch directly into Garrett's throat. Stumbling out the way and gripping his throat, Garrett falls to one knee in the sand and a choked noise leaves him. Running over, I uselessly smooth my hands over his shoulders, screaming his name while he struggles to draw a proper breath.

I hear the first punch land behind me, twisting to see Axel mercilessly beating a weakened Huxley on the ground. The pair scuffle but it's clear to see a mile off who has the upper hand. Shadows from the flames dance over Axel's back, the heat seeming to intensify with the shift of mood in the air. Dax intervenes, heroically throwing himself in the middle to push Axel back. After a few seconds, he stops resisting and strides over to soothe Garrett, who has returned to breathing normally again.

We all pass glances around the flickering flames, no one knowing what to say about our ruined campfire. I avoid Dax's blue eyes completely, scared to see his reaction to the news. Garrett finally manages to speak, his tone low and directed solely at Huxley.

"Just so we are clear, I get tested after every partner believe it or not. And Axel has more resilience in his little finger than you do in your entire body, so look in the mirror before you open your mouth." Pulling Axel with him, the pair stand and walk back to the house, taking their blanket with them. Huxley also storms off, but he chooses to walk into the darkness down the beach.

Pushing myself onto the log with Meg, we sit in a silent

triangle with Dax. Luckily, the fire is hiding the blush covering my entire face, my level of embarrassment hitting the Richter scale. I mean, one-night stands aren't uncommon in my book but to have three lovers in one space, talk about awkward. Dax is busy fiddling with a strand of his afro while Meg clicks her tongue.

"It's getting a bit chilly, huh? I'm gonna go find a hoodie," Meg hops up suddenly. She winks down at me even though I'm begging her with my eyes to stay. Smirking, she slinks off while I throw a mental dagger right into the centre of her back. Cow. Dax slowly moves around to the log I'm on, edging closer to me. I keep my focus on the burning logs, unease rippling beneath my skin. Once he's barely a few centimetres away, I chance a look and hate the empathy etched into his features.

"You must think I'm such a slut," I sigh, hiding my face in my hands. The following silence confirms my suspicions, which hurts more than I thought it would. I've never given much of a shit how people perceive me, but with Dax it's different. He's different. The fire is beginning to die out, so Dax reaches over to poke it with a long stick, shifting the logs to stoke the flames back to life. When he sits back onto the log, I notice he's nudged up more to my side.

"I think we are all living in difficult times, with uncovering the truth of your lineage, armed men trying to kidnap you and the dynamic of our group crumbling - we all need a release. I don't judge you for being human. I hope you know I'm always here for you too." Pulling a sweaty palm away from my face, Dax links his fingers with mine and stares at me with understanding eyes.

"Dax, I don't do relationships. You know that, right? I won't be able to return your affections." Rubbing his thumb across the back of my hand, he looks at me sheepishly.

"I wouldn't ask for anything in return, I'd just like to chance to be yours."

I know he's trying to comfort me, but instead a flicker of panic rises within. Dax is perfect boyfriend material, but I'm not that type of girl. I can't handle commitment, nor would I be able to give him the life he would want. I can imagine him feeding me strawberries on a hillside picnic, me playing cheerleader on the side lines of his basketball games, being the girl under his arm sitting in a movie theatre. But when it comes down to love, I'm hollow inside. My life has no worth to me, so it's unfair to expect it to mean something to him.

Releasing his hand, I stand and step away. Concern crosses his features, his fingers reaching for me as I shift away from them. "I'm sorry, I can't," is all I manage to say, turning and bolting towards the house. Running until I push the door of our bedroom closed behind me, I flop onto the bed beside Meg and let the tears fall. Her hand lies on my back, an initial flinch shuddering through me until I remember I'm not that girl anymore.

"What happened?" Meg whispers in my ear, shifting down to hug me close. I can't speak, only sobs bubbling out of my lips against the mattress. I've been content with myself for years, only needing Meg and my extra-curricular activities to give me a reason to wake up each day. But the look in Dax's eyes just now, the promise of a life he longs to give me has only resonated with my soul that I'm not enough. I'm still broken, unable to easily fall in and out of love because I know losing someone like him would be it for me.

I cry until my chest aches and the tears dry up, Meg holding me gently the entire time. I ache, inside and out at the taunting images floating around my mind of a life I can't have.

"Talk to me," Meg pleads once I've gone silent. I could fake being asleep, but she'd only revisit this conversation in the morning.

"It's Dax. He wants...me." I whisper, shifting my head to the side. My eyes sting and my cheeks feel puffy, although it's nothing Meg hasn't seen a thousand times before.

"Aves, I know we've spoke about this but-"

"But I can't be with him. I don't want to leave anyone behind." I interrupt her, knowing I'm in the mood to be easily persuaded. She'd have me running into his arms in minutes if I forget my morals. Life is pain and anguish, no one makes it through unscathed. The best way to be is to hide away and enjoy what I can.

"Why does it have to be so black and white? Life is colourful and vibrant. You've earnt the right to a happy future." I scoff to myself, not ready to have this argument again.

"It's never been clearer than now that shit follows me wherever I go. He's better off with a normal girl who can love him the way he deserves. I'm better off alone." She knows I mean other than her, evident by the way she squeezes me tighter. "I want to go home. Back to how it was."

"I don't think you truly mean that. Whether you're ready to admit it to yourself or not, you've bonded with all of those guys, even Wyatt at one point. You know better than anyone you can't have the good without the bad, and individually each one of the men downstairs are good for you."

Leaning back against the headboard, I watch Meg slip out of the door with a tray in her hands. She's brought breakfast and lunch to me in bed, not that I've had much appetite, but she has demanded I join the rest of them for dinner. The thought of seeing anyone else is making my stomach tie in knots, my head and my heart battling for control over my emotions. Staring out of the angled window, I watch the clouds roll by lazily in a bright blue sky. The sun passed over a while ago so I know it's afternoon without needing a clock nearby.

My legs are starting to twitch, my fingers feeling itchy. The walls are closing in on me, the oxygen in the room growing stuffy. I need to leave this room. Pulling out some jeans and an olive-green hoodie, I'm halfway through dressing when Meg returns.

"We're going for a walk," is all I need to say. No questions asked, Meg replaces her denim shorts for tracksuit pants and ties one of her college jackets around her waist. I shove my hair into a messy bun on top of my head to match hers and push my feet into a pair of white Converse. Inhaling deeply, I turn the door handle and step into the hallway. Meg is hot of my heels so I can't turn to run back, forcing me down the two staircases.

A conversation on the sofa stops as I reach the living room, four pairs of eyes twisting to look at me. I can't keep the blush at bay but smile and wave easily as I stride over to the front door. Unable to even look in Dax's direction through sheer embarrassment, I keep my fringe at an angle to block the view of him and leave the house. Breathing in deeply, the fresh air fills my lungs and soothes some of my worries.

Linking my arm with Meg's, we venture into the forest without the need for words. Diverting from the rocky path, we step through overgrown shrubs to lose ourselves in a sea of green. The overhead canopy shades us from the sun's heat, a much-needed coolness draping over my skin. I trail my fingers along the rough bark of impossibly thick tree trunks and stop every so often to smell the perfumed scent of a beautifully bloomed flower. Vines coil around overhanging branches like snakes hidden amongst the foliage, watching us pass underneath.

Looking over to Meg, she flashes me a wide smile which I can't help to reciprocate. Pulling her to a halt, even though we are in the middle of a muddy patch of soil, I drag her in for a hug. Winding my arms around her neck, I press my cheek against hers. "I love you," I breathe. She's the one who's always been here for me, the one I never worry about leaving me. My twin, and most of the time, my only lifeline.

A loud rustle in the bushes jolts me, twisting to locate the source. Meg's posture has also straightened as we stare between the masses of tree trunks surrounding us. A twig snaps on the opposite side of the small clearing we've found ourselves in, causing my heart to jack hammer in my chest. Gripping her hand tightly, I start to walk as calmly as my shaking legs will carry me between the trees and away from the noises. A sound similar to a grunt comes from too close and forces us into a run.

Never breaking our hold on each other, Meg and I leap over branches and plants like hurdles, never slowing. In my mind, the noises grow louder and the rustles edge closer. My ankle snags on a root sticking out of the ground which loses me precious seconds to shake out of. Large leaves slap us on the way past, my calves beginning to burn as I push through them. Sweat slips down my forehead and into my eyes, but I don't feel hot thanks to the fear frozen in my veins.

There's a stitch forming in my side, but Meg won't let me slow. She yanks me along at a speed my feet can barely keep up with, slipping on mud and landing on the uneven ground at angles. A crack from behind makes us scream, the house coming into view as we push our legs even further to a maximum speed. Crashing through the door, I collapse on the ground heaving and coughing. Shadowed figures surround me as I curl up in a ball and find my face. Hands grab my arms, hoisting me to my feet with a yelp.

"Are you okay? What happened?" Huxley's chocolate brown eyes scan me with pure panic trapped inside them. His blonde waves tickle my chest as he looms over me, waiting for an answer I don't have. Gathering I'm safe from whatever was out there, I throw myself into his arms and bury my face into his chest. His arms slip around my body, holding me almost painfully tight but I don't mind.

Meg's pants shift into a breathy laughter that fills the air, a sound so foreign for the moment, I turn to see if she's completely lost the plot. Bent at her waist clutching her side, she's pointing outside the open door. A bobcat is sitting on the edge of the forest, staring in at us curiously. A pale brown coat with a mix of tiger stripes and leopard sports cover his body, his face similar to an average house cat with longer whiskers. Twitching his pointed ears, he darts back into the bushes, disappearing from view with a rustling sound following him.

Sagging against Huxley, I shake my head at my own foolishness. The tension has also left his body but he continues to stroke my hair, the closeness I was worried we would never have again returning. "Well," I muffle against his chest, "at least I've done my share of exercise for the day."

# *Wyatt*

Screams jolt me from my new hobby of staring at the ceiling, my feet hitting the floor beside my bed as I vault from the mattress. Running along the hallway on tiptoes, I peer around the corner of the staircase to see everyone gathered at the bottom. Meg's hysterical laughter confuses me, Avery's buried in a cocoon of Huxley's affection. After peering outside for a moment longer, Garrett and Axel shut the front door and usher everyone into the kitchen for a dinner they've prepared. Surely it's no coincidence after finally being able to contact Ray, the girls are fleeing the forest screaming but I haven't thought his men could get here so fast.

Slinking back to my room, I stuff my feet into the only pair of sneakers Ray had brought for me, black Nike's with gold laces to match the tick. Pulling a black hoodie over my head and leaving the hood up, I creep back towards the stairs and press my back against the wall as I slither down. Looking between the wooden slats, I see everyone sitting with their backs to me except for Dax and Hux. Frowning, I hover halfway down the steps unsure of what to do.

"I'm gonna grab a drink, anyone else want one?" Dax offers, rising from his seat and moving towards the fridge. Hux's concentration is centred on the burger he's dissecting, so I edge further down the steps and shoot through the front door before he notices. Relaxing on a long breath, I run into the woods as daylight begins to dim. Sticking to the rocky path, I keep up the pace until I'm well over a mile from the house. Blowing down inside the neck hole of my hoodie, I now regret wearing the damn thing since there's a furnace trapped inside.

Stopping to look around, dense greenery tainted by dusk stretch either side of me, only broken by the hundreds of looming tree trunks. I have no idea which way to go, or even if the henchmen I'm looking for are even here. Kicking a rock from side to side with my left foot, I pull my phone out of my pocket and switch on the flashlight. Somehow the empty setting seems eerier now that I hold a bright light in my hand, shadows hanging over my shoulder until I spin to banish them. A trick of my mind sees silhouettes darting between trunks in my peripheral vision.

Full beam headlights suddenly blind me, searing my retinas so hard I can't stop seeing spots after they are turned off. Hefty chuckles mix with the chirping of crickets and buzzing of insects, the whole forest waking up to mock me. Opening the door of a concealed vehicle, the hulking bodyguard I recognise, originally from the ambush at the mansion and later at Ray's home, steps into the shrubs dressed all in black. The light within the car comes to life, illuminating the interior while the entire outside is hidden by a leafy netting. A box of mesh sits hidden between a gap in the tree trunks, masses of springs and leaves tucked into the gaps. Now that I am looking at it, the disguise is pretty obvious, but it does the trick.

Impatiently waiting for me by the door, I rush over to join the one I've nicknamed Rhino in my head, thanks to his unfortunately lumpy forehead. He's a huge man in his late 40s with dark brown eyes and a nasty habit of biting his fingernails. Moving around to the passenger side, I fumble in the dark for the handle before locating it and slipping inside. Hearing muttering in the back seat, I twist to see a pair of heavily muscled brutes in the backseat I haven't seen before. Also wearing full black with ski masks in their hands, they stare blankly at me which isn't surprising, I wouldn't imagine they have much going on upstairs. Judging by their similar buzzcuts and scarred skin, these guys seem more like the hit now, think never type. Slamming his door shut, Rhino keeps his focus forward and exhales loudly, clearly bored of being in my company already.

"How'd you guys get here so fast?" I break the silence first, needing to know how they've had time to construct a camouflage cover and by the smell of charred wood, have a stake out BBQ. The inside light goes dark so Rhino reaches up to flick it back on, the constant flashes straining my eyes and starting to give me a headache.

"We chartered in by jet," he grumbles, tapping his thumb on his thigh. My mouth opens with a long-winded whine about how I had to drive three days straight and catch naps in laybys, but the words die on my tongue. These goons have clearly worked for Ray for a long time, probably done a lot of shit I don't even want to know about. And to be fair, I've been given a better opportunity than them – one job and I'm done, able to enjoy Ray's luxurious lifestyle without lifting a finger. No wonder Rhino seems pissed as hell, jealously doesn't look good on anyone.

"So, what's the plan then?" I move on swiftly. Glancing over when he doesn't respond, Rhino's eyes are glued on the windscreen as a tic pulses in his cheek. It's now pitch-black outside, so nothing to distract myself with as the silence drags on.

"Ray said it's your call," he finally grinds out. Ahh, I see why my presence is such a strain to him now. The newbie is in charge. Pushing my tongue into my cheek, trying to refrain from laughing mechanically and placing my fingers together like the villain in every spy movie ever, I think through the best options for a smooth double kidnapping. Not that I've ever really thought about it before.

I need the twins (ugh) away from the others, secluded and easily cornered. Especially now I know how deep their connections with Avery run, I'm surer than ever they will happily put themselves in the way of danger for her. The trickiest bit is the lack of cell phone signal around here so I can't contact Rhino when the perfect opportunity arises. Resting my chin on my fist, I click my tongue against the roof of my mouth until Rhino flicks open a switchblade and holds it above my dick with a closed fist.

"Well since you guys scared the shit out of them earlier, we'll have to wait for the dust to settle until they venture out alone again. Since I can't contact any of you, someone will have to hide out nearby so I can give a signal for the right time. Plan is - grab the girls and get the fuck out of dodge. I'll follow in the Sedan." Grumbles fill the car, this time from the back seat.

"How long is that going to take? We can just storm the house now and take them by force," Dipstick number one moans. Catching his eye in the rear-view mirror, I straighten my spine to sit upright in my seat. The boss doesn't slouch, he commands attention and respect which is exactly what I'm going to get.

"Ray promised me no one would get hurt, again." I slide my eyes to Rhino's brown ones, annoyance filtering through me that they sent a new recruit to an armed ambush. Huxley has been healing for weeks, and since his wounds are now on the inside, he still has a long road ahead. "We try to draw the girls into a trap first. If any of my... the guys intervene after that, that's on them." I think that's fair enough, there's only so much I can do if they are desperate to be Avery's hero.

"Fine." Rhino's deep voice says sharply. "There's a thick hedge beneath your window, we scoped out during your campfire. Flash your phone's light down when the time is *right*." The incline of his bumpy head and emphasis on the last word mocking my order. Turning in his seat, the leather squeaking in protest, his top lip lifts on one side in a snarl. Leaning across me, he pops open the glove compartment to pull out a bottle, dumping it in my lap. There's no label, just a dark bronze container with liquid sloshing around inside.

"Chloroform, in case it all goes tits up. Two days are all we are prepared to wait. After that, we take the house by force and I pity anyone who dares to cross us when we do."

Dragging my feet, I turn the final corner to reveal the three-story beach house. Almost every window has a warm glow radiating from within, figures passing by and laughter leaking out. Scowling, I stop the final distance telling myself I'll be back with dear Rachel by the weekend. I don't realise I'm not alone until I'm almost at the front stone steps. Huxley's wavy hair hangs in front of him limply, his head hidden beneath his palms. Shoving my hands into the adjoining pocket on my hoodie, I cover the bottle as best I can and take a seat beside him.

My presence seems to spook him just as much, his glazed eyes darting over to mine as if I've pulled him from a trance. Offering the best side smile I can muster, he huffs and looks back down to his bare feet. In just a pair of shorts and t-shirt, it's a wonder he isn't cold now the night's air has dropped considerably. But I'm fully aware how it feels to be trapped inside, no weather or physical pain can penetrate the barriers of our suffering.

"She's really something," he speaks unexpectedly, grabbing my shifting attention. "I didn't really believe you all these years, but I understand now. She's like a dark angel, desperately trying to fly free from the depths of hell but the demons keep dragging her back down."

My eyebrows rise, unable to stop visualizing the analogy he must have spent all evening thinking about. Her blonde hair whipping around her face as she struggles to kick off the shadowed monsters clawing at her ankles. Huge black feathered wings protruding from her scarred back, her outstretched fingertips grazing the earth's surface. Except in my version, I'm the demon scraping his clawed nails into her calf and yanking her back where she belongs.

"Maybe she deserves to be there," I mumble. His eyes snap back to mine, first with disbelief and then revulsion. Scoffing, Hux rises to his feet and glares down at me like a piece of shit beneath his heel.

"You really believe that, don't you?" Not bothering to answer since I'm too tired for this argument neither of us will win, I also stand and walk inside. A heated game of Scrabble is happening across the room, forfeits being dealt for hyphenated words as I pass by to reach the fridge. A bowl of pasta is covered in cellophane and waiting for me, like every night when I hadn't joined the rest for dinner. I don't know who's been saving it from Garrett on my behalf and I don't really care enough to question it.

Taking the bowl and a fork, I proceed to ignore everyone huddled around the dining table to retreat to my room like the hermit I've become. Closing the door with my back, I drop onto the bed with a sigh. My head is pounding now, anticipation to have this all finished threatening to crack my skull with the level of pressure I'm feeling. Ray put me in charge, a test I'm sure to prove my worth but also the chance to show him I was the right choice. For once, I'll have done something right.

Stabbing the pasta with my fork, the corners of the room start to blur and close in, as they do around this time every night when my vitamins begin to wear off. Tonight, I'm tempted to take another set but Rachel specifically told me, only two a day. Closing my eyes, I can smell her sweet perfume, feel her soft hair across my neck from when she hugged me goodbye. The stress that's been weighing me down shifts ever so slightly to give way to a rush of excitement that I'll see her again soon. Just a day or two more and I'm long gone.

# Huxley

Reclining in the porch swing, I let the momentum gently sway me back and forth, my toes dragging gently across the wooden floorboards. The sunrise is especially beautiful this morning, the sun appearing pink through the strokes of reds and oranges. Feathered clouds are being pulled towards the horizon as if the sun is their magnet, drawing them closer to a point they'll never reach. But none of that, not even the glistening sea and occasional leap of a dolphin, are what brought me out here.

I couldn't sleep, worrying about Wyatt's comment when I heard scuffling outside my bedroom door. Following the sound, I found the pair across the sand stretching and chatting in hushed tones. I'd been happy to take the room without the sea view up to now, but maybe I'll suggest it's time to switch. Not because I'm perving over two hot young women in Lycra who are currently bending over, watching them is soothing me. I feel the strain of each powerful muscle they stretch as if it were my own, the wash of calm relaxing Avery's posture filtering through me as well. The fact her actions are able to have an impact on parts of me I didn't know still existed, there's the true beauty of this scene.

I thought as soon as my wound healed, I'd be back to my old self. The longer it takes to find myself again, the more I hate who I'm becoming. It shouldn't be this difficult to be happy. To close the void the bullet ripped open which has now grown and festered into a place my nightmares live. But in this moment, watching her keep the demon at bay with ease, I have something I'd given up on trying to find. Hope.

Crashes and chattering from inside announce the arrival of more household members, irritation working its way back into my chest as they ruin the peacefulness. Screeching of a boiling kettle, the fridge banging closed, plates clanging and deep rumbles of chuckling. Scraping my piercing against the roof of my mouth, I try to hold onto the serenity with both hands, but it's fled. My body starts to tremble as the darkness pulls me back into its tight grip. A faint screaming rings around my skull, my subconscious desperately trying to claw it's way free but there's no use. A numbness seeps through me, the raw emotions I'd felt swallowed down once again. All that's left is a bitter taste in my mouth and an empty shell.

The back-door flies open, a larger audience stepping onto the porch to enjoy my view. Bobbing in excitement, Garrett throws himself over the railing and runs across the sand in only a pair of knee-length swim shorts. Steering away from the sea, he grabs Avery around the waist and flings her aside to stand before a puzzled looking Meg. His actions are clear to me now I know the full truth, Garrett loses interest after taking a girl to his bed. Although I believe he stills lusts for Avery, not that I can blame him, but I can hate him for it, there's a new shiny toy around for him to play with. Meg. And up to this point, she hasn't seemed particularly interested. Tapping her on the shoulder, he bolts in the opposite directions shouting, "Tag!"

For a moment she remains rooted to the spot, until a wide smile spreads across her face as she lunges forward to attack Avery. Shoving her twin back into the sand after she'd just managed to get to her feet, Meg's running spurs Axel and Dax from the porch to run onto the beach. Seeming to avoid facing Dax, Avery chases Axel and Meg who took off in the same direction. Not one to be left out, Garrett also speeds towards them too, only to be tagged when Avery senses his presence behind her and quickly turns back. Shooting for Dax, Garrett's legs thump powerfully in time with his arms as he gains on him in no time. Delivering a backhanded slap to his ass, Dax jolts and yelps although he hasn't stopped smiling, like the rest of them. They make it look effortless, when I'm unable to rise from my seat, the heaviness of my limbs weighing me down.

The group run back and forth like the sand is a football pitch, diving and skidding with more than one victory dance. Axel is gunning for Meg, the sun's glow reflecting off his scalp reminding me of a basketball as he runs at top speed. At the last moment, Garrett jumps into the way to receive the 'tag', acting chivalrous but I know he doesn't have it in him. Twisting to a helpless Meg, his wide smile looks full on Joker and his eyes are laced with menace as he bends to throw her over his shoulder. Racing straight into the depths of the sea, she screams and thumps his back but there's no stopping him from diving into the oncoming wave and taking her with him. Leaving them to it, everyone else starts to retreat inside speaking of breakfast but my eyes are glued on the pair in the water.

Having breeched the surface, Meg uses her legs to kick water into his face in an attempt to swim away. Ploughing through the spray, he catches her ankle and drags her into his body. Holding her close, a loud whistle rings across the space which has Axel pausing in the doorway. Garrett signals for him to join them with his hand but Axel waves him off, turning back to enter the house with a look of hurt flashing across his face. Not seeming to care, Garrett dips his head down and takes Meg's mouth hostage with his. Their silhouettes grind against each other, Meg's back arching and nails clawing at his shoulders. Not wanting to know what's going on beneath the surface, I finally pull myself up from the seat and make my way inside.

Avery is by my side in seconds, sliding her arms around my waist and smiling up at me. Managing a hint of a smirk for her, she leads me to the table and gently pushes me down into a seat. Now I see what this ambush was about. A plate of toast smothered in jam is placed in front of me within seconds, alongside a coffee I'm not sure was originally meant for me since I don't usually take mine so dark, but I'll take it. Caffeine has become my best friend as of lately.

Across the table, Axel is pushing cereal around his bowl with the back of his spoon, lost in thought. If he seriously thought Garrett would be faithful to him, he's deluded and I have no sympathy. Where I'm trying to fight the all-consuming anguish taking over my soul, Garrett accepted his, a long time ago. His outer bullshit is a rouse, luring women into bed so he can vent his frustrations sexually and say they were begging for it.

Managing to force down a whole slice of toast by the time Avery joins me with her own, her fingers trail along my arm in praise and I suddenly feel like a puppy being trained. What's more annoying is how I'm not too bothered by it, just enjoying her sole attention. Dax slips in on her other side, looking over at us longingly but she keeps her head turned away from him. This time my smirk is almost genuine, the tables beginning to turn back in my favour.

Breaking the moment, Meg slops through the backdoor with Garrett right behind her. Dragging her athletic vest over her flushed face and dumping it by the washing machine, she stands in her sports bra appearing agitated. The plum coloured leggings glued to her lower half appears black as water drips onto the lino flooring. "I swear he was a fish in a previous life," she grumbles, her nostrils flaring and teeth grinding as she stomps across the kitchen towards the staircase.

Garrett rounds the table once she's disappeared from view, sliding his wet arm around Axel's tense shoulders. Shrugging him off, Axel leaves his breakfast and the table without saying a word. Garrett's slack jaw and panicked eyes are a balm to my stress, relishing that, for once, something has managed to affect him. Although not for long, dropping his sodden ass into the recently vacated seat, he begins to eat the soggy cereal with an easy smile back in place.

Torn between wanting to stay close to Avery but needing to be as far away from Garrett's incredibly noisy chewing, I push myself upright and thank her for my breakfast before slinking back outside. Despite barely doing anything this morning, I feel like I've started a journey to conquer an internal mountain and returning to my room would slide me back to the bottom. Not stopping on the porch like usual, I venture towards the sea for the first time since arriving here.

The softness of the sand welcomes my bare feet, squishing between my toes with each step onward. My navy gym shorts waft around my thighs in a light breeze that also pushes my t-shirt against my body. The body I can't bare to look at right now, but one step at a time. As soon as I can find the energy to exert myself again, I'll be exercising three times a day to get back to my original size. Not for appearances but because I miss the delicious burn and next morning ache only peak fitness can provide.

Finding myself at the edge of the sea, I take one last step to allow the warming water to smooth over my feet. Like the wave that crashed to push the tide out to me, a dam within my core breaks and crumbles. I can't hold back a gasp as a physical wash of relief floods my system, cleansing my pores and boosting me up the mountain I was just visualising. For the first time, I'm able to see the peak, a bright glow leaking out from behind it.

Glancing around me, footprints moulded into the sand start to wash away in the expanding tide. A fresh canvas is left behind as the water retreats, gracing me with an opportunity to add in my own next time. A perfectly blue sky hangs above cementing the start of a new day, a clean slate I can thrust myself into. Needing to share the buzzing in my veins with the one person in the world I can stand to be around, I turn to run back towards the house. An image in the sand grabs my attention, a large heart drawn with a nearby stick showcasing the words 'Avery + Gaxel' inside. Grimacing, I make sure to smash my foot through the centre on my way passed.

Avery has just finished washing up as I re-enter the kitchen, taking her by the hand and pulling her upstairs. As soon as my foot hits the top step, raised voices filter from under Garrett and Axel's bedroom door. Unashamedly, I relax my hold on Avery's hand to walk the length of the corridor slower than necessary.

"What's gotten into you?" Garrett's muffled voice sounds over scuffling of feet on the floorboards inside.

"You know what has. I'm not getting into this right now."

"This is 'cause I was messing around with Meg, isn't it? I called for you-"

"I'm not a dog, Garrett!" Axel's voice booms, making me halt to hear how this plays out. "I don't give a shit what you do, but don't give me some speech about changing unless you mean it!" A door within slams loudly, Avery flinching from the noise that vibrates through the flooring.

"Axel, come out of the bathroom. You know this is just the way I am." I can imagine from the longing in his tone, Garrett is slumped against the door like a lovesick teenager which brings a smile to my face. Finally, something is affecting the asshole and it's making my fucking day.

"When am I ever going to be enough for you?" The smile is wiped right back off again from Axel's response. He should have known what he was getting into but still, if there ever was a man that deserved to find happiness, love even – it would be him.

Sensing that's enough, Avery drags me along and forces me into my room. Her giggle is music to my eyes as we enter, reminding me of the revelation I had on the beach. Spinning and using her back to close the door, I push myself against her lithe body and steal a kiss. Surprised for a second, she melts into my torso and pulls me back down by the nape, crashing her lips against mine. Sweetness drips into my mouth as her tongue skates across mine, turning the blood in my veins to honey. Holding her face in my hands, I take every drop she is offering until I'm panting.

Her bright blue eyes are sparkling as I pull back, biting down on her full bottom lip while I try to control my sudden urges. A part of me had been worried my Johnson would no longer work after all this time, but the stiff bulge in my shorts has proved me happily wrong.

"What's got into you?" Her tone is light, her words escaping on a chuckle. Drawing her towards the bed, I pull her down for a hug since I don't want to get too far ahead of myself but need her close. I've already run a marathon compared to where I was last night, I don't want to push myself any further so soon. Her body curls into the side of mine, her golden hair spilling across my shoulder.

"I feel… better. A tiny bit." I pull her closer and breathe in her vanilla scent that I've missed. "I don't think the nightmares will be able to find me tonight. No more replays of that afternoon, the masked man with different coloured eyes and a scar in his eyebrow diving at me-" Avery's body stiffens all of her sudden, her fingers digging into my chest as she begins to shake. Pulling her upright, the pure horror in her gaze sends lightening bolts of panic into my gut.

"You never mentioned those details before," her voice quivers. "Not in the police reports or to me…" A tear escapes her eye which I quickly catch with my thumb. Her breathing grows rapid, terrified puffs leaving her trembling lips. Tilting her chin up to face me, I beg her to tell me what's wrong while apologising for upsetting her. I don't understand how I've hurt her again but I have, and that's enough to plunge me back into the depths of my self-loathing.

"I can't believe it was him. Fredrick Walters. The man who abused me, who I hoped I'd never be near again." She twists her head from my light grip, shunning me with her back. "He was the one that shot you."

# Avery

Meg wraps herself around my body, making me flinch. I've been so distracted by my thoughts whilst staring into the rippling sea, I hadn't even realised night had fallen. The waves spilling towards me and recoiling back has a hypnotic effect, pulling me into a trance where none of the secrets and pain exist. If it really is him, the one I fear the most is closer than I thought and was in my damn house, then I don't know what to believe anymore. Has my whole life been a setup, a convenience in some revenge plot against my parents?

Squeezing me tightly, I lean my head on top of Meg's, pulling on her strength to refill my own. At least we found each other again, that's a blessing I can hold onto. My twin completes me, where I finish, she begins and I'll never spend a day of my life without her again. Curling my arms around the soft jumper she's wearing, we stare into the distance in silence together. The sky is incredibly dark tonight, a thick layer of cloud covering the moon and stars from shining down upon us. My eyes prick up, noticing how deathly quiet the beach is. Even the birds are hiding in their trees, the entire world waiting in anticipation for something to happen.

Figuring we should turn in for the night, hoping the morning brings a healthy dose of resolve with it, I link my fingers between Meg's and slowly spin her towards the house. The moon breaks through the clouds, a spotlight shining down in the distance like a warning siren from space. In the brief illumination, a darkened figure becomes visible amongst the tree line beside the porch. Even from here, I know that silhouette isn't one I recognise – the rounded middle and slightly hunched shoulders reminding me of an upright gorilla.

Every nerve ending numbs, a shudder rolling through me as Meg's head shoots up too. Gripping my hand tight enough to bruise, she puts one foot in front of the other to slowly pull me forward. The only rational part of my brain that still works can sense trouble waits for us at the edge of the beach, but I also know our best shot to avoid whoever it is lies inside the house in the form of five guys. I believe even Wyatt would put aside his personal vendetta if I were truly in danger. Acting as calm as I am able, I stroll beside Meg pretending we haven't seen the unnerving shape that's hidden from view since the moon has been concealed by the clouds again.

Steering off to the opposite side of the porch, a scuffle of leaves in our new direction makes my blood freeze in my veins. Only ten feet left to go, nine, eight. Gorilla guy lunges for me from the left, a shriek leaving my lips as he approaches rapidly in my peripheral vision. A similar shape darts from the right, running for Meg as we bolt towards the back door. My foot hits the first wooden step when I'm yanked backwards into a wall of muscle. His sausage fingers cover my mouth, a sharp sting digging into my side. Meg has managed to dodge her attacker, making it past the porch swing before she notices I've been caught.

Pleading for her to run with my eyes, although I know she won't, I kick and thrash wildly. My shoe connects with a shin, the resulting grunt and shift causing his hand to lift from my mouth a smidge. Taking full advantage of the opportunity, I lean forward and throw my head backwards into his face. A deafening crack beside my ear makes my stomach roll as I'm dropped to the sand. Scrambling, I leap and catch the edge of the timber railing with my fingertips, quickly pulling myself up and over. Pushing Meg through the back door forcefully, I scream at the top of my lungs as the men barge inside after us.

Garrett slams the fridge closed, his eyes wide as saucers as Axel hops down from the kitchen counter. Without hesitation, they dive at the men chasing us, allowing us time to flee towards the stairs. Squeezing Meg's hand tightly in mine, we can't help to glance back. Axel's fists are already covered with blood, his inner beast coming to the surface to pummel his attacker relentlessly. With his amber eyes blazing and teeth bared, he appears to be more animal than human in this moment.

Not having the same luck with his opponent, Garrett's head spins with the force of a punch cracking across his cheek. Fear has me trapped in its clutches with each hit Garrett takes for me, his eye already swelling. With a thump that floors his foe, Axel runs over to step between his lover and an oncoming kick to his abdomen. Taking it with merely a grunt, Axel's shoulders bunch as he advances to return the favour.

Remembering to flee, we round the banister as the front door is kicked inwards and slams to the ground. A monster of a man, the biggest one yet, steps onto the fallen wood and sneers at me. Through the gap of a ski mask, his brown eyes are laced with a hatred that I don't understand. Backing up, a heavy weight ploughs through us from behind, Huxley launching himself from the bottom step straight onto the thug.

Meg falls to the floor from the movement, her legs scrambling to regain her footing with my help, yanking her up by the jumper. Looking beyond her frightened expression, I see Garrett and Axel have managed to push the rest of the gorilla gang back outside, punches flying violently on the other side of the windows. Dax appears behind me on the stairs, his hand coiling beneath my arm and pulling me up the steps. Meg's fingers are torn from mine on a scream, her hair twisted around the thug's fist. Huxley is sprawled across the floor, struggling to get back up as Meg is dragged across the room.

"Get her to the study," Meg shouts at Dax, as if I'm not

here. My heart jackhammers in my chest, desperately trying to help her but Dax's grip is relentless. Pulling me up the steps forcefully, I twist and reach for her even though it's pointless. "I can't leave you!" I scream, tears freefalling from my eyes.

Grabbing a lamp from the small table in the corner on the way past, Meg swings it behind her like a hammer throw champion. Catching her attacker in the temple, she manages to scramble from his grip to close the gap between us. Pulling me close, she kisses my cheek and stares into my eyes with urgency. "They don't know about me. Go to the panic room, I'll be right there." Before I can respond, she moves over to help Huxley to his feet, checking him over for injuries. Finally allowing Dax to draw me up the staircase, my heart cracks with each step away from her but she's right. She'll be fine and can join us in a minute.

Making it onto the landing, battle cries filtering through the floorboards from beneath, we dash towards the study's open door. A slam at the end of the corridor has my head whipping around to see Wyatt emerging from his bedroom, his emerald eyes zeroing in on me with malice etched into their green depths. Not wasting another second, I enter the room and wrench out the book Meg showed me as far as it will go. The clicks release on the other wall, Dax's eyes already noticing the slight shadow against the cream paint and opening the door for me to run into. Flying across the panic room, I open the laptop and key in the password to see what the fuck is going on downstairs.

Slamming has me whipping around, the locks sliding back into place making me gasp. Dax is standing in front of the release button, his stance wide and ready for the inevitable fight I'm going to give him. "What the fuck are you doing? Meg's out there!" I scream. His eyes dart to the floor, scratching his scalp so his afro is bouncing viciously in the pale lighting. Crossing the small room and shoving him with my palms, he barely moves, his hands raising to hold me back by the shoulders.

"I'm sorry Avery, I can't let anything happen to you. You heard Meg, they're not here for her. Everyone is doing what they must to protect you, as am I." His voice is low and even, considering I'm throwing my weight against him. I don't want to hurt him but if he comes between me and my twin, I won't hold back. Channelling my self-defence lessons, I step back for him to lower his arms before swinging a punch into his abdomen. It didn't pack the whack I wanted but it's still enough for him to take a step back and his piercing blue eyes to widen in shock.

"Dax, I won't tell you again. Get out of my way. She could be hurt!" Ducking low, he makes the mistake of trying to protect his crown jewels while I shoot up to catch his jaw with my knuckles. Thrusting my shoulder into his chest, I manage to nudge him a sidestep over in the right direction. All I need is an opening to slam my palm on the red button on the wall by his head, or to piss him off enough that he'll throw me out willingly. I like Dax, more than I care to admit out loud, but I will drop him for Meg any day of the week.

Hurling another punch towards his chest, he catches my fist in his large hand this time. Grabbing my other wrist forcefully, he quickly spins me around so my arms are crossed over my own body and trapping me in a cage I can't fight my way out of. Shouting and struggling against his grip, he pushes his body flush against the back of mine and lies his cheek on my head.

"I care too much to let you leave." He breathes into my ear. Floods of tears are streaming from my eyes, burning a trail down my cheeks in the process. My nostrils flare, my voice dripping with venom.

"If something happens to her, I'll never forgive you. There'll be no coming back for us after this," I try in a last-ditch attempt to hit him where I know none of my punches could have reached.

"I know," he whispers, his voice full of grief and understanding. Slowly, his fingers unpeel from my wrists until I'm fully released. Twisting, I suddenly feel a tug of discomfort at my side. Hissing, I press a hand above my hip for it to come away red. Looking through a tear in my t-shirt, I notice a slight incision from where a knife must have been pushing against me by thug number one. Dax falls to his knees, lifting the material to inspect it but I push him away. It's just a scratch and I have more important things to worry about right now, like how others are putting their lives on the line to protect me.

Refocusing my attention, my spine is taut despite my limbs feeling slack as I slump across the room to take a seat in front of the laptop. I feel Dax's presence over my shoulder before his arm slides around my chest, not in restraint but in comfort. And a part of me kind of hates him for it. Watching the screen intently, my hands rise to hold onto his arm, digging my nails into his flesh with an equal need of reassurance and to make him suffer for trapping me here. My eyes drag from window to window, desperately trying to find Meg and my... friends. No, not friends. These guys welcomed me into their group and it's time I admitted I've let them all into the one place I promised no one would never be able to infiltrate. My heart.

# Wyatt

No, no, no! My feet pound across the hallway, turning into a run. Rounding the doorway, I find the study is completely empty like I feared it would be. Slamming my fist into the door, my hand flies through the wood up to my wrist. The sting of splinters penetrates my knuckles but there's no time to worry about that. How in hell did she manage to get to the study? I set it up perfectly, finding Ray's men the second Meg left to join her sister by the water's edge and then slinking back to my room to remain the innocent party. What these men are gifted with in muscle, they sure as fuck lack in intelligence.

Pacing back and forth in the hallway, trying to figure out how I'm going to get her now, a scream from downstairs distracts me. I'd been so focused on finally getting Avery to beg me for her life, I'd forgotten all about Meg. Rushing down the corridor and skidding to a halt at the top of the staircase, I run down to see Meg being held high in the air by her throat. The owner of the hand is Rhino, his fingertips squeezing tightly enough to make her wheeze, as if he's forgotten Ray's one instruction to bring her back alive.

An idea barely forms in my mind as I implement it, rushing at him and diving into his side. Only by taking him by surprise, he is knocked off balance enough for me to ram my shoulder into his gut and shove him over the back of the sofa. Jumping over after him, I land on his stomach with my knees, making him wheeze beneath his black mask.

"What's your fucking problem, Weasel?" How sweet, he gave me a pet name too. Seeing Meg has fled to behind Huxley in the corner of the kitchen, I lean down to speak into his ear.

"Trust me," I hiss through my teeth. "I have a plan. We need both of them." As my words register, Rhino seems to relax slightly although his brown eyes are still shooting daggers into mine. Sitting upright, his fist suddenly flies into my face, catching my cheek as I turn at the last second. Knocking me from his body, my side slams into the coffee table on my way to the floor. "What the fuck?" I groan in pain, holding my throbbing face.

"Just making it look believable," he smirks, his eyes crinkling in the corners. Glancing around the edge of the sofa, we still haven't been noticed so I refocus on the twatbag grinning at me.

"Just play dead already, I need to use her to lure Avery out." He grumbles beneath his breath but obeys anyway, making a dramatic show of collapsing and twitching every few seconds for absolutely no one else's benefit but his own. Shaking my head, I leave the failed actor on the floor and scramble to my feet. Huxley is eyeing the fight happening through the window on the porch, pulling Meg along as he edges towards the back door, no doubt looking for a clear shot to get her out of the house. If she manages to flee in the darkness of the forest or take one of the vehicles out front, I'll lose her for sure.

"Meg!" I whisper loudly, running up to her. Huxley puffs out his chest and widens his stance as he moves between us. Fighting the instinct to roll my eyes, I keep my features as slack as I can manage with a possible broken cheek bone. "Come with me, we need to get you away from here." I hold out my hand as she peers around Hux, her pale blue eyes frowning at my open palm as if it were on fire. Distrust lines every inch of her face, her eyes flicking up to glare at me.

"Hurry! There's no time for our feud bullshit right now. Avery's waiting for you in the study," I stare at her with my most genuine look, or at least I hope that's what she sees. After hesitating for a further second, she slowly slides her hand in mine. Ignoring the velvet softness I shouldn't even notice right now, if ever, I gently tug her towards the stairs. Seeming content with my caring act, Hux strides outside to join the fight. A pang of guilt pulses through my body, hoping Ray's men go easy on him.

Going against every instinct in my body not to crush her hand in my grip and drag her screaming, we eventually enter the study so I'm able to release her. She takes an instinctual step towards the bookcase, then stops and turns to face me. "You can leave now," she challenges, crossing her arms and narrowing her eyes in suspicion. My heckles rise, a physical tightening I have to push down before I can respond.

"Look, I know things have been difficult. But I want to make sure you're safe, both of you." I attempt despite the look in her eyes saying she's withdrawing for me. Stepping into centre of room, Meg crosses her arms defiantly.

"If you're so concerned with helping all of a sudden, go help your brothers." I glance back at the door, anguish slicing through me before I remember the real goal here. I didn't intend for tonight to go down like this but if the guys want to risk themselves for these cretins, that's their issue. This has to happen, tonight. And my 'brothers' will know the truth about me soon anyway so might it as well be now.

"Show me where the hidden door is," I bark, the hardness I've been struggling to keep at bay falling back over my eyes. Her expression doesn't shift in the slightest showing she was never fooled by my act and might as well tattoo 'I told you so' across her forehead. "It doesn't have to be this way; I only want her." I lie, knowing she's not getting away either way. Meg's eyes remain on mine, a bitchy tilt to her eyebrows as if she thinks she can beat me.

Pushing my hand into my tracksuit pants pocket, I grasp the white cloth I doused in chloroform like Rhino insisted – not thinking I'd needed to get my hands dirty but glad I'd taken the precaution now. Whipping the rag free, I dive towards her in a flash. Dodging me at the last second, I crash to the ground as Meg falls to the side and attempts to crawl away. Grabbing her ankle, I yank her backwards and leer over her, her hand gripping my forearm with surprising strength as I try to push the cloth onto her mouth.

Kicking me in the stomach with her free foot, her lithe body rolls and jumps up before I recover. Rounding behind my back, her arm slinks around my neck as she attempts a sleeper's hold which only makes me laugh. Reaching back, I grip her nape and throw her over my shoulder. Flipping her onto her back, her head landing in my lap and distracting my thoughts momentarily, I don't anticipate her fist punching upwards. Smashing into my chin hard enough so my head snaps back, I growl in my first flare of real anger. Up to this point, our fight had been akin to foreplay to me but now, the games are over.

Allowing her to roll onto her stomach, I twist over to mount her back. Yanking a fist full of her silky hair back, she's squeals like a piglet ready for the slaughter. Placing the cloth down for a second, I slip my free hand around her long neck to savour the moment. Water droplets splash onto my arm as she still attempts to buck me off. "Keep going, I'm really getting off on this," I sneer. She immediately goes still as I anticipated, abandoning her only chance of an escape to not let me have the last laugh. But I will, and it'll be glorious.

"Why? Why are you doing this?" She croaks out, her throat bobbing beneath my palm as she swallows. Gripping a little tighter, I lean forward to whisper into her ear. For once, I'll give her the truth.

"I'm taking back what I'm owed." Her lips part to answer as I grab the cloth and cover the lower half of her face with it, her head flopping forward a moment later. My hand remains around her neck for a second longer, my thumb acting on his own accord to stroke her fluttering pulse. Releasing her and sitting back on the floor to admire my work, a faint scream I recognise sounds from somewhere beyond this room. A smile drags my lips up, figuring Avery's snuck out through a different exit only to be captured anyway.

Slipping my arms beneath Meg's dead weight, I lift her over my shoulder and exit the room. My mind insists on repeating our fight over and over, her skill and strength becoming more impressive with each mental replay. Marching down the stairs, everything's gone quiet on the lower level. Finding only the two dipshits, Rhino nowhere to be seen, hovering around the kitchen waiting for me, I stride over to place Meg into the arms of the closest one. Ignoring the pull of my chest at the sudden lack of warmth, I follow them towards the back door. Across the door mat, Huxley's still form is inconveniently in the way. Judging by the rise and fall of his chest and lack of visible injuries, I'm going to guess he more than likely passed out from lack of nutrition than anything else.

Stepping over his body, my foot creaks on a floorboard of the porch as the fresh night's air fills my lungs. My task is done, I'm free to leave this life behind and it feels incredible. About to take another step, a small sob reaches my ears. Letting curiosity get the better of me, I round the corner to see Garrett hunched over Axel, cradling his head in his arms. Glancing up at me, the glow from inside reveals the glistening streaks lining his cheeks.

"Wyatt! Please, you gotta help. He needs medical attention." Axel's skin is deathly pale, his body a little too still but that's not the worrying part. The blade handle protruding from his lower abdomen is, it's black handle glinting in the faint light with a scripted gold R.P engraved into the side. Fucking idiots. Squinting back towards the darkness of the forest, I see Rhino skid the black Sedan around. Popping the trunk, where no doubt Avery is too, the goofball holding Meg flops her into the back and closes it with a loud slam. Once everyone has entered the vehicle, Rhino flicks on the headlights suddenly to light their way and speeds off into the woodlands with a screech.

Crossing the porch, I kneel beside Axel and take his hand. It should have never come to this. If they'd just stayed away, if they'd not fallen for Avery's charms like I constantly warned them not to, none of this would have happened. They'd be in Waversea and I'd be long gone without them knowing what had happened to me. "I'm so sorry, brother," I whisper so quietly, Garrett didn't even hear between his sobbing. I've never seen him shed a single tear, and now he can't stop. How did he fall so far from his high horse? I'd be disappointed if I still cared. Wrapping my hand around the dagger's handle, I take a long exhale.

"Wait, Wyatt-" I whip the blade free in a swift movement, Axel's body jerking involuntarily. His eyelids flicker in time with the rapid flutter in his neck that is beginning to slow in the faint artificial light. Blood spews from his gut, the thick liquid jerking me between the hallucinations I've been struggling with and reality. Garrett yells, whipping his top off to press down on the open gash. "Noooo! Why would you do that?!" He shouts at me, leaning all his weight onto the wound, not that it'll help. More tears leak from his eyes, his weakness making me feel nauseous as he stares at me in shock and disgust.

"Couldn't leave any evidence," I shrug, rising to my feet. I stand for another moment to watch the strange display. Axel's chest is barely rising anymore, but Garrett is still pushing on his wound as if he can force his own lifeforce into his lover. Garrett will thank me one day, when he remembers he doesn't do monogamy for a reason. Everyone leaves eventually. Screams of every curse word Garrett can think of are bellowed towards my retreating back, although none of them come close to what I think about myself. I know when I close my eyes, the numbness I currently feel will ebb away and the reality of tonight will weigh on me like a thousand bricks.

Ignoring the 'I hate you' and 'I'm gonna kill you for this' echoing throughout the night as I round the front of the house, I see a hunched shadow beside the vehicle Ray let me borrow. Her outline isn't defined, more of a smoky shape around her scraggly hair. She's changed slightly, her skeleton visible in the form of black bones, each one grinding against the other as she shifts on her feet. Scratching her nails against the back tyre, I smirk and roll my eyes. Walking past, I whistle to grab her attention, those orbs of green in her dark skull focusing on me.

Slipping into the driver's seat, I glance back at the house shrouded in shadows. All of the laughter I'd heard whilst here has left, only an empty shell of misery remaining. Which is what I wanted, right? Mentally saying one last goodbye to the men inside, it dawns on me I'll never see any of them again. I wouldn't have survived this long without them, but the truth of my character had to come out in the end and what I need now is a real family.

Twisting the key, the engine roars and the headlights illuminate the forest. I'd better hurry to catch up with the others, wanting to be the one to present my good work to Ray. The eerie shadow settles into the passenger seat, her head cocking like a bird as she stares at me. Her fingers reach over to rest on top of mine on the shift stick, icy coldness seeping beneath my skin at her touch. The chill runs up my arm, blossoming in my chest and freezing over what's left of my blackened heart.

"Come on mom, time to go home."

*The last of The Shadowed Souls Series will be available later this year, Dangerously Damaged!*

# Thanks!

Thank you for reading the second novel in The Shadowed Souls Trilogy! Be sure to follow me on Amazon and Goodreads to find out when the last in the series becomes available for preorder. Also, head over to my Facebook group 'Cole's Reading Moles' and instagram '@abigail_cole_author' for announcements, giveaways, reveals and more! See you there.

# Acknowledgement

I would like to express a special thank you to all of the wonderful ladies who have helped me on this journey so far. Each one has given invaluble help to make these novels the best they can be and I'll always be grateful for their support. To Teresea and Kirsty for proof reading, and Gemma, Danielle and Denise for being my Beta Readers. Also, for all the bloggers and reviewers who have been promoting on my behalf - I hope this book was everything you hoped it would be. All of you are helping to bring my dream of becoming an author to reality.

Printed in Poland
by Amazon Fulfillment
Poland Sp. z o.o., Wrocław

61231636R00148